SISTER IN TROUBLE

S.A MCEWEN

First published in Australia 2022

Copyright © S.A. McEwen 2022

ISBN: 9780645211030 (ebook)

ISBN: 9780645211054 (paperback)

Editor: Erica Russikoff, Erica Edits

Cover Design: Elizabeth Mackey

Disclaimer

SISTER IN TROUBLE

S.A MCEWEN

For Marion.
Thank you for decades of love and support.
YOU'RE a treasure x

PROLOGUE

SYDNEY, Australia

March 2006

The woman hurries along the cliff top.

It's late. The sky is a murky black, tiny pinheads of stars invisible through the gloom and city smog.

The moon, though, is luminous.

She's later than she meant to be.

Her step quickens.

The moon casts long shadows across the path. Something moves, and she gasps; but it's just a cloud passing over the moon, making the shadows squirm and morph like cartoonish ghosts.

Still. There's something creepy about this path in the dark.

Far, far below, she can hear the waves crashing into the rocks. The sound is ominous. In the daylight she has walked this path many times, and the sound of the ocean is magic to her, soothing and wild at the same time. But tonight, in the dark, she shivers.

There's still no rail between her and the cliffs in some places, despite numerous complaints to the council.

Not for the first time, she thinks how easy it would be to fall.

To die.

To push someone.

She breaks into a run.

It's ridiculous; she's thirty-something years old, spooking at shadows like a child afraid of monsters.

Maybe monsters are real, though.

She thinks about her husband, and her step falters for a moment. Then she braces herself and hurries on.

It's just the headlands.

She knows them like the back of her hand.

She's lived nearby her whole life.

She's scrambled over ledges and slipped under overhangs more times than she can count, or more often than would be considered strictly safe and sensible.

Of course she's fine out here.

Up ahead, out of sight, someone moves in the shadows.

They've been listening to the crashing of the waves, too.

They know this path as well as she does. Where the gravel is looser, and poses a slipping risk.

Where the path skirts dangerously close to the cliff tops, without a rail.

All the places people have been lost, and all the good places to hide.

1

Monday

December 2021

Adele rocks back on her heels, wiping a hand across her mouth.

How ridiculous, she thinks.

She fishes in a pocket for a tissue and wipes her chin absentmindedly.

Her movements are so familiar, she doesn't have to make decisions about them. She doesn't think about them at all. She could do this in her sleep, in fact, even after all these years of not doing it at all. So her body carries on with this particular ritual, while her mind meanders almost whimsically.

She hears the crunch of leaves and twigs outside, and cocks her head, listening.

For the second time this week, she's seen a man loitering around the headlands. Adele walks along here most days, enjoying the flex of her glutes as she takes great strides up the inclines, then enjoying a rest and the view from the top at

Marks Park. The waves crashing violently into the rocks below her have been the soundtrack to her exercise regime for years.

She's still not used to the memorial.

Did anyone really think about that choice? she wonders, for the three-hundredth time. Sure, sure, she gets it. She knows it's terribly privileged to not have to think about being beaten up or murdered just because of who you happen to fancy. But it jars her every time. Every single walk, every single day, she sees it and has to think about all the gay men murdered in this spot over the course of decades. And it's just, well, so *glum*. It's so seedy and sad and terribly depressing. And of course, thinking about murdered people inevitably brings her back to Celia.

Another crackle outside the toilet.

Adele isn't worried. There are a lot of people out. It's overcast and gloomy, but that doesn't stop the runners or the tourists. For a while, the activity in this area seemed too much to stop at the public toilets and purge there—she had worried that someone would hear her, confront her. But no one ever had.

What would they say, anyway? "Are you sick? Do you need help? Can I call someone?" That's what they'd say. Not, *"Do you have an eating disorder, ma'am? You're a mother, for God's sake! What is* wrong *with you? Are you completely insane?"*

No, no one would say anything, no one would even consider for a moment that a forty-something-year-old woman, well-dressed and serene-looking, would stop on her power walk around the headlands and choose to vomit in the public toilets. It was too ridiculous. Eating disorders were for teenagers, weren't they?

So maybe there's a man outside the toilets, now.

Let him loiter, Adele thinks.

Worse things have happened to her than a creepy man accosting her at public toilets.

Still, she doesn't leave immediately. She takes a drink from her water bottle, still locked inside her cubicle. She'd really like to lie down, and wonders if the grass is dry outside. She'll go check in a minute. She is finding it very hard to get motivated today. Motivated for anything.

Oh, she knows this is ridiculous. What would Peter say if he knew? Darling Peter. He'd be horrified. He always thinks so highly of her. She's still not quite sure why he loves her. She's always thought of herself as a bit of a fixer-upper, and he's always thought she was a prized, fully renovated mansion on the Italian coast.

She cocks her head again. She can hear a commotion in the distance, the dull chug of a helicopter. People shouting.

She wonders if someone has fallen down the cliffs. They have railings now, warning signs. There're still gaps though. Some parts of the track make her heart skip a beat, the danger feels so close, so tangible.

How many people died here, before?

Before Celia.

Life has been roughly divided along these lines: before Celia vanished, and after.

In the distance, a siren wails.

2

February 2006 (five weeks before Celia disappeared)

Celia lies in bed, pretending to be asleep.

She can hear Albert fussing in the bathroom, muttering and moving things around loudly enough that it's apparent he wants Celia to wake up and solve his problem.

She keeps her eyes resolutely closed.

Inside, she reviews the list of things she needs to get done today.

There's the appointment with the gynaecologist. She really should invite Albert to come with her, but she really doesn't want to. Sometimes it's just easier, more efficient when she's by herself. There's less *fuss*. There's more proficiency and less emotion and that is just the way Celia likes it.

She'll walk the coastal track around the headlands. She ought to invite Adele, who keeps suggesting they exercise together, but Celia knows she won't. Powering around the gravel track is her thinking time, and she has a lot to think about.

"Darling, I'm sorry to wake you." Albert's voice is soft,

gentle. "But I can't find my shaving cream and I'm going to be late for work."

Albert works twenty minutes away at Darlinghurst Clinic General Practice. He's been a GP there for as long as Celia has known him—the better part of fourteen years. She'd seen him around her entire childhood, of course, but she tells people that they met, properly, in her final year of high school, and he swept her off her feet.

Now, Celia wishes her feet had been a little more steady. She'd been flaky at school, more interested in boys than study, and had no idea what she wanted to do with herself after school. Being pursued by a hot young doctor seemed like an end in itself. And now, well, she has her own little art gallery, and she's good with art, she has a good eye, people like her, they trust her. But it was all funded by Albert, and Celia wishes she had made something that was entirely hers. Her skill, her passion, her success (though to be fair, when she dwells on this notion, she can't actually think what that might be, and she feels a little swell of resentment, as though twenty-year-old Albert had stolen something from future Celia, somehow—the opportunity to nurture those things, perhaps).

She wants something physical that is visible and hers alone. *Something she could take with her if she needed to leave.*

The thought pops into her head unbidden and she swats it away, irritated, then rolls over and looks at her husband. He smiles at her apologetically. He's still a handsome man, but he's let his weight go a little. A round stomach pokes out in front of him, not really noticeable in a shirt and slacks, but very prominent naked. It's distasteful to Celia, who is as slim and toned as the day they met, and it feels like an affront somehow —that she looks after herself, takes care of her attractiveness, and he...doesn't.

Doesn't he care how he appears to her? That he is attractive to her?

"You showered in the en suite on the weekend, remember?" she tells him now. "You probably left it in there."

"Of course!" Albert's face brightens. He leans over and kisses her on the lips. "Thanks, angel."

Celia watches him bustle out of their bedroom, his saggy bottom filling her with dismay.

It's just the baby-making, she thinks to herself. They've been trying to fall pregnant for over a year now, and Celia is impatient. Her doctor isn't very worried. He tells her it often takes couples a year or more. But the relentlessness of pinpointing ovulation and having missionary sex on demand for those few days a month has turned Celia off sex altogether. That and Albert's paunch.

They've just started IVF, which is oddly a relief to Celia. It seems much more organised. More under control. Which is a ridiculous misconception—if the last twelve months has showed her anything, it is that baby-making is one area of her life that is completely, utterly outside her control.

Maybe she doesn't even really want a baby, she thinks now, startling herself.

Then she texts her sister: I'm not feeling well. Could you fill in for me at the gallery today?

She knows she shouldn't. Her therapist has told her that feelings and actions and thoughts all impact each other; that doing things she enjoys will lift her mood. But she only listens to some of the things her therapist tells her. Some of her reflections about Celia and life in general are deeply irritating, and Celia puts those aside with amazing alacrity.

No, the reason she shouldn't text her sister is that she knows she asks a little too much of Adele. She knows that if she asks, Adele jumps. It's sweet and flattering and also...quite convenient. Celia asks things of Adele that she knows she, Celia, would never do for Adele if the situation were reversed.

But Adele likes helping, doesn't she? She's one of those people who likes to be of service, she gets a real little boost from it. Being the helper. Being *indispensable.* So really, maybe Celia was doing Adele the favour here.

She smirks to herself, and snuggles back down into her bed.

Later, when Albert comes to say goodbye, she tells him she's not feeling well, and he fusses and worries over her, and it annoys her so much she wishes she'd said nothing.

Why is it that everything he does annoys her these days?

If he'd left without a fuss she would have been equally annoyed, as though it showed a lack of care, a lack of love. Honestly, sometimes she thinks she just enjoys being in a huff about one thing or another. She doesn't know what is wrong with her at the moment. Everything seems to exist underneath a gloomy black cloud and nothing she does or doesn't do seems to shift it.

Adele texts her back, and they confirm times and tasks required, and Celia smiles to herself. The cloud, apparently, shifts a little when things get done, items get ticked off. *When people do what she wants them to do,* a little voice murmurs inside her head. But her satisfaction is interrupted by banging on the front door, and her smile vanishes.

For a moment, she considers ignoring it, closing her eyes firmly against the intrusion, but a part of her is also curious. It's too early for a parcel, too early for much of anything. No one in their right mind would knock on someone's door at seven o'clock in the morning and expect to get a sunny reception. People are getting ready for work, getting children ready for day care or school. Shouting at them to find their shoes, or finish their breakfast, or something.

If they had children, that is.

The thought of children brings back Celia's cloudy mood with a vengeance. Her frown deepens further. But she swings her legs out of bed and pulls her bathrobe on, and patters down the hall.

Bang, bang, bang.

"I'm coming," she mutters to herself, her irritation soothed by some good firm stomping as she moves down the hallway. And also soothed by a little buzz of anticipation.

Are my days so dull, she wonders to herself, *that I should be so hopeful about who might be on the other side of my door at this time of the morning?*

Pulling her robe tighter, she turns the lock and swings open the door.

And steps backward in alarm.

3

Monday

December 2021

Adele barely registers the furtive shape stepping back behind a tree outside the toilets when she is accosted by Melissa.

Melissa lives on Adele's street, and her face is lit up with horrified excitement. She grabs Adele by the arm and starts leading her back toward the cliffs.

"Something's going on down there," she whispers loudly in Adele's ear, not even pausing to say hello.

Adele wonders if she smells odd (a drink of water only goes so far in cleaning one's palate), and tries to pull slightly away from her friend, but Melissa is having none of it. She leans in even closer, her stage-whisper somehow distasteful to Adele. Perhaps it's her thinly veiled excitement. "They've found something, I bet! Another body, probably."

Adele wonders if it is possible that Melissa has forgotten that the police once searched these very cliffs for her sister's body, and that as such, sharing excitement with Adele about finding human remains there might be inappropriate or insensitive.

Perhaps, given they never found a trace of Celia, and given that it was fifteen years ago, that wasn't fair. Perhaps it was reasonable that other people forgot.

Nevertheless, Adele lets the silence hang. She wonders if Melissa will remember. But Melissa chatters on, oblivious.

Melissa and Adele went to school together, and though grudgingly Adele might admit that Melissa is her closest friend, in this moment, she wishes Melissa would unclamp her arm, quieten down, and well, quite frankly, bugger off. Let her enjoy her morning walk and morning purge in peace.

But her irritation is interrupted when Adele thinks she sees something out of the corner of her eye and she stops suddenly, remembering the loitering man. To her satisfaction, Melissa is unbalanced, and jerks to a halt beside her, letting out a surprised gasp. Adele ignores her, staring intently at the line of trees behind her, but she can't see anything.

If there is a body at the cliffs, maybe a lurking man is more sinister than she allowed.

She turns back to Melissa and permits herself to be led to the cliff top. A chopper hovers above them, and Adele cranes her neck. *Police, or a news crew?* She can't tell from this angle, but even as she stares, uniformed police officers emerge to their left and start ordering everyone back.

Swarming, Adele thinks, the solitary word flashing into her consciousness and out again. She watches them spill out from all directions, police tape appearing in long lines out of nowhere, it seemed to her. Onlookers were being gently herded away. It looked both orderly and chaotic at the same time—the sheer volume of them. Where had they all arrived from so suddenly?

"We need to get you to move behind the tape, please, ladies," a young constable says, his voice stern, his face fresh, and Adele starts to obediently move away, but Melissa looks at him eagerly. "What's going on, Officer? What have you found? Is it a body?"

The constable doesn't answer, just gestures for them to move along, and Adele suddenly tells him, her voice urgent: "My sister disappeared here fifteen years ago. Could it be...?" The sentence is left hanging, and out of the corner of her eye she sees Melissa's hand fly to her mouth.

Even Adele doesn't know what she is asking. Divers scoured the area, where it was safe to do so, which to be fair wasn't everywhere of interest. The bottom of the cliffs were violent, ferocious. In low tide, they could do a bit, but none of it was what Adele would call thorough.

They did their best. But there was a reason these cliffs were notorious. There was a reason bodies disappeared and were never found. When it all started coming out about the gay hate killings, someone had said—who was it? One of the police? A reporter?—that these cliffs were "the perfect murder weapon." *Didn't they find one victim ten years after he was reported missing, some bones finally working their way out after apparently being pushed deep inside some cracks in the cliffs, an unfortunate side effect of the relentless, violent waves?*

A criminal didn't even have to try to hide his victim. The surf would do it for him here, it seemed.

Adele has no doubt that her sister met her end here.

Her bones are probably deep inside a crevice down there, uncared for, not laid to rest.

Adele hasn't been able to rest, either.

Oh, it's better now. For a while it consumed her. Needing answers. Needing someone to blame. But that was normal, wasn't it?

She had put it aside, she had gotten on with her life. But it was always there. The questions. The wonderings. The blame.

Albert, though, seemed to have been able to rest. Celia's

slimy, smarmy husband had carried on with his perfectly charmed life, and avoided justice for Celia's murder (Adele is certain of it) for over fifteen years.

In the cafe across the road, Melissa stumbles her apologies, but Adele waves them away.

She hardly expects everyone else to ruminate on Celia and her killer the way that she, Adele, does.

The young constable gave them no information.

But could this be it?

Finally, some resolution?

Some justice?

For a while, immediately after Celia went missing, Adele had visited the local station almost daily. She'd remember something, something that might be relevant, usually something that incriminated Albert (an argument, a turn of phrase which seemed glaringly suspicious in hindsight).

The detectives never saw it that way, though. All they saw was a bitter sister, full of unreasonable hatred and rage. No one else ever had a bad word to say about Albert. He was well-loved, "a pillar of the community," as the saying goes. A local GP, looking after the people of Darlinghurst for many years before Celia disappeared and even more after. The community rallied around him. He claimed money was missing from their accounts (though it was just withdrawals here and there, no big lump sum around the time Celia disappeared, so it seemed just a convenient way to use some normal, everyday spending to try to incriminate Celia).

There was the fraudulent GoFundMe, too.

It was widely accepted that Celia had done a runner, and Adele had gone crazy with grief.

Except, Adele knew that Celia never ran from anything.

Celia was a fighter, not a runner. She would fight tooth and nail until the end. She liked to win too much to flee from anything.

And Adele wasn't crazy with grief. It was something far more complicated and unsettling than that.

No, Adele wasn't crazy with grief.

She was crazy with guilt, and maybe a little bit of rage.

Later that day, Adele walks into the police station on Roscoe Street with her head held high. She knows what they think of her. Her desperate scrabbling. Her need to find a culprit, someone to blame.

She wasn't always entirely lucid or rational when she spoke to them, she will give them that. She still can't quite account for the Adele that materialised around that time, most notably around the police involved in the case. Her capacity for anger. How primed she was to fight. She wasn't really sure who it was she was fighting, or even what she was fighting for. Celia's name, her memory to be unsullied? The police, to make them do their job? Her own feelings, which were so big, and so difficult, and so unmanageable?

But the police didn't really look into Albert as a murder suspect, either. So the low opinion went both ways.

Now, she speaks primly. "I'd like to talk to Detective Mulgrave, please." Mulgrave was her main contact in those early days. He was opinionated and arrogant and Adele disliked him immensely.

The woman behind the glass looks momentarily confused. "Oh. He retired last year. Is there something I can help you with?"

Adele is temporarily stumped. She doesn't want to have to explain it all again. She didn't like Mulgrave, but he knew exactly where she was coming from. He didn't agree with her or believe her or even particularly like her. But he knew the case. He knew all the little pieces of evidence Adele had tried to provide, over the years.

But maybe a new person, with fresh eyes, was actually a godsend.

"Yes. I'm here about what happened at the Tamarama Cliffs this morning. My sister went missing there fifteen years ago. If remains were found..." Her voice trails off, and she shakes herself in irritation. Even she doesn't know what she is asking. She wants someone just to tell her. To put it all right. To make sense of it, to close that chapter, to help her put it all behind her. To say, "Of course, you will be the first to know. We have all your details at the ready. We will take care of everything. Don't you worry about a thing."

"There will be a cold case on my sister. I think you concluded she had run away. But no one has heard from her since. Her bank accounts and passport have never been used. I always thought someone pushed her off the cliffs. If there is new evidence, I'd like to be informed."

The officer makes a few notes, and smiles. "Of course. Why don't you give me your details, and I'll pass them on to the relevant person, and—"

"No, thank you." Adele's voice is firm. She will not be fobbed off by this young nobody. "I'd like to speak to someone. I am happy to wait. I've been waiting for fifteen years, you know. What's another hour or two." Her voice is starting to get that shrill note again, that tone that makes people start to shift uncomfortably, and not quite meet her eye. Adele takes a deep breath, and leans on the counter—as though some physical assistance might also support her mind, the ever-so-subtle fraying around the edges. She feels it like effervescence; little tiny bubbles fizzing and spitting around the edges of her sanity.

The officer looks uncertain. "We don't have any information, yet. It will likely be a while before we have anything we can release. And I don't have anyone here who can talk to you any time soon."

Adele feels the old familiar rage rising in her, support of the countertop or not. Almost against her will, she can feel her chest puffing out, her eyes narrowing, as though she is pulling herself up to be just a little bit taller, a little bit more intimidating than she has ever actually been in her entire life.

Why is no one interested in justice except for her? Why can't they see what is right in front of them?

But before the bubbling rage manages to escape, she feels a gentle hand on her arm, and a familiar voice whispers, "Easy, tiger," in her ear, and Peter's face, always so reassuring, fills her vision.

Somehow he manages to simultaneously take her seriously and make her laugh a little at herself.

I know why you're here. I know how much it still hurts, his face seems to say.

But also: *Come on, crazy lady. Let's not harass the police again just yet.*

Or maybe: *Let's put your time to better use.*

It was true. How much time and energy had been lost to this already?

Adele lets Peter lead her away. She doesn't even look back. It doesn't even matter which of the above he's saying. His mere presence soothes her inner turmoil away.

Peter will sort it out. It's always a bit better if she leaves things to him. She gets too agitated, she knows. She doesn't always make sense. She comes across as whiny, or aggressive, her voice too high-pitched, her face too brittle, her reasoning not all that reasonable.

It's just, it's her *sister.*

And if it was your sister who was missing, and her loathsome husband living a happy, charmed life without her, making terrible accusations about her, sullying her memory, then how could you know how it affected a person, how it warped your vision, how it messed with reality?

When she looks back, Adele knows she became tunnel-visioned about convicting Albert of something. She knows she lost her mind a little bit.

But her sister was missing and no one was finding her, no one was solving it, and wouldn't anyone go a little bit crazy if it was them?

If it was their sister?

Especially if, perhaps, maybe, you worried that you were the reason that she was gone?

4

---

*A*FTER

Monday

December 2021

Harrison pauses in the hallway, and his shoulders slump.

"I'm telling you, they've found something down there." His mother's voice has that slightly manic quality to it, a tone he hasn't heard in so long he'd almost forgotten about it.

Almost.

He had been heading down to the kitchen to fix himself a snack. He's on the verge of turning eighteen, and fixing yourself a snack before going out to meet your mates is the soundtrack to his life right now. He just has a few more exams to get through, then it's summer holidays, Christmas, university.

Maybe.

He's applied for a Bachelor of Commerce at University of Technology Sydney. He's also applied for a Bachelor of Arts at the University of Melbourne.

He hasn't told his parents that last location. He knows exactly what his mother would think of the distance it would put between them.

Now, he weighs up his options. If he continues into the kitchen, his mother will see him. And she may well be distracted on the phone right now, but as soon as she hangs up, she's going to tell him things. Things he probably doesn't want to hear.

But if he goes back to his room to wait it out, see if she'll go to her room or go out, he might be late. The special someone he wants to hang out with might see someone brighter, shinier, more handsome. Timing is everything when you're nearly eighteen. You don't want to be so early you look too eager. But if you're too late, people have formed groups, or worse, pairs.

Paired off in cozy couples to snuggle under trees and sip warm beer.

He's paused there in indecision, and he doesn't really mean to listen, but as he tries to decide whether to press on or retreat, he can't help but overhear what Adele is saying. He can tell it's his Aunt Bethany on the other end. And he can tell that they're talking about Aunt Celia. Even though Aunt Celia hasn't been much of a topic in their household for years now, she had been such a feature for such a long time, the rhythms of the conversations are ingrained in his subconscious. The self-righteous, slightly panicked tension in his mother. The soothing, look-for-the-silver-lining, terrible attempts at good cheer of his aunt.

At one time it was so consuming that he hated Aunt Celia. That was all he ever heard about. Celia, Celia, Celia. Albert, Albert, Albert. He can't remember either of them in real life, but he can remember a bubbling, childish jealousy that they were all his mother ever talked about and cared about for a while.

Not childish. That's what his friend Tom tells him.

He has a point. You're allowed to have childish feelings when you're a child, right? Harrison's first memory is of being cold, wind whipping around him at the top of the cliffs that he grew up on, his mother snapping at him furiously, and a bunch of yellow papers tearing out of his hands and out to sea.

He asked his mother about it once, and she told him, without hesitation, that no such event ever occurred. "You must have dreamt that, darling," she'd said, squeezing his waist, her eyes full of love, and he faltered for a moment. It *was* crazy, wasn't it? That someone would ask a three-year-old child to help put up posters about their missing aunt on a freezing cold day on top of a cliff? A cliff with no railings? A cliff where dozens of people had died? And then shout at that child when they accidentally let the posters blow away?

And yet, he has seen those posters. There's still a handful in a drawer somewhere in this very house. And they are definitely yellow. The face staring out from them is definitely the face he has pictured in that memory for all these years.

But maybe he saw them, later, and overlaid them onto that memory?

Memories are tricky. People always think they're so reliable, without taking into account their own capacity to want a different narrative, a different truth, and how that might slowly chip away at a memory over the years, wearing it so smooth that eventually it looks nothing like the original.

Anyway, it was all in the past now. Harrison hadn't heard much mention of Aunt Celia in this house for at least a few years. It was like finally the waters had settled into something calm and peaceful. Adele seemed content. She still ran Aunt Celia's art gallery (sold, eventually, to someone else, but Adele stayed on), she walked around the headlands (after refusing to go near them for years, he believes), she volunteered at Harrison's school tutoring "troubled" kids, and complained about the things all his friends' mothers complained about: teenage sons, muddy boots left all over the house, worries about whether their kids would ever be able to afford to leave home, and now, with the pandemic, worry about whether life would ever go back to normal again.

And now, here Harrison was in the hallway, and Adele was almost certainly talking to Aunt Bethany about Aunt Celia, with the overzealous clip in her tone that suggested she was about to take some sort of action, and Harrison was overcome with resentment.

He just wanted to go out and have a good snog, or more, maybe, and forget about lockdowns, forget about exams, just have a little fun for an hour or two (it was a Monday, after all— he'd hardly be out late).

"Of course it could be her! And even if it's not, it's just like living it all over again! Remembering! The horror of it! The thought of her going over that cliff, terrified, in the dark..." At this point, Adele spins around flamboyantly gesturing with an arm the arc someone might take over the edge of a cliff, and stops short when she sees Harrison in the hallway. She stares at him for a moment, then turns back around, her voice dropping.

Harrison resolutely starts toward the fridge, pulling out some ham and cheese and slathering butter on some fancy sourdough bread as fast as he can. With his phone already in his pocket, it's easy enough to change his plans, have his snack on the road, and he grasps his sandwich in one hand and strides purposefully for the door.

"I'm going to Tom's for an hour. See you later, Mum!"

He doesn't even wait for her response.

And he's far too preoccupied with his own goals to remember that she isn't the first person he's heard talking about Aunt Celia this week.

"You're late."

Harrison swings around at the sound of the voice. It sounds

like chocolate and whiskey and languid mornings in bed entangled in arms and legs and sheets—two of which Harrison has never technically experienced, but it doesn't stop this particular voice conjuring up the images and warmth and desire that Harrison expects they might exude.

"I was trying to avoid my mother. I actually thought I was early. I ate on the way instead of at home."

"Well, maybe you are early. Maybe waiting for you just felt hard."

Harrison squints up at the familiar face (it has hovered above and around him in his very exciting and rather graphic fantasies for weeks now), the warmth of being desired new and exciting and consuming...and illicit. On his morning walks, Harrison has wondered, in fact, how much of this crush is true desire and how much is the exhilaration of wanting something a little bit taboo. He hasn't come to any conclusion on the matter and he doesn't much care. Whatever it is, it feels good, and he's a seventeen-year-old male, and he doesn't want to be a virgin anymore, and this might be as close as he's come to sex in a very long time (trying to be a teenager and get it on with anyone was difficult enough, without throwing pandemics and lockdowns and social distancing into the mix), and to hell with what it means or whether it's a good idea.

He smiles, self-consciously, and moves a little closer.

It may well be a Monday night, but he's never had so much freedom as he does right now. Adele has been very strict about study. Then there was basketball, which Harrison played a few nights a week, and by the time both of these things were done, there wasn't much time for much else. He thinks Adele may have orchestrated it that way, but he doesn't mind. He usually chats to Tom in hangouts while he studies, and they usually walk home from school together too. And there's plenty of mucking around with the basketball boys, as well. Harrison has never felt like he's missing out. He has always felt like he's gotten exactly enough of what he needs.

Until now.

Now, he has every intention of staying out much longer than an hour. He knows his mother will text him to check in once it's dark, but she won't worry like she once did. He's excelled all the way through school, he's won awards on the basketball court, he can see her relaxing before his very eyes. Letting him slip away into adulthood, patting herself on the back at how well she and his dad have launched him into the world. He has friends, he has work experience, he has goals and savings even. He's the only one of his friends who could go out and buy a car if he wanted to, or fund a gap year of travel, pending the pandemic, of course.

He's never given his parents any serious trouble. "He's just an easy kid," he's heard Adele telling people for years.

An easy kid.

Well, he might be about to turn that on its head. Throw a little hand grenade into that perception. But even now, Harrison doesn't think it will go that badly.

Adele lost her sister, then she lost her mind (everyone said so, these aren't *his* words). But Harrison thinks she's found her equilibrium. He's not worried about the fallout from this little secret.

Well, he wasn't.

Until people started talking again about bloody Aunt Celia.

5

February 2006 (four weeks before Celia disappeared)

Celia settles herself on the plush couch, rearranging the cushions until she feels just so.

She has one behind her, one beside her, and one on her lap to rest her hands on.

"It looks like you're building a fort around yourself over there," her therapist had said the first time she did it, and Celia supposed she was right, that was exactly what she was doing. Buffering herself. Creating a barrier. A nice, soft, fluffy barrier.

Her therapist, Evan (a silly name for a woman if ever Celia heard one), ought to be used to it. Not just because she was a thin, wiry little woman, with hard angles and a severe bun, who might just scare her patients a little and send them searching for fluffy barriers—but also just because of the nature of her profession. *Didn't everyone come in wanting to protect their little secrets, protect their soft underbellies? Was it possible that some people just walked in and spilled everything out, carelessly?*

Celia finds the thought distasteful.

Like Albert's paunch. She chuckles to herself, and Evan raises an eyebrow.

"I would think it's sensible to size you up a little, check that we're a good fit, before showing you all my vulnerable parts," she had replied, cool, appraising. Yes, yes, most people came to therapy to get help, to get answers, to learn how to find the answers inside themselves, even.

But that was not what Celia needed.

Celia needed something else.

"How has your week been?" Evan asks her, and Celia ponders this before answering.

At the start, she had felt as though she needed to give A grade answers immediately every time Evan asked her a question. Silences, stretching outward interminably, seemed like a waste of very expensive minutes. They also felt like she was failing somehow. It was an unfamiliar feeling, unexpected and unpleasant.

Now, she's acclimatised. She lets the thoughts roll around in her mind before opening her mouth.

The days of preparing for therapy were long gone, too. Having bullet points of what she wanted to talk about.

"It's been a bad week," she says, eventually.

Evan waits.

"With Albert, I mean."

Evan continues to wait.

"In fact, I think it's getting to the point...I mean. I think perhaps it might be time to do something about it."

When Albert returns from work that night, Celia is wearing the soft pink dress that he likes, and pulling a roast chicken out of the oven.

He comes over and presses his lips to hers, and gazes into her eyes.

"How was your day, darling? Tell me everything."

And Celia did, sort of—telling him about running into Adele's friend Melissa at the shops (she had a little baby bump, Celia didn't mention that), about the call from Bethany (the black sheep of the family, she'd randomly taken a job on a cruise ship and would be gone for a year, but after only a week was calling Celia amidst despair and vomit. She was horribly seasick and hated the ship with violent passion already). She told him about the argument with Adele, who wanted to host lunch for their mother's birthday next week, but Celia always hosted it and their house was bigger, after all, so wouldn't everyone be more comfortable with them? Wasn't that their *tradition*, even?

Adele did have Harrison, who was two, or was it three, and Adele did always seem to bring so much *stuff* with her now, bags and bags of stuff, and Celia really couldn't see quite why she needed to bring so much stuff for him. Didn't kids like to just bang on pots and pans? And just because Adele had a kid and it was more convenient for her to host at her place now (Harrison seemed to need so many naps still, wasn't he too old for that?), well that was Adele's choice, wasn't it? Celia didn't see why everything should have to revolve around children. Especially other people's children. She was still in that blissfully unaware stage of life where she was thinking about children, planning to have children, but had no idea whatsoever how one's life changed after children. She had no understanding of just how judgemental she was about other people's parenting, and how much she would cringe at all the things she declared to herself that she would never do, should they ever get the child they were trying for.

Or maybe she wouldn't, because that would require some insight, some self-reflection, and they weren't two of Celia's greatest strengths. She looked forward with laser focus, but what had already happened, well, it was done, so why bother?

Albert nodded and hummed, one hand affectionately on her waist the entire time. Celia felt a little crowded by it. Sometimes she wondered if Albert had read somewhere about how a devoted husband was supposed to act. It always seemed like he had turned the volume up one notch too far. Attentiveness taken to something a little unnatural. Affection just a little too close, and little too touchy. Concern for her well-being just a bit over the top, too much to be truly authentic. A bit *annoying,* if she was really honest with herself. She wished he'd take all of his perceived good husband qualities and just turn them down a little bit.

She wished he'd go to the pub with his friends just once in a while and forget the time and not come home till 4 a.m. and she could yell at him the next day for spending the grocery money on whiskey and forgetting to pick up the dry cleaning.

No, that wasn't true, she didn't wish that at all.

It was just sometimes she seemed trapped inside this strange caricature of a marriage, which looked perfect from the outside, and she couldn't really say exactly what the problem was, only that she had this sinking, nagging feeling that there was a problem, somewhere, and it didn't feel *right.*

"I booked you into a day spa session on Thursday," Albert says now, massaging her shoulders gently. "I thought it might help you relax before our appointment on Friday."

For some reason, Celia takes exception to the phrase "our." There was nothing jointly shared about it, except the desire to end up with a baby, and Celia was not even one hundred percent sure that that was a joint desire anymore, either.

But it was her body, her uterus, her vagina, her taking the drugs, her getting poked and prodded and measured and assessed (*this was her second appointment this week! So much time, so much effort*), all while Albert sat by glowing and beaming about what a good job he was doing looking after his wife as they tried to conceive a baby.

Distasteful.

There was that word again. Popping up here, there, and everywhere at present.

"I actually was planning lunch with Adele on Thursday, darling. I do wish you'd ask me, not just book things for me."

Albert pouted. "I was just trying to help," he said, and walked off into the lounge, stiff and sulky.

Had it always been like this?

Celia thinks perhaps in the early years, she had loved how Albert took charge of everything. He was so sure of his opinion about everything, from where to eat, to what to drink, to what she should wear. It was quite intoxicating to let someone else take care of every last thing (particularly when he also paid for it). Except now, when she was actually rather interested in taking the reins back, she found that Albert was a little unrelenting about relinquishing them.

"I've texted Adele!" Albert called out, sounding satisfied. "She's happy to reschedule lunch. She knows how important this cycle is for us."

It was the last of their embryos, though "last" was probably a stretch given only two from their first round of treatment had been viable for transfer, which was a disappointingly low number and felt very close to failure to Celia. She was used to numbers she was involved with being much more satisfying. More able to be flaunted. Success was who she was, at least in her own mind—she never failed to get what she wanted, and the gallery was certainly very profitable—and this was all feeling very problematic.

Also, if this one didn't take, they'd have to harvest some more eggs, and getting viable ones had been quite tricky the last time.

Not to mention invasive, and time-consuming, and generally depressing.

"I was looking forward to lunch." Now Celia was pouting and sulking. She actually hadn't been looking forward to lunch; all Adele talked about was Harrison, it was exhausting and boring, and also yes it made her feel jealous and left out, but still. If anyone was going to be cancelling lunch plans, it should be her, Celia, not Albert on her behalf.

"Let's just get this implantation done. Then *I'll* take you out to lunch," Albert tells her, and Celia sees that he really doesn't get any of it, at all.

But it doesn't matter, because she didn't tell him everything about her day. She didn't tell him about therapy (she's never told him about therapy), and she didn't tell him about the visitors she had that morning. And she certainly didn't tell him the fledgling plan that is starting to take shape in her mind, of exactly what she can do about it.

6

Tuesday

December 2021

"They never recovered the money. But the sister still insists the husband did it."

Bethany stops her cautious creeping toward the bathroom, frozen.

The coffee churns uneasily in her stomach. She gave up caffeine years ago, but this morning, something had made her order a full cream latte, on a whim, and now she feels jittery and sick. She's edging toward the bathroom like a severely hungover person, or someone elderly enough that they are worried about falling down, their hips giving way in a spectacular, embarrassing, and terribly painful fashion.

"Well, we'll know soon enough. Can they even get DNA or identify a body if it's been in the ocean for fifteen years?"

"Teeth, I reckon." The couple look too old and frail to be gleefully discussing recovered bodies over their coffees and cheesecake. They look like they should be the ones tottering to the bathroom, not Bethany. "Anyway, there's plenty of other people it could be. I reckon there's still some missing men in those cliffs that we'll never know about."

The headlands were home to a string of homicides over a period of decades. A gay beat, it was also a grimly convenient place to target gay men if you happened to be homophobic and vile, and Bethany comforts herself with the thought that it's probably just another gay guy whose body the police have found. Then she startles herself so much with her insensitivity that she stops her slow advance toward the bathroom for the second time, and feels horribly guilty as well as horribly sick.

Oh, it was all ghastly, and she forces herself to carry on. The police will let them know if there's anything relevant to Celia in this latest development. There's no point worrying about it. Adele will do enough of that.

Adele will do enough for the both of them.

Bethany has already had a phone call, had to try to calm her sister down. Although really, it's for her own benefit, not Adele's. She needs Adele to be calm and positive, so that her distress and rancour don't accidentally rub off on her, Bethany, and disrupt all the things she's put in place to cope all these years. Even if she agrees with Adele, which she doesn't often, but if she does—well, sometimes she takes the opposite stance anyway. Just to keep Adele's hysteria at bay.

Yes, they just need to wait for the police to work things out, and not go jumping to conclusions. Statistically speaking, it's far more likely to be more gay hate at play here, and the police will let them know soon enough.

She doesn't have a lot of faith in their abilities, though.

They found out not much of anything last time. Nothing about the GoFundMe, supposedly set up by Adele to help them with the costs of cancer treatment for Celia. Except, Celia didn't have cancer and she didn't have any problems with money. And Adele clearly had no idea what a GoFundMe was, let alone how to set up a fraudulent one.

No one had cashed in the fund, anyway. It had all been returned to (irate) donors, and because of complex technical things like VPNs (which the whole family had agreed they didn't understand, and very much doubted Celia did, either) the police had declared they couldn't track who or where it had been set up.

"The husband claimed the wife was behind that FundMe account," the woman was saying to the man when Bethany returned from the bathroom. "That she took off with the money. I gave to that FundMe."

"GoFundMe," the man corrected. "I was there, remember? But didn't our money get returned? So I don't think the wife went anywhere with it."

"He did say she was a bit sly about money. That he thought there should be more in their joint accounts. I bet the body isn't hers. I bet she's living somewhere nice and sunny, near the sea, laughing at us all," the woman continued, and Bethany has to agree with her. Celia was always so happy and smug and Albert was always so attentive and loving (*overdone and kind of sickly and self-interested, but at base still genuine*, Bethany thinks), and she never saw a single thing that would make her think *homicide*.

Still, Celia had *already* been living somewhere nice and sunny, near the sea. What advantage could there possibly have been to relocating somewhere else, with one hundredth of the funds, and a life sentence of needing to hide? It didn't really make any sense.

No family, either, in that life, though whether Celia would view that as a positive or negative, Bethany isn't sure.

She makes her way to the cashier to pay, thinking that the alternative narrative didn't make any sense, either, though. She doesn't particularly like Albert, but she doesn't think he's got it in him to push his wife off a cliff.

The GoFundMe though, that part she couldn't for the life of

her put to rest; it niggled and haunted and irritated her. Adele thought Celia was a victim of family violence, and it was to be her nest egg to escape with—but if that was the case, she would have cashed in on it; the fact that she didn't disproved Adele's theory as far as Bethany was concerned. Adele would say that Celia was murdered before she had the chance, that Albert had found out her plan and killed her off, but that was just ludicrous. Bethany always took the stance that though Celia was clever, there was no chance she could work out VPNs, hide her identity, and pull the whole thing off with no one being any the wiser. Especially because—Celia was essentially lazy. She'd never do anything herself that she could get someone else to do for her.

No, if anyone was going to do something like that, it would be her, Bethany, and it was vaguely irritating that no one even considered that *she* could have helped Celia set up such a thing. Her sisters thought she was so ditzy, so off-with-the-fairies, such a hippie and a do-gooder, but she could set up a GoFundMe no one would ever be able to trace with her eyes closed. She's had plenty of practice with using technology to keep things hidden. If she was in charge, nothing would ever come to light unless she allowed it to do so. It annoys her that her family don't know this about her. She was always "the dreamer" to them, a label they'd assigned her when she was about five years old, goddammit, like daydreaming instead of learning to read was such an odd choice for a five-year-old! And she'd never been able to shake the label since.

Despite that, she thinks the police will never find anything out about Celia's whereabouts. They couldn't even dig up the most obvious motive at the time. Which, obviously, *Bethany* didn't believe was a motive, or she would have told someone. It didn't make sense, it was the wrong way around. It *wasn't* a motive.

But if anyone knew about it, they might make out it was a

motive. It was a stretch, it was extreme, and Bethany once again wonders if she should have told someone. But it was too risky, and it wasn't relevant.

But she still can't believe the police never found out about it.

Maybe Adele was right. Maybe they were hopeless, and blinded by Albert's wealth and social standing.

Anyway, it's lucky for her they couldn't work out even the simplest thing, the thing that muddied all the waters, the thing that couldn't be explained or justified or understood.

Like, say, Albert sleeping with his sister-in-law.

7

Tuesday

December 2021

Peter hands Adele a double scoop of pistachio ice cream and lemon sorbet (an unlikely pairing which he once questioned religiously every time she ordered, but now orders for her without blinking, even when the teenage workers behind the counter do a double-take) and takes her other hand in his big, warm one as they stroll away from the ice cream van and back toward the cliffs.

Darling Peter.

It's far too cold for ice cream, and ice cream causes Adele some other issues anyway, but she loves her husband dearly for his relentlessness when it comes to looking out for her well-being.

"They'll call us if there's anything we need to know," he says, looking straight ahead, allowing Adele a little space to compose herself. She loves how he manages to make her feel completely seen, and then responds in a way that also makes her feel calm.

Yes, she's feeling that familiar agitation, that familiar panic about what happened to Celia. But he manages to convey that he sees it and gets it, and what they should do about it, all with so little fuss. Plus, an ice cream.

What a man, Adele thinks as she licks at the edges of her cone.

How did she get so lucky?

She had met Peter toward the end of her studies—a meandering Arts degree, without much purpose and without much effort, if she was perfectly honest with herself. She had no idea what she wanted to do with her life, and wasn't always entirely sure she wanted to *have* a life, either. Life seemed so big, and hard, and...*interminable.*

It just seemed to stretch out in front of her, on and on and on.

So many days to fill, so many meals to purge, and it was all quite exhausting, really.

And then Peter appeared, and he was the yin to her yang, as the saying goes. He was so relaxed. So easygoing. So warm and content. They did fun things. They joined a hiking group and travelled to far-flung places to walk for weeks at a time, carrying everything they needed on their backs. They went on a cruise ship and went bungee jumping in New Zealand. They ate at nice restaurants and Adele started to worry less and purge less in equal measure.

Peter was studying astronomy (Adele did not even know that that was a thing) and to this day Adele doesn't really quite grasp what it is he does, but he wears a suit to work every day (even still, through lockdowns and working from home) and he looks handsome and kind and as steady as a rock.

Adele moves a little closer to him, so their shoulders almost touch. She likes being close to Peter.

Only Peter really understands her relationship with Celia. Bethany doesn't. Her parents don't. But then, how can you articulate family dynamics to the people who are part of it? Family dynamics are tricky. Things get embedded in so deeply, so immovably. And Adele *knows* it is irrational, she knows it's no one's fault. On some level she even knows that she has to fight so hard for Celia's memory, for her case, because Celia really wasn't a very good sister to her at all. But to admit that is too much, even to herself. She skirts around the idea, and shies away from it, unable to face it or unpack it. She lets herself believe what everyone does, an understanding at the surface level: she is just defending her sister's memory, trying to find justice.

But even though she doesn't think about it in sentences, in words, she feels like Peter understands it. And being the yin to her yang, she leaves it with him. So she doesn't have to look at it. Not yet.

Once, long ago, before Celia disappeared, they'd been talking about the gallery, and Adele had been saying how grateful she was for the work, for the way Celia included her, and offered her work first, and he'd looked at her steadily, and said, "But she's really doing it for herself. You can see that, right?" She'd been in a fluster because Celia had asked her to fill in at the last minute. Something had come up, something Celia had glossed over, and Adele had read between the lines— they were trying to fall pregnant, though there was no "falling" about it. Falling sounds accidental, whimsical, easy. What Celia and Albert were doing was exhausting, and painful, and never-ending. So when Celia skirted around the why, Adele had immediately understood. It was something medical. Something important.

Adele had had her own plans that day, a special lunch at a fancy restaurant with Peter. It was their wedding anniversary and they had a low-key day planned. So Peter was put out, but he took it in his stride, because he understood her relationship with her sister. That this was not about putting Celia before him; it was about Adele's own sense of self. Her perceptions about who she was. What a good sister would do, even though these standards only ever seemed to apply to Adele, and not to Celia. Occasionally he would point something out to her, and Adele would shift uncomfortably, his perception sitting incongruously next to her own.

Like that day. Adele had expected to hear *something* from her sister. How the appointment went. Or even just a thank you for helping out on a hard day. But she didn't hear from Celia. What she did see, though, was pictures on Facebook of Celia with a man and a woman Adele didn't recognise. They were at a restaurant overlooking the Sydney Harbour Bridge, laughing and drinking expensive-looking cocktails.

Perhaps she'd gone out after her appointment to make herself feel better, Adele had reasoned to herself.

She never asked Celia.

She did start to look at her with slightly different eyes, though.

Peter's eyes. Peter, who was so fair, so reasonable, so calm and funny. Peter, who was so good at reading people. She trusted his judgement more than she trusted her own.

And what Peter seemed to think, what Peter drew her attention to gently every now and then, was that Celia asked a lot from people, a lot from Adele, without ever giving anything back, or ever seeming to really care for other people very much at all.

———

Without really intending to, they end up at the headlands, looking out across the Pacific Ocean. A sharp wind whips Adele's hair around her face and she holds her ice cream aloft, trying to keep her hair free from it.

Peter leads her to a bench and holds his hand out for the ice cream, and Adele hands it to him, and reties her hair back away from her face.

She smiles at her husband.

Then she stares at the cliff edge in front of her.

The last place Celia was known to be alive. If you believe her text messages, which the police don't, necessarily.

They think that Celia was last seen when she left her house at about eight o'clock. Albert claimed she went for a walk, and never came back. *"In the dark?!"* Adele had shrieked, because it was ludicrous, wasn't it? Who went out to exercise in the dark on the headlands?

It wasn't really dark, though. It was autumn, but it still felt like summer, the days long and ponderous, the sun and the smell of salt and hot chips lingering around the headlands well into the evening. But still. It wasn't Celia's habit to exercise at night. And Adele knows for a fact that Celia was at home that night, later than eight o'clock.

She came out, though, later.

Adele knows that too.

Celia texted her, after all. So why would Albert lie?

There's something else Adele knows, too, though, that she hasn't admitted to anyone, that's she's only just starting to admit to herself. That's taken her fifteen years to feel safe enough to consider, free from Celia and her subtle, toxic influence: that her life actually got a great deal better the night that Celia disappeared.

That her life is actually a great deal better without Celia in it.

8

Tuesday

December 2021

Marilyn Montana watches the by-line on her television screen with a deep sense of fear and regret.

She thinks she might be ready to make the phone call.

She regrets taking her husband's surname the same way she does every time she thinks about making an official phone call to someone important. She sounds like a busty stripper, not a librarian. But that's not her main regret at this moment.

She wasn't always a librarian. She used to be a social worker, before she got tired and burnt out and depressed. Her husband, Marty, still tells her she should have changed the type of work she did within social work, rather than retraining completely, but she always reminds him that they met training to be librarians, so his suggestion would have cost him a wife. So now they're Marilyn and Marty Montana and Marilyn winces every time they're introduced to anyone. *Why did she take his name?* She didn't even think about it at the time, but now it seems terribly patriarchal and senseless. The effort of changing her name was stupendous. Hours and hours of her life wasted filling out forms and getting copies certified and being on hold on the phone. When her previous name was a perfectly good name and would have saved her this relentless and monumental cringing every time she realised she would have to provide her details to someone on the other end of a formal phone call.

You really would have thought she'd be used to it by now. She and Marty have been together for thirteen years and married for twelve.

It was a whirlwind romance, as they say, and also their son is thirteen, and though Marilyn didn't much care about having kids out of wedlock, her mother most certainly did.

Sighing, Marilyn puts aside her knitting. Knitting reminds her of her grandmother, who has long since passed on, but taught Marilyn the basics when she was a little girl, and recently, when Marilyn had started to feel like something was missing, like some dissatisfaction was creeping into her life (*you have a teenager!* her mother had retorted, as though it were obvious Marilyn should feel discontent) Marty had bought her some needles and some bright, cheerful wool, and handed them to her grinning like the cat that got the cream, and it was so sweet that he remembered her stories about her grandmother, that Marilyn had started knitting immediately, with zero interest in knitting whatsoever.

But Marty knew her well. Now, she's like an addict. Getting her fix in every night. Just a few more lines. It's so soothing. So satisfying. Watching something materialise out of nothing right in front of her eyes. Something beautiful. Well, okay, something quite ugly for the first few attempts. But that only spurred her on more. She *would* make her grandmother proud, dammit!

She sighs, and grimaces, and picks up the phone. She's looked the number up several times already (*she doesn't need to call triple zero, for God's sake! But how do you talk to the police without calling the emergency number, or going in?)* and has it written in her diary, underlined several times, so it's right there. Easy enough to call, in theory.

She stares at the number for a few more seconds, then Marilyn calls the local police station.

They have a normal landline, just like everybody else. Or not, these days, Marilyn supposes. Even her mother has ditched her landline now, it's mobile or nothing, which is surprisingly progressive, given the hullabaloo about getting pregnant before she was married (it was the new century, for God's sake!). Unfortunately her mother usually forgets to charge her mobile, so Marilyn can never get on to her, and she's had a minor stroke recently, it's all very worrying and unacceptable.

Marilyn makes a mental note to do something about reconnecting her mother's landline this very day.

Then she's yanked back to her current problem. "Can I help you?" The voice on the other end of the line is terse and Marilyn bumbles straight in, fearing both that she is wasting the time of an important police officer, and also that she has done absolutely the very wrong thing by not wasting their time with this information fifteen years before.

"I'd like to talk to someone about Celia Armstrong. About the body found near the cliffs."

The by-line running under the news said as much: *Remains found at the base of the Tamarama Cliffs, the site of numerous gay hate murders in the 80s and 90s. Locals speculate it could be Celia Armstrong, who went missing in the area in 2006.* Earlier, the full coverage had cut away to an interview with Celia's sister, dug out from the archives, already looking low resolution and out of date.

In the interview, the wind was whipping around her face, the Pacific Ocean in the background. *Did they really interview Adele at the site her sister supposedly vanished, and may have been murdered?* Marilyn had wondered. On her screen, Adele leapt out at her, strident and hostile, something unnatural about the pitch of her voice. She was almost shouting—that the police weren't taking enough action, it had been four weeks and there was no progress. Something about the footage makes Marilyn recoil.

Now, Marty waits in the hallway, not realising he's holding his breath. There's a pause as the officer says something to Marilyn. Then:

"Well, I don't really know if it's anything, and I didn't notice at the time, it was only much later that it came to me, and I should have come forward then, and I don't know why I'm calling now to be honest, because I'm sure it's nothing, it's just that, well at that time, I worked as an intake worker at Bondi Community Centre, as a family violence worker, and I had an intake appointment with a woman who never showed up. And it was that same week that Celia disappeared. And the name didn't match—it was a Celia Smith. So like I said, I didn't think much of it. Of course I should have thought something of it! Smith is the fake name everyone gives, isn't it? If it's a Smith in a family violence service, it's almost certainly fake. Or just... well, it's a common name, too, isn't it? So it might not be fake! It might just be common. It's statistically...well. Never mind. But it was only later, there was a vigil, on her birthday, you know? Celia Armstrong's birthday. And it was the birth date of the woman who no-showed. The Celia Smith who never showed up. We collect a few basic details. Name, birth date, phone number, we try to get an address but often we don't. And I only remembered the birth date because it's my son's birthday, so I remembered the date. I commented on it when she made the appointment. And it seemed like—"

There is a long pause.

"Yes. I see." Marilyn's voice is small and frightened. She always was a straight A student. Marty knows how the feeling of doing something wrong has haunted her. But Albert was their family GP. She has always waved it away, it was just a coincidence, they had no-shows all the time, it was the nature of the work, it was hard to leave a violent relationship, things came up, you had to trust women to know what was right for them, to know their own safety inside out, to know when it was safe to talk or not safe to talk. To be ready to make that space, to have that opening ready when the right time came (except that they always needed more funding, more workers, how could you hold a space at the right time when there was never any funding and appointments were booked out months in advance?!)

"I can come down now."

You couldn't just send a police car around for a welfare check every time someone didn't show up—you risked putting them in more danger. Enraging a violent partner who was probably well-practiced at looking reasonable, at deceiving people. You called the number at the times they had specified were safe to call. And anyway, the Celia who called did not supply an address. Marty knows all this, Marilyn has told him it all anxiously, more than once. He knows it's how she justifies it to herself.

Not doing more.

He doesn't know whether she should have done more. He's not a social worker, he's a librarian. He's also a devoted husband, so he had comforted Marilyn and made murmuring sounds of agreement. He trusts and believes she knows what she is doing.

And also, Albert was their GP! He was warm and friendly and down-to-earth. A bit pompous, a bit self-important, but GPs *are* important, so you could hardly blame him. There is no way Albert could possibly have been a violent husband! Marty cannot imagine it. You might as well try to convince him that Albert is a fish.

Nevertheless, somewhere along the way, without actually discussing it, they had changed to a new doctor, and never mentioned it again.

At the time, Marilyn had tried to call the number Celia Smith had left several times. Marty knows this, too. It always just said, "This call cannot be connected."

Either she had given a fake number, or someone had cancelled her mobile phone service.

Either way, the Bondi Community Centre had never heard from Celia ever again.

And perhaps, no one else ever had, either.

9

Before

March 2006 (three weeks before Celia disappeared)

"Be careful, Harrison!"

Celia's voice is slightly shriller than she had intended it to be, but the child was a loose cannon. He careened around the house like he was being chased by twelve ninjas, and Celia had a whole heap of fine ceramics on display this week. It was by an artist from the gallery, and Celia was thinking about buying the whole set. It looked like magic in her expansive house, with its huge windows and grand white walls.

She didn't want it broken before she'd even made up her mind.

Albert ruffled Harrison's hair affectionately. "Slow down, Donatello," he stage-whispered to him, winking at Celia. "Remember to do your reconnaissance of the scene."

Celia is not impressed. Albert may well be more practiced at talking to kids, but she's pretty sure three-year-olds aren't watching the *Ninja Turtles*. His attempt to diffuse the situation and protect her ceramics irritates her somehow.

Albert isn't particularly keen on the bruised-peach hues of the bowls and vases, but he leaves the house decorating up to Celia. He never even complains about the cost.

"Where's Mum?" Adele is short, and Celia is conciliatory. After all, she got her way with the lunch. Everyone is coming to her house, just like always, and she has a roast in the oven and an impressive (store-bought) pavlova out on the kitchen bench, fruit draped around it appealingly. She feels quite proud of her efforts, and also a little bit bad about insisting that she host. Adele looks tired, and appears to have given up keeping tabs on her child—hence the careening around the house.

Celia studies her younger sister. It could be her revenge— letting Harrison break the odd expensive vase. But it's not Adele's style. She does just look genuinely haggard.

"She'll be here any moment," Celia replies, bright and cheerful. "Why don't you go sit out the back with Beth? There's some champagne on ice, and Harrison could play in the yard?" Her voice is hopeful, but Adele turns and walks toward the back door without another word.

Down the hallway, there is a great crash—Harrison hitting the wall so hard a painting rattles, and shrieking with laughter —but Adele does not even break her stride.

Bethany has already opened the champagne, and smiles up at Adele lazily.

"What a view," she sighs, as though this is the first time she's seen it, when in reality, she makes the same comment every time they gather here.

Which is all the time, Adele thinks grimly.

Still. It is beautiful. Adele and Peter live a couple of streets back, and walk the same tracks, shop at the same shops...but they don't have this view over the ocean.

They don't own a multimillion-dollar house.

Adele shakes herself. She doesn't know why it's all annoying her so much today. It's actually rather nice not to have to host, not to have to cook anything. Celia, always the expansive hostess, had waved away all Adele's suggestions. "You're coming to mine, why don't you just do nothing and let me look after it all," Celia has said, and for once Adele did exactly that. Usually, she'd still go to the markets, find some nice cheeses and charcuterie. Adele notes that there are none of these things out to snack on, and it gives her some satisfaction that Celia probably still expected her to provide them, despite her protests. Celia liked to look and sound generous and kind, without always necessarily wanting to follow through with actually being so.

Pouring herself a glass of what she hoped was something expensive, Adele flops down next to Bethany on a recliner.

"They're going to put a pool here, did Cee tell you?" Bethany is still gazing dreamily out to sea, her genuine pleasure and joy for Celia throwing Adele's bitter little thoughts into stark contrast.

Was Bethany always so nice?

"How wonderful for them," she says, bitchily, but if Bethany notices, she lets it wash over her without comment. She always was the dreamer, so happy for other people, so... unfocused. If Adele ever wanted to bitch about someone, she turned to Peter. Bethany just never bought in to the family arguments.

At least, Adele didn't think she did. Maybe Bethany and Celia got together and bitched about her. This thought had never occurred to Adele before and it unsettles her more than she cares for.

"I bet it was Celia's idea," she says, glancing at Bethany sideways. "Celia always manages to get what she wants, don't you think?" If Bethany was the dreamer of the family, Celia was the clever one. *Clever, pushing gently at the edges of manipulative,* Adele thinks.

Clever enough to be good at it.

Bethany doesn't bite though, just sips on her champagne and sighs happily. "Imagine family get-togethers once the pool is in. Harrison will love it. Even Dad might enjoy himself."

Adele doubts that very much. Her father is a man of very few words, and there is no chance whatsoever he will be frolicking in a swimming pool with the family. Not even with his only grandchild. Playing is not something John has ever been interested in, and Adele does not think he is going to start now.

"Adele!" Celia's voice startles both of them, and they turn to see her marching down the path, pushing Harrison in front of her roughly, and Adele sits up abruptly. Champagne slops over the edge of her flute, onto her jeans. "Shit," she mutters, then stands up, placing her glass down next to her.

"You okay, sweetie?" she asks Harrison, searching his eyes. He looks frightened, and shocked, and runs and buries his face between her legs.

"He broke a piece from the gallery," Celia says through gritted teeth. "And I have asked him and asked him to not run inside and he won't listen. So you can keep him out here with you, okay." It is not a question, and Adele glares at her sister.

"Perhaps if you'd let me host at my place, your precious designer home wouldn't be disrupted by the pesky realities of having a child around," she can't help shooting back, hoping that Celia feels the barb, feels her lack of children acutely, and then is ashamed of her cruelty. She crouches down to Harrison's level and turns her back on her sister. She doesn't want to see Celia's response or if her remark landed the way she had intended it. She just wants to make sure her child is okay.

"You okay, sweetie?" she asks Harrison again, and he nods uncertainly. "We need to remember to walk inside, not run, okay? But you can run around out here as much as you like. What do you think?" Harrison relaxes visibly, relieved he is not going to get into trouble. Aunt Celia *had* shrieked at him so many times not to run inside, but her house was so much bigger than his house, and there were so many great places to hide and gallop, that it was almost impossible to remember from moment to moment.

Although the giant crash and the shards of orange scattered across the gleaming white floor might certainly help him remember for a while.

That and a few other things.

Like the twist of pain in his arm, and the gaping chasm of terror that opened up between that moment, and the moment he was back with his mother.

They ate on the back lawn, and the conversation was strained.

Adele's mother, Jocelyn Stonwald, was a small, wiry woman who never sat still. She hovered around the periphery of the table, jumping up to top up glasses and fetch serviettes from the kitchen.

"For God's sake, Mum, sit down!" Adele hollered at one point, and the table fell silent. Adele had meant it to say, "It's your birthday! Let us look after you!" but it had sounded more like a rebuke, an irritation. Celia glared at her from across the table.

Adele turned to Bethany, ignoring her sister. It felt like a new power, ignoring Celia. Adele realises she has never done it before. She's always so worried about doing the right thing, about hurting people's feelings. She even manages to worry about *other* people hurting people's feelings and is ever ready to step in, make everyone feel better. *It's an over-sensitivity*, she thinks. When did she become so hypervigilant to other people?

It was a constant awareness, at the forefront of her mind. Who looked uncomfortable, who looked upset, who needed checking in with, what she could do to remedy the situation. If she'd said or done the wrong thing.

It was exhausting, it took time and effort and headspace and commitment, and Adele feels a sudden bitterness that nobody ever did any checking in or soothing or remedying for *her*. Something nags at her, on the edges of her consciousness, about purging and looking after people, and it feels important and illuminating, but as she tries to grab at it, it slips away, a strange sensation of hollowness and awareness at once.

"How did you get back home, anyway?" she asks Bethany, vowing to think about it more later. "I thought you'd be halfway across the ocean by now."

"No, we were travelling all the way up the coast. Lots of the guests on board were foreigners, it wasn't like Melbourne was the beginning."

Bethany had had a great farewell dinner before heading off to Melbourne to start her job three weeks before. No one had expected to see her for the best part of a year. But if she was dismayed about (another) failure, she didn't show it. "I just got off when we docked at the Sunshine Coast and caught a bus back down."

"So what will you do now?" Adele wishes she could keep the resentment out of her voice. What does it matter to her what Bethany did or didn't do? Except she was staying with Jocelyn and John again, and though she meant well, she was so vague and so helpless and hopeless that Adele knew Jocelyn would be running around after her, exhausting herself. And then inevitably calling on her, Adele, when she fell apart and needed help.

"You know Mum has just had an iron infusion," she adds, not waiting for Bethany to answer. "It might be good that you're with her. You could help her out with things. Make sure she slows down, rests."

Bethany nods enthusiastically. Adele wonders if she genuinely means it, or if she knows she will never actually get around to helping Jocelyn with anything. Beth will talk and dream and plot and plan with their mother, and not notice that Jocelyn has cooked three meals and cleaned the entire house around her in the meantime.

For the first time in a long time, Adele feels very strongly that she doesn't want to be around these people. She wants to take Peter and Harrison by the hands and walk right out of this damn perfect garden and maybe never come back again. From Celia, with her pretence that family mattered, all while being self-centred and smug; from Bethany, and her dreamy, unfocused eyes and failure to help with anything at all; and even from her parents, with Jocelyn trying so hard all the time to be the perfect mother when she had never been that, not even for a moment, and Adele was exhausted from the effort of helping Jocelyn to maintain the self-delusion.

And her father, well. John was virtually invisible. He made no noise, he showed no interest, and it really mattered not one little jot if he was with them at all.

It all suddenly seemed like such a giant lie, such a pointless fabrication or parody of family, that Adele wanted to shield her family of choice from it—*dear God, please let Peter and her and Harrison never end up like this!* But she also, for the first time, felt forcefully, unequivocally, that she rejected this family, once and for all.

It had never actually occurred to her before that she didn't have to stay connected to them if all they did was vex and wound her. She could get up, right now, just stand up and declare that they were leaving. She could make some grand statement, or let her exit be statement enough. She could walk away.

The thought is intoxicating.

"Would you please pass the chicken, Dell?" her father asks her gruffly, interrupting her fanciful daydream and her rage, and Adele immediately falls back into her usual place at the table—acquiescing, a little bit subservient, and always wanting to please.

She passes the chicken, and doesn't say a word.

10

Tuesday

December 2021

Does he remember, even?

Adele peers at Albert. He's pushing his trolley jauntily, without a care in the world. If he's worried about the morbid discovery on the cliffs, he's not showing it.

She rarely runs in to him. So rarely that she didn't ever seriously consider moving away. In the immediate aftermath, yes, she talked to Peter about it. Hysterically, perhaps. Not wanting to be near that man. But they didn't move in the same circles. This is only the third time Adele has seen Albert at the supermarket. He probably gets everything delivered, like she does. Just on the odd occasion, she forgets something and has to face the crowds at their local market or here, in the collection of shops and hairdressers and bottle-o's.

The sight of Albert makes her stomach turn, even after all this time.

Adele was drunk, that night. She had felt like she couldn't

move, like she was trapped inside her body, glued to the mattress in the spare bedroom, paralysed.

But she remembers. Every touch, every look.

And every memory makes her shudder. Blanch, even.

But none so much as that last look. Not from Albert. He'd finished, and rolled off her, letting out a huge fart, and then immediately passing out. If Adele had thought she was repulsed before, she was almost retching after that.

No, it wasn't him leering at her, or the eager way he looked at her after every touch, every thrust, expecting to see rapture, never once doubting there'd be anything else. His ego was staggering. Through her stupor, she was sure she'd grimaced once, sobriety creeping through a small crack, horrifying her with what she was doing, and he'd met her eyes, and God knows what he thought he saw, but apparently it wasn't her disgust, at him and at herself. He'd thrust into her harder, and looked so smug, so self-satisfied, like she should be grateful that he deigned to slip his dick into her, or that he perceived her to be loving it, his puny little dick and his grotesque grunting. He'd grinned stupidly at her, pumping away, whispering something that sounded like, "I always wanted you, too, Addy."

No one called her Addy except Celia. Did Albert know how much she hated that nickname? Was he taunting her?

"Noooo," she'd slurred, and wished she had the strength to push him off her, but her limbs weren't working, they felt like spaghetti, like she was conscious but not conscious at the same time.

"Yesssss," he'd purred back at her, and he'd cum—inside her!—and rolled off her, and was snoring and farting almost immediately. The whole thing was burned into her brain like the worst of the worst memories, which was so unfair, wasn't that the only saving grace of being so drunk, that you couldn't remember things, that you could forget your worst moments, your worst, most unforgivable behaviour?

So his gaze lived on in her memories, yes.

But it was the eyes through the crack in the door that she sees, through the days and through the decades.

She was so drunk. She should never have been getting drunk with Albert in the first place. She should have known better. *Should have should have should have*...but through all her self-recriminations, another little voice, a voice she quite likes, says: "Yes, but who wants to have sex with an almost unconscious woman?"

And the other question remains, what she doesn't know, what she can never be sure of, is—did Celia see them?

Celia was supposed to be at the gallery. Adele and Bethany had come around for dinner, but Celia was held up, an opening that was dragging on, she said to start without her, and Adele and Albert had certainly started on the wine, but they'd never gotten around to making dinner.

Bethany, at some point, must have excused herself and disappeared. Albert would never have had sex with her if Bethany was in the next room, would he? Which only left Celia, coming home.

Was it Celia, peering through the crack in the door?

And did what she see have anything to do with why she's now gone?

It was the week before the vanishing. How could it be a coincidence?

Everyone thought her hostility was misplaced. Even Bethany had tried to gently turn her away from it. They'd been sitting in Adele's kitchen a week after Celia had disappeared.

"Why are you so sure Albert has something to do with it?"

"It's always the husband. Women disappear, it's the husband."

"But he adores Celia. You've seen him. The man is broken."

And Adele could hardly say that she'd slept with Albert just last week, could she? That he wasn't nearly as devoted as he appeared.

That there was something cold, something calculated in the way he'd fucked her. The way he'd looked at her. Like she was an...experiment. Or a challenge.

It was as close as Adele had ever come to feeling like a notch on a bedpost, and something about it—besides the obvious—was deeply, profoundly unsettling.

Over time, Adele could see that she could have gone to the police. She'd never experienced drunkenness like that before or since, and perhaps it was to alleviate her conscience (she was well aware that that could be the case), but she also was fairly confident that Albert had slipped something into her drink. He was a doctor, after all. He'd admitted he'd always wanted her. And there was that quality to her stupor that Adele was sure wasn't alcohol. Like she was sort of awake, but had lost control of her limbs. Like she had no strength.

Had Albert convinced her that she consented at the time?

With another fifteen years' experience under her belt, Adele now calls it the night that Albert raped her. And yet, still, after all this time, it's shame and guilt that come first, almost winding her with their force and magnitude, whenever she thinks about Albert.

Did she lead him on?

Did she drunkenly suggest it?

Was it her fault?

She's never told anyone about it, ever. Not Bethany. Not the police. And certainly not Peter, who was at home looking after Harrison that night, and who looked after her so beautifully for the two days following that her hangover lasted.

"I'm so glad you had a good night with your sisters," he'd said, his kind face so earnestly delighted (Adele had withdrawn from them almost completely after Jocelyn's birthday, and that dinner had been Celia trying extra hard to make it up to her, and while Peter was not Celia's greatest fan, he was definitely Adele's greatest fan, and he would support whatever she wanted, even dinner with her sisters), that she just couldn't bear to think about it for one more single minute.

But did Albert having sex with her make him more guilty, or less?

Maybe Celia did see them, and maybe she really did just run away.

11

AFTER

Tuesday

December 2021

Can you come out?

Harrison lights up instantaneously. Like the text message was a light switch and bang, he was on.

They'd only seen each other yesterday! Someone was keen.

Harrison grins to himself.

Not really, he replies. *I'm studying, and I promised Mum I'd help her with something in the garden.*

He hits send and then cringes. He sounds so...young. A mummy's boy. Doing his homework and helping his mummy.

But his phone lights up again immediately: *So helpful. I'll imagine you wielding a chainsaw topless, shall I?*

Harrison blushes.

Don't tell me. Let me imagine, the next text comes through, with a suggestive winking emoji, and Harrison blushes some more. He doesn't quite know how to respond. How to *be*. He's never liked anyone quite so much and it's discombobulating. He had thought that he somehow managed to skip that awkward teenage phase, where you don't quite know where your limbs go or what to say to people. But perhaps he had just never cared enough about who was watching. Right now, he was as self-conscious and fumbling as a thirteen-year-old.

Happy imagining, he texts back, copying the suggestive emoji, then turns and face plants on his bed, groaning. And spends the next hour doing no study whatsoever, but agonising over what he might have said or should have said, wondering if the silence means that his last message was too cocky, too sexual, too bland, too *something.*

He's so *young.* That's the problem. When your lover is older (lover! The word slips in without Harrison even hesitating, and fills him with shivers and thrills) you can't help but worry about your age. *Is he too inexperienced? Too immature? Too...gangly and teenage-like?*

He doesn't even notice that Adele never comes to get him to dig out the seedlings that have sprung up under the ungainly crepe myrtle in the backyard (more a hand shovel than a chainsaw kind of job, really, but he's not going to correct anyone).

He pays no heed to the news floating around his house, weighing his mother down with both renewed hope and accumulated despair, that the remains found at the bottom of the cliffs have not been identified, but are believed to be the remains of a female aged between twenty-five and thirty-five, and efforts to identify them are ongoing. However, the statement released reveals that the victim had two broken and subsequently healed radius bones, which would help in the identification process, and with which they had ruled out the victim being missing local woman, Celia Armstrong (who did otherwise fit the description).

And he has completely forgotten what his lover had just last week told him, about seeing Celia and Albert fighting on the cliffs around the time that Celia disappeared, but had turned away and left before seeing how that argument ended...and did Harrison think telling his parents would be a good idea?

Later, it will seem impossible to have forgotten such a thing, but in the moment, in the thrall and crush and exhilaration of first love, anything outside that is immediately rendered worthless to his over-excited brain, and given not one ounce of attention, however much someone else might love to hear it.

That and the fact that he is primed to shut out anything to do with Celia, because Celia not only stole his mother from him for a good few years, because he had to compete with a missing woman for his mother's attention, but also because pre-memory, in his bones, an imprinted sense of danger, something out of reach, words not remembered but not forgotten, send him scurrying away from Celia toward something warmer and more light.

12

After

Wednesday

December 2021

In the front of the house, Jocelyn fusses around Adele's kitchen so busily that Adele wants to scream.

"Mum, you don't need to clean my kitchen. I thought you just wanted a nice cup of tea."

It will take Jocelyn half the day to get to the point if Adele doesn't help her. There will definitely be a point to her visit, and Adele is absolutely sure that it is very clear in Jocelyn's mind, but for some reason she can never just come out and say it, especially if it's controversial.

"The body isn't her," Adele goes on, taking a guess that that is what is on her mother's radar. Or perhaps she herself just wants to talk about it. It's surprisingly disappointing, which is an absolutely awful and terrifying thing to think. If the body is not Celia, then there is still a chance that Celia is alive and well somewhere, perfectly happy.

But if it was Celia, then Adele could finally close that door.

It's like an open wound, that never quite heals over.

What happened to Celia?

Did Adele contribute to it?

For the first time, Adele can see the link between her relentless campaigning for justice and her sense of guilt. Why had she never joined those dots before? Peter had certainly tried to gently talk to her about it. She remembers one time, where he held her through a fit of tears (and they were like a fit —loud, violent, physical), then asked her softly: "Do you ever wonder if perhaps you're so upset not because you miss Celia, but because you don't?" And of course Adele had turned on him like a viper, his suggestion so vile and ugly it was just another thing to fill her with rage.

But after the rage subsided, and the months and years passed, she had realised that he was right.

She and Celia had not had a good relationship. Celia took advantage of Adele. And Adele had to take some responsibility for that: she was such a people pleaser. A *pathological accommodator,* Peter had called her once—lovingly, absolutely. But also with razor-sharp insight. She accommodated everyone else's needs even to her own detriment. She found it hard to say no. On the rare occasion she did say no, she felt so guilty and worried so much about how she was perceived and indeed, how she perceived herself, that it took up more energy than just saying yes and doing the damn thing, whatever it was, would have done.

But on the flip side, Celia kept asking. Celia was always taking.

Celia was never giving back.

And it was horrible to admit it, even to herself—but Adele's life without Celia in it looked much the same, on an emotional level, as her life with Celia in it. That's how little support and connection Celia actually offered.

In fact, life without Celia also meant life without endless requests and demands on her time and attention. Yes, yes, Celia always asked so nicely. So nicely sometimes Adele ended up thinking doing Celia a favour was her, Adele's, idea. And it was definitely only once Celia had disappeared from her life that Adele could actually start to see how much she gave to Celia, how put upon she was. *Why did she never notice when it was happening?*

Now, Jocelyn looks surprised. "You didn't actually expect it would be, did you?"

Celia had never had broken forearms, so that was that.

Adele feels confused. "Yes, of course I thought it could be. Didn't you?"

Jocelyn doesn't meet Adele's eyes. "No, I didn't. It's so long ago, darling. I like to think she's off somewhere having a nice life. She's not here, and we all have to go on without her. What will finding a body change?"

Adele is so shocked by this that she just stares at her mother. For some reason, she had thought Jocelyn's feelings would be a more amplified version of her own. How could Jocelyn sleep at night, not knowing what had happened to her daughter?

And yet apparently she had found a way to live with it. So much so that finding remains at the cliffs barely caused her to stumble, let alone break her stride.

"What did you want to talk about then?" Adele says, abruptly. She is finding this conversation remarkably upsetting. Adele had always known her mother was a master at rejecting emotions, but this was something else.

How could Jocelyn just give up like that? Celia might not have been a great sister, but siblings always have rivalries, don't they? What could possibly make Jocelyn less distraught about all this than Adele? How was it possible that Jocelyn could move past it?

The alternative—being waylaid by it forever, and never getting back to life—seems somehow like a better option than this casual acceptance, this absence of strong feelings. Not better for Jocelyn, Adele can see that; but more understandable to Adele.

"Why do I need to want to talk about something?" Jocelyn is miffed, but Adele doesn't care. "Can't I just want to see my daughter?"

Adele sits and stares at her mother, eyes steely, refusing to speak. Enjoying genuine time together, just for the sake of it, has never been part of their relationship. Usually, Adele would cave first, allow her mother the delusion. But today, she just can't seem to make herself play her assigned role.

Eventually, the silence is too much for Jocelyn. She sighs. "The police called. As part of their investigations, they found that a domestic violence service had a no-show from a Celia the week she disappeared. They were asking questions. It's probably moot now, given the body isn't her. But they wanted to know if we'd seen anything, or were ever worried." Jocelyn looks uncomfortable, her eyes sliding away from Adele's again, as she adds: "I told them that we weren't."

"*What?!*" Adele explodes. She had been sitting listening thinking, *at last. At last someone is looking at Albert.* And then Jocelyn had gone and turned them away! "You know he controlled everything. He controlled their money. He controlled what they did. It's a classic sign."

"Yes but he never kept her from us. He never hit her. He never withheld money. He just liked to see where it was all going. *I* do that, darling. With Daddy. That's not abuse, that's knowing who is better with finances in the relationship, that's protecting your partnership, not abusing it."

Adele thinks of her father, so quiet and...hen-pecked? And is not so sure. She loves her mother, she really does, but Jocelyn is not an easy person to live with, and never has been. Jocelyn likes everything just so. Just right. Done her way. She gets an idea in her head and sticks to it rigidly, brittle little lines around her mouth forming if anyone should dare to offer an alternate approach. And God forbid they talk about it.

No, if Jocelyn is upset, she gets her fixed little frown, she bangs around the house making sure everyone knows how hurt or angry she is, but she will never say a word. She will never discuss it. Once, Peter had ventured to say, "You seem upset, Jocelyn. What's on your mind, we'll work it out?" and the entire family had stared at him like he was completely insane, because talking and understanding and compromising was not how they did things in this family.

Jocelyn had slammed down her teacup, splitting it neatly in two, and stalked out of the room, and Adele's sisters had melted away. "What?" Peter had said to Adele, eyebrows raised, genuinely baffled by what he had done to spark such a reaction, and Adele had loved him even more.

She still cleaned up the mess, though.

It was almost their private joke now. Peter continued to do this for the next fifteen years, and Jocelyn continued to go off in a huff. Adele continued to clean up the mess. She was the fixer, after all. Kind, sensitive, making everything all right. Making everyone feel okay about themselves. Peter's words changed absolutely nothing, except Adele's love for her husband. He would not be broken by her family. He would not become rigid and bad at communicating along with them. He would not accept this as the status quo. He was relentlessly normal and well-adjusted in the face of whatever it was her family did when they got together.

"Anyway, that's not why I'm here," Jocelyn continues now, irritably, as though she hadn't just stoked the fire her daughter had been trying to coax to life for decades, then promptly doused it with water.

Adele sits up suddenly, her eyes a little wild. "What if Celia *did* break her arms, Mum! What if *Albert* broke them! He's a *doctor,* for God's sake! If anyone could fix a break and keep it from us, it would be Albert. What about that time they went to Italy for two months? It could easily have happened there. Celia could have been ashamed, she could have believed it was an accident, she could have kept it from us, and we'd never even have known!"

Adele can feel the familiar unsteadiness, the tunnel vision, everything else falling away. It's ridiculous, she knows she has come further than this, but it's habitual, rushing to help Celia, to make everything all right for Celia, to make excuses for Celia. Even after fifteen years, it hasn't gone away. As though if she can find an explanation, or rationale for Celia's behaviour, then the world is the right way up again.

"Nonsense, we were video calling the whole time they were away, remember? It was such a novelty, it had just come in, Celia loved it. You must remember! I worried about how much it was costing them, but she always waved my concerns away. *Literally.* So, we would have noticed a broken arm, for sure. You're clutching at straws, darling." Jocelyn looks annoyed, and exasperated. "Would you prefer it if this body *was* your sister?" she adds, her voice rising several octaves, something jarring and familiar in her tone, an implied accusation Adele can't quite put her finger on, like she isn't enough, or there's something *wrong* with her, just for having feelings, for trying to process them.

Adele puts her head in her hands, and rests her elbows on her dining table. She suddenly feels very tired. She has a sudden urge to binge and purge, and wants Jocelyn to leave. No one else is home. She could be done and feel better in an hour.

When Jocelyn first discovered Adele's purging—she was just thirteen, and she didn't tell her mother, but she'd been purging for a whole lot longer than she admitted—it was impossibly hard to make Jocelyn understand. Adele didn't really understand herself. But she knew enough to know that the personal trainer and the dietician her mother brought in to help her "manage her worries about her body" weren't going to help her in the slightest. "It's not about my weight," she'd tried to gently protest, and it was true, Adele was just a normal-sized teenager, and she didn't need to try to slim down at all.

No, it was about how it settled her mind. The focus of it. The finding, and hoarding the right foods. The pressure in her head. The fizzing, edgy, unsettled feelings that made her unable to cope, unable to think. How the purging made her *mind* weightless, not her body. How all her thoughts settled into something normal, something coherent, afterward. For a while.

She wasn't immune to what the world asked of her. You'd have to be blind to not feel some pressure to be thin, and sleek, and toned. And Adele did want that, she wanted that very badly, it was absolutely internalised as worthiness in her young mind. And with therapy she had come to understand they were connected. But they didn't feel connected, at the time.

"You couldn't control the things that were making you feel unlovable," her therapist had once told her. *"So you tried to control the one thing you feel you can control in order to be loved. How you looked."*

Adele had turned this around and around in her mind for a long time, and finally decided that that may well be true. But what felt truer, in her bones, was that sometimes, she just needed her mind to shut up, and purging was, however short-lived, a road map to peace and quiet for a little while. The best way she ever managed to describe it was as an addiction. It was just like blotting the world out with booze, except instead of booze, it was this ritual. Find food. Eat it. Purge. She even felt drunk, afterwards. She would never trust herself to drive, to make decisions, to remember things after a bout of purging. Something happened in her mind that was completely out of control, which did not fit at all with her therapist's narrative that she was trying to gain control when her life felt most out of control. No, it felt more like she was deliberately throwing control away, and revelling in feeling completely unruly and ungovernable for a little while.

It still didn't make any sense, but why would it? It was a completely nonsensical thing to do at any time.

At forty-five, with her life going just fine, it was completely, utterly insane.

Why was it rearing its ugly head again this week?

But she's pulled out of her reverie, her wondering just how worried she should be about this relapse, by Jocelyn's next words:

"Anyway, I wanted to talk to you about something else."

13

March 2006 (two weeks before Celia disappeared)

Celia thinks about calling Adele, or Bethany, and doesn't.

When did things change so much that she wouldn't call her sisters when she needed help?

Adele would just be smug that her marriage was in trouble. Especially after that lunch. Now was definitely not a good time to call Adele. And Bethany, well there was something secretive about Bethany. Something Celia didn't trust. She couldn't put her finger on it, but she was sure something was going on with her that made Celia wary. You needed information before confiding in people. You needed to know where they were in their lives. What might influence their reactions.

Usually, Celia would make it her business to find out. But she has enough problems of her own without adding Bethany's to them. And with Bethany, she'd more likely than not need help. Request input. She'd never had a proper job (Celia manages to forget that her "proper" job had consisted solely of Albert buying her an art gallery as soon as she left school; with everything already working like clockwork, and with wonderful employees already on hand, it did not require very much input from Celia at all) and never had a proper boyfriend, and was always leaning on people. It looked so needy. Celia found that distasteful, too.

Celia thinks back to the men on her doorstep (*was "men" the right description? One of them looked disturbingly young*). It felt like months had passed, not just a week or two. She's impressed by her own calm thoughtfulness. Not needy, not reactive. She had felt mildly unwell before she got out of bed that day, and she certainly felt unwell after their visit. But she held it close to her chest, and thought about it.

It couldn't be true, could it? Albert was pompous, and arrogant, and he liked getting his own way. But *bisexual?* She really couldn't believe it. She certainly couldn't believe that she had missed it somehow. And she could believe even less that he had ripped off that young man for a mere two hundred dollars.

They'd looked so aggressive. She had been frightened, momentarily. But she had quickly realised that they were more afraid than she was. And so obviously camp, just *flaunting* it, with tight leather pants and stud-covered singlets. *The hair, my God,* she thinks. *How long did it take them to get that hair every morning?*

So they'd all stood at her front door, staring at each other. One of them, the older one, was cracking a belt together like he was in some ridiculous sitcom, trying to intimidate her, except she thinks he had it confused with something from a porn movie, and it seemed overtly sexual, not threatening. And she may well have been intimidated if they had been straight (*was that sexist? Or homophobic?* Celia really doesn't know) but they looked kind of hopeless and...vulnerable.

"Can I help you?" she'd said, when she had recovered herself, and her heart rate had slowed back down.

"Yes. We're looking for Albert."

"That's my husband. And he's not here, he's at work. Can I

help you with...whatever it is?" she had spoken gingerly, really not sure that there was anything she could help these two punks with.

"Yes." The older one had stepped into the doorway, the way he leant on the frame had actually intimidated Celia, and she had taken a step back, her heart starting to hammer in her chest again. "Albert ripped off my friend here, for sexual services provided last week. And we had to do a little digging around to find him, but find him we did. You know it's called rape by deception, right? Dan could press charges."

Celia had still not caught up with the reality facing her. It did not even enter her mind that Albert had paid anyone, let alone a *man,* for sexual services.

She stared at them blankly. "I'm sorry...?"

The talker seemed to have suddenly taken pity on her. He looked uncertain. "Your husband hired my friend Dan here for sex last week. They agreed on three hundred dollars. But two of the notes in the envelope were photocopies. Dan should have checked, it's true. But your husband also shouldn't be a lying little shit. Not if he wants to keep his homosexual activities a secret from his wife, that is. They always think we won't find them, or that we'll be too ashamed to follow it up," he'd gone on, muttering this last bit over his shoulder to Dan, and he seemed to Celia more resigned than frustrated or even angry. Resigned that this was the stuff they just had to do.

Celia, for her part, felt nothing; they obviously had the wrong Albert. "Look, I don't know what you think happened. But my husband likes women. You've come to the wrong place. Or maybe someone gave his name because they thought that would be funny. Or maybe—"

But the first guy had spoken over the top of her, indicating a photo on the wall behind Celia. "That him?" he'd said.

It was a photo of Celia and Albert on their wedding day. Celia's smile was radiant. It truly was the best day of her life.

The possibilities stretched out in front of her, magnificent. Albert had just inherited a considerable sum from his father's passing, and bought their house and her gallery. He is smiling his devastatingly handsome smile, his eyes half-closed, whispering something in Celia's ear, filling her with joy and laughter. He's slimmer, but looks much the same.

"Yes," said Dan, and Celia simply did not accept this could be true.

"No," she'd said, her voice firm. Albert was a bit controlling, a bit of an ass sometimes, but he was not a liar. He was not a cheat. Celia is sure she knows exactly what makes her husband tick, and this has never even entered her mind as a possibility. It was more believable that these men were trying to scam her. She stamped her foot in indignation. "I will not stand for this! In my own home. You ought to be ashamed of yourselves. And if you think I'm going to be blackmailed about some story you've made up—"

Here, though, Dan had held up his phone. "Is this his number?" he'd asked. And for one irrational moment, Celia had wished that Albert had had the foresight to get a burner phone if he was going to text such distasteful things to young boys, so she could live in plausible deniability, so she would not have to confront this horror, and respond to it.

She had closed her eyes, and hadn't needed to confirm it. It was clear that she had recognised the number, and the men—Jonno and Dan—had thought she was traumatised by the contents of the text message.

"What do you need?" she'd asked, her voice flat, and Dan and Jonno will later discuss how surprisingly respectful Celia was, given the circumstances. Usually, they are blamed for everything, as though if sex workers didn't exist, these men would be delightfully faithful husbands for their entire lives.

But at the time, Jonno had just told Celia that they'd like the two hundred dollars, plus an extra fifty for their trouble. He

hadn't actually expected her to comply. They had thought they
would find Albert, and he would be so freaked out they had
found his home address (people often think sex workers are
stupid, too, that they wouldn't have the resources to track a
person down who'd committed a crime against them) that he
would hand over the money owed. And even if he didn't, the
police may not take sex workers getting stolen from very
seriously, but they certainly take the passing on of fraudulent
money very seriously indeed. And this dude, who clearly could
afford to pay...well, Jonno would have gone to the police about
him just out of spite.

But he was older and more jaded than Dan. Dan still
believed that people were basically good.

Still. As Celia had peeled notes from her wallet, her face
blank, Jonno had felt a desperate need to make her feel better.
He felt bad that they hammed up their gayness (it really was
just meant to make Albert—had he been home—want to get
them off his doorstep quick smart, usually it was just T-shirts
and jeans, and Jonno felt weirdly exposed and too big, too
imposing all at once). "It's more common than you think," he'd
said, stumbling over his words. "It doesn't mean he doesn't
love you, or want to be married. Or even that he's gay.
Sometimes men just want to experiment. Try something new."
His words sounded hollow. It was the truth; he had many
clients who were happily married to women with no desire to
ever leave their wives. They just liked a little dick on the side
sometimes.

But he also knew that, when your world was turned upside
down by something so shocking you could barely conceive of it,
such words are hardly going to make everything go back to
normal, and be okay.

Now, Celia lies on a recliner on her back deck.

She usually lies here picturing the swimming pool, how
she'll style the new deck.

But now she's lying here, thinking about that giant jerk of a husband, and feeling not pain, or betrayal, or despair.

She's mulled over it, looked at it from this way and that, thought through her options, and felt surprisingly calm the entire time. But something's been brewing inside her, apparently, because as she lies on the deck, what Celia feels is a rage so great, she thinks when Albert comes home, she might actually even kill him.

14

Wednesday

December 2021

Adele stares at her mother.

She can't be serious, can she?

"Has he mentioned it to you?"

Adele thinks of her son, his beautiful lanky frame, his quick, perfect smile. She'd always fretted about girls in his room. He was smart, well-rounded...but accidents happen. A teen pregnancy is supposed to be something that mothers of daughters worried about, but Adele gives them a good run for their money. The thought of Harrison making that kind of mistake catches somewhere in her abdomen. But now that she thinks about it, there haven't been any girls in his room in a long time.

There haven't been any boys, though, either.

"Are you sure it was Harrison?"

"I think I know what my only grandson looks like, Adele."

Adele tries to read her mother. She, Adele, is shocked, but more at her own failure to notice than anything else. Every other kid in school is bi or gay or trans or *something* these days. It hardly seems worth mentioning.

Until it's your child.

(Is she being homophobic or transphobic again? She just means that it's so *normal* now. But she supposes "normal" to middle class, left-leaning people doesn't mean it isn't hard, or painful, or fraught with bigotry. She's not trying to *minimise* suffering, for God's sake!)

Eventually Adele realises she is arguing with herself, and Jocelyn doesn't seem particularly perturbed about the information she has just imparted.

"Will Peter be okay with this?" Jocelyn asks, as she continues to fuss around a teapot. Adele has not used a teapot for about twenty years, and makes a mental note to throw this one away. She's been wanting to do a spring clean for about five years now, and could use some more space in the cupboards.

"Of course," she bristles. She still can't get her head around her mother seeing Harrison kissing a man at a bus stop. Really kissing. It seems so flamboyant, which is not a word she would have used to describe her son.

"Parents aren't always, you know," Jocelyn goes on. "Even Albert, you know, we all wondered about him."

Adele's head snaps up. "What do you mean?"

"Oh, it was before you knew him." Jocelyn waves the memory away like it doesn't matter, and brings the teapot, cups, and biscuits balanced on a tray that Adele also has not used for a decade. No wonder making tea has taken so long; Jocelyn must have been rifling so far back in cupboards she'd nearly gotten lost.

"We remember his parents from the parents' council when Celia started school. Albert was so camp back then. I would never in a million years have thought he'd marry my daughter. It was right around the time everything was happening on the cliffs, and Albert's father was very against that lifestyle.

Someone told him to keep Albert off those cliffs at night, and he flew right off the handle. Had this dad up against the wall, ranting and raving, banging him against the wall, over and over. The guy was just suggesting, keep your camp kid safe. There was no malice in it. Well, maybe there was a bit of malice. It wasn't really talked about back then. But Roger was *wild*. Of course we were all wrong, Albert was just one of those kids with feminine characteristics. Not gay, as we now know." Jocelyn smiled and bit into her biscuit. "I would never have picked Roger for someone who wouldn't accept a gay son. He was a GP too, seemed very liberal and laid back. He was our doctor, for a while. But after that night, I just felt a bit... uncomfortable. It was John who pulled him off the poor guy. We started going somewhere else."

"You thought Albert was *gay?*" Adele can't wrap her head around this. Albert has seemed a lot of things, but not gay. She would never have thought it in a million years.

And yet...and yet. Something niggles at her, something familiar somehow, something unsettling, that she wants to grasp and examine but also wants to shy away from, a type of nausea or anxiety that is easier to shelve than to dwell on.

"Well, he was just a kid. I guess they're all awkward at that stage, really."

Adele isn't quite sure which surprise to focus on first. That Harrison was kissing a man. That Jocelyn had thought Albert was gay, and the wave of discomfort that passed through her. That Jocelyn might seriously consider awkwardness equated to homosexuality. Or that Jocelyn wasn't perturbed by this, and was pleased that Celia married him (Adele thinks that whatever Jocelyn might say about it now, her mother was probably a terribly judgemental woman in her youth. She suspects being unfazed by a gay grandson is a new, carefully curated approach to the world, definitely no more than a few years old).

"Did Celia know?"

"Of course not. That was years before Celia and Albert started dating. He'd grown into a man by then. Very masculine. All the girls fancied him. Celia was the lucky one, I guess."

"Yeah. Lucky." Adele grimaces.

"You know what, it never even crossed my mind when they started dating," Jocelyn goes on, oblivious to the rage in Adele's voice. "I only thought of it now because of Harrison."

What Jocelyn doesn't add is the way her heart had lurched when Roger had attacked the other father, not because she was worried for the man, but because of how it had made her worried for Albert.

The rage and disgust she'd seen on Roger's face.

The rabid denial his son could be gay, or even effeminate.

The desire to punch that thought out of an acquaintance's mind.

What would he do to obliterate it out of Albert's?

She has forgotten her distaste about the idea of homosexuality, the relief that it wasn't an accusation being levelled at her children, the real reason they changed GP—that she found not just Roger's rage uncomfortable, but his son's sexuality, she just didn't want to be near any of it, she didn't want to think about it. They changed GP so it could be out of sight, out of mind. Not that she would ever have admitted that to herself.

So her memories are not entirely to be trusted, but what she does remember, whether it was true or not true, what Jocelyn remembers thinking is, that poor boy.

That poor, poor boy.

15

March 2006 (two weeks before Celia disappeared)

Celia doesn't mess around once she makes up her mind.

When Albert gets home from work, she is sitting at the dining room table, drumming her fingers against the impeccable wood surface.

She hasn't made dinner, she hasn't made herself look pretty, and she hasn't really worked out what it is she wants to say.

"I'm home, darling," he calls from the hallway, and she can hear him hanging up his coat, emptying his pockets into the key bowl on the coat rack.

She waits, fingers drumming, drumming.

"Celia?" he calls, padding through to the kitchen. Celia takes some satisfaction in the fact that he'll notice the lack of delicious aromas welcoming him home. He's old-fashioned that way. Celia does all the cooking. It seemed a small price to pay for this marriage, this house, the endless money.

"Are you still sick, darling? You must be, the kitchen's empty!" He's trying to sound worried about her, but he's probably more worried about what he's going to have for dinner.

She can hear him padding along in his socks, checking the bedroom, then making his way back down to where she sits.

"Celia! Are you okay? I was worried."

"I'm perfectly fine, thank you, Albert. I just had a little shock today, that's all." This was not strictly true—the shock had been several weeks ago now, but Celia had been sitting on it, examining it from different angles, wondering what to do about it. But Albert didn't need to know that.

"Oh no! What happened?" Albert pulls out a chair beside her, reaching for her hand. He looks the picture of the concerned husband, worry etched in to his brow, warm eyes looking at her, beseeching her to tell him everything. So he can fix it. Albert likes fixing things for Celia.

No, that's not true, Celia thinks. Albert likes being *seen* to fix things for Celia. For everyone.

Albert likes making sure people know that he fixed the things. It's never an end in itself. It has to be witnessed for Albert to take pleasure in it.

"Some young men visited, right after you left actually. Quite the sight, they were." Celia watches her husband with interest. She is still surprised by how little this hurts, how *not* upset she is. Is it because she herself no longer really wants sex with Albert? Or is it because it is something concrete, something she can say—*this! This is what's wrong.* Unlike the other stuff, the stuff she can't quite articulate, can't quite put her finger on.

There's no evidence, that's the problem. She can tell Evan, "Albert does all the right things. He says all the right things. I just get the feeling that sometimes, for no reason, he does something subtle and unkind *just for fun.* And it's so elusive and so small I can't even ask him without sounding like a crazy person."

She thinks about the example she'd given Evan—the phone call she overheard: It was after hours, and Albert had gone into his study with his mobile. Celia presumed it was a patient he was following up with. And she hadn't been listening—she respects privacy, mostly, and also she can't think of anything less interesting that the health worries of an ageing population. Albert's work gets less and less interesting to her with every year that passes.

But as she was passing, she heard something that seemed strange to her, and she may have loitered just a *little* bit longer than necessary, re-ordering the coats and hats on the hat stand outside the study door.

Albert had that soft, caring, overly empathic tone that he used with patients.

I care so much.

I'm the best doctor you'll ever see.

Tell me all your secrets.

That's what she imagined he was aiming for with the tone. Cloying, that is how it sounded to her. If Evan ever tried that tone on Celia, she would probably punch her in the face.

"Unfortunately, the tests have returned some bad news. I've just received them back, and called you straight away. The spot on the shoulder *is* melanoma. I've booked you in for an appointment tomorrow to talk about it further and decide on next steps. But we'll want to check if it's spread to the lymph nodes ASAP. I'm so sorry. But we'll get you through this. We'll be right with you the whole way."

In itself, it wasn't very strange. It was exactly what you might expect, in fact, from your caring and considerate GP.

Except that, Celia had taken the call on Albert's mobile while he was in the shower two hours earlier (they didn't have a landline and Celia saw it was the clinic calling, so she thought it must be important, and picked up the call). Pam, his receptionist, was working late, and chatted to Celia for a few minutes. And when Celia said that she'd get Albert to call Pam back when he was out of the bathroom, Pam had said: "Oh, no need. It's an urgent biopsy result he was waiting on, but I can tell you without identifying the patient, it's good news, so he doesn't need any more details. He knows who it is, he's promised he'll call them as soon as he knows. But it's definitely not melanoma. Can you just ask him to call the patient? They're expecting his call."

And yet here he was, calling his patient, not immediately, but two hours later, to tell them a result that didn't exist?

Evan had suggested that this wasn't a small thing, that this was very clearly something that Celia could confront Albert about without sounding like a crazy person, and Celia had felt irritated. Evan didn't *get it*. A few years earlier, she tried to explain, Celia would have confronted him. She might even have been worried—had she muddled up the message? Or she might have assumed it was another result, that Pam had called about another patient. But Albert's phone had been on the dining table with them all through dinner, and abandoned there when they went to watch the news. Celia was one hundred percent certain that no one had called Albert, and that Albert was in the study, lying to his patient.

She is also one hundred percent certain that he will sail through this fabrication in some way where he either saves the day ("You're all clear! Nothing in the lymph nodes! We'll just check your skin every six months from now on, okay?") or admits his mistake sometime soon, fumbling, apologetic, so chagrined.

In public.

Celia wonders aloud to Evan about how Albert presents in private. What he looked like, in his office, after he hangs up the call. *Is he laughing? Gleeful? Aroused?*

She wonders about the sort of person who takes some purposeless, inexplicable pleasure in another person's distress.

But she tries to explain to Evan—the times they had argued in the past, about smaller lies, strange and pointless lies, he'd been so outraged, so certain that Celia had gotten things wrong, so believably distraught that she could think such a thing of him, that she herself believed him for such a long time. Now, she knows better. But she couldn't quite make anyone else see. Albert could talk himself out of anything. And she was so *tired* of it all by the time she overheard that phone call, she didn't say a word.

That's what she'd said to Evan.

But this. Gay sex workers on her doorstep!

This is an explanation.

It's an *excuse.*

After this, she could do whatever she liked. She could leave and no one would need a reason, no one would question her. She isn't quite sure how the finances would work out but surely she would be entitled to *something?*

Anyway. Celia isn't approaching this conversation feeling like she is going slightly crazy. She is much calmer than she would have otherwise expected, especially after that frustrating conversation with Evan, trying to explain it, and how agitated and unheard she had felt. The unsatisfactory, unacceptable turn that conversation had taken. Evan would have been proud of her, in fact, if it hadn't been for that intolerable ending to their session.

No, this is concrete, and large, and visible, and really just utterly perfect.

"Dan and Jonno. Very polite young men. But they were looking for the two hundred dollars you owed Dan, to replace the fraudulent ones you had supplied for the service you received." Celia cocks her head to the side, curious, detached.

"I didn't know you liked a bit of dick on the side, darling."

And it was so unexpected, whatever Celia thought of Albert, whatever she worried about and tried to untangle, she never, ever, ever thought that he would hit her.

So when his fist shoots out across the table and connects with her breast, she is so utterly shocked and blindsided that she forgets to even feel afraid.

16

Thursday

December 2021

I know your secret.

The sheet of paper is pinned to the door with an aggressively large nail, and Adele's laugh freezes on her face.

She and Peter have just returned from a walk around the headlands. Adele had scoured the land for the elusive figure she keeps seeing, or imagines she keeps seeing. Is it nerves, with everything about Celia coming to the forefront of her consciousness again?

You'd certainly have to be a fool to be doing anything sinister on the cliff tops these days. There had been so much publicity recently about all the deaths and the memorial, and then the police presence as they recovered the remains this week. No, she's probably imagining things, her nerves taut and flighty, seeing shadows where there aren't any.

And if she does see a man lurking again, she will damn well go and grab him by his shirtfront and demand some answers.

Well, no, she probably won't do that. It's a nice fantasy, though.

Now, she and Peter stare at the note in shocked silence. Neither of them moves.

"Should we call the police?" Adele asks, eventually, her voice disconcertingly small.

"And say what? It's hardly a threat." Peter is brisk, and a little irritated, which unsettles Adele. She relies on him to make things okay, but he seems just as rattled as her. But then he gives himself a little shake and seems to right himself.

"Don't touch it. I'll put it in a plastic sheet, just in case. It's probably about Harry." Peter actually now looks angry. Adele had told him about her mother's revelations, and they had stared at each other in kind of surprised wonder. How had they not known this about their boy?

They'd talked at length about whether to say something. Perhaps it was respectful to let him tell them when he was ready.

"But what if he thinks we won't like it?" Adele had said. "Kids can get this stuff wrong." She thinks about all the stuff she got wrong about her parents, and feels a little wave of bitterness wash over her.

"But we've always been careful to say 'boy or girl' when we talk about if he's bringing someone home, or marrying someone. He cannot possibly believe we'd have anything negative to say."

"Why hasn't he told us then?"

Eventually they agreed that maybe he'd be reticent about telling them about a love interest, regardless of their gender. They would bring it up with gentle humour as soon as possible. Something easy, off-hand, an invitation to tell them more or not, just to ensure it was very clear that they were perfectly happy with whoever Harrison dated, so long as they were a nice person.

But now there was this note on the door, and something churns inside Adele. Suddenly, all those deaths at the cliffs take on a much darker, much more personal meaning. Of course she cared before. Of *course* she did. But now she can imagine it being her son that might be targeted, and maybe the deaths had stopped (*have they? how would they know? bodies can disappear for fifteen years, it seems*) but had the hate? Someone pinning a note on your door was not a friendly gesture. There might not be a direct threat, but it was there. It was implied. And Adele feels a desperate urge to find Harrison and lock him up inside and never let him out again.

Except, someone knows where he lives.

Her heart starts thumping harder in her chest.

"Peter." She doesn't know what she wants to say. All these thoughts, she wants Peter to intuit them, to know them, but she doesn't think she can manage to get them out of her mouth.

Peter looks at her grimly. He understands. Adele lets herself breathe. *In, out. In, out.*

They unlock the door, and Peter goes to get a plastic envelope to store the evidence in. And Adele walks very fast to Harrison's room. She knocks on the door, but there is only silence from the other side.

"Hon? It's me. Can we talk for a minute?" It's no use, though, Adele can feel that Harrison isn't home. She is attuned to his presence, the largeness of him, the warmth, the life force.

She opens his door anyway.

His room is neat, neater than a teenage boy's really ought to be. His bed is made, his textbooks are stacked neatly on the desk. There are no clothes on the floor, the cupboard doors fully shut. The only thing out of place is the bin, knocked onto its side under his desk.

Out of habit, Adele goes to straighten it. She can't remember the last time she's done anything in Harrison's room.

He washes his own clothes, his own bedding. He empties his own trash. He irons his own shirts.

She feels a sudden pang. Her boy is independent. He is ready to go out into the world.

Will the world be good to him?

Adele sits heavily on the corner of his bed, her shoulders slumping. She looks into the bin absentmindedly as she sets it straight.

And gasps.

There's a torn corner of a note. It's been torn into many pieces, but staring up at her are the letters SE, in the same rough black block letters as the note on her front door.

Secret, again?

"Peter," she calls, but her voice is so faint, even she barely registers it. The room swims a little bit. Peter was with her this morning, she didn't even purge, but she feels light-headed, that swirly mistiness that comes over her mind afterward, where she can't think quite straight but doesn't have to focus too much on her worries, either.

She's done it too often, it's too habitual, her body is confused. This sick feeling about threatening notes, her worry about Harrison, and she doesn't even want to, but her body seems to be saying, "*This is what we do, lady. This is how we cope,*" and before she can even rescue the note, she hurls up her breakfast all over Harrison's bin, and whatever awful message might be lurking in there.

17

BEFORE

March 2006 (one week before Celia disappeared)

"I don't mean to pry, but..." Albert says, and then proceeds to pry.

Bethany rolls her eyes when he turns back to the fridge.

Yes, you do, she thinks to herself. She's used to Albert wanting to be seen as important, and caring, and relentlessly respectful.

She shouldn't be here. But she can't help herself.

At first, she felt special and singled out by Albert, that he wanted to confide in her, talk to her about his problems with Celia. Bethany was never seen as a grown-up in the family, always the baby, always the dreamer, her ideas never taken seriously (to be fair, her last idea *had* been quite ridiculous and it was probably to be expected that she was ridiculed somewhat for it. Everyone knew she got seasick, she could never go out on the little boat Albert kept at some fancy boathouse up the coast. What on earth had she been thinking, signing up for a year-long job on a cruise ship? Also, her quarters were cramped and the work was *hard*—much harder than she was used to working).

But when Albert started asking if he could talk to her, she had puffed up like a happy little self-important puppy.

Yes, yes, throw the ball to me!

It's embarrassing to think about, now. But not completely surprising. She wonders how many different times and ways she has tried to break out of her prescribed corner in their family. *Dreamy.* Bethany is fairly sure she has been the opposite of dreamy for years. Her family would be shocked, in fact, at how un-dreamy and hard-nailed she has become. But they still see her the way they always have. They see exactly what they want to see. *You're not really allowed to change in families*, she thinks.

So of course, when it felt like Albert saw her as the understanding one, or the sensitive one, she'd jumped at it. She wanted to be seen as she actually was, not as some pre-teen child who wasn't very good at concentrating.

She's been on medication for ADHD for some time now. It was a right pain trying to get diagnosed without her parents verifying her symptoms. Even as an adult, you're supposed to have a family member interviewed to provide independent information about your childhood, and there was no way Bethany was going to involve any member of her family in her private affairs. God, she could just imagine the spike in their perceptions about her being dreamy after that. She would never hear the end of it for her entire life.

But the medication had helped. Her work with her occupational therapist had helped too. She had all sorts of strategies in place to help her stay focused, and if only her family knew some of things she had pulled off, they would die of shock.

Not just because of the amount of concentration and complexity involved, either.

Bethany smirks to herself.

So yes, she was a little too enthusiastic when Albert recruited her as a confidante. Her hopeless desire to be seen differently within her family is embarrassing to her, a little flare of shame that she can't quite pinpoint. It goes against all her perceptions about herself: being wily, and clever, and hard-nosed.

She had felt smug and superior, playing the role they expected her to play, because it was easier, and things in families get so entrenched, it's like an intricate dance that they all do when they get together, everyone knows their steps, even when they don't want to do them, they're carried along by the sheer force of family dynamics. Adele organises and fixes and worries, even when she resents it; Bethany dreams and takes no responsibility; Celia comes up with grand plans and manipulates things to get her own way; and no one even *minds*, it's just the way it goes. It was as normal as breathing.

And then the first moment someone treated her differently, she responded without hesitation. It's the immediacy of it that shocks her so. It was like she threw everything aside, swept it all away for a chance to be seen, without even a moment's thought or consideration. It's distasteful to her, and uncomfortable and awful and desperate: but the truth of it that she saw for the first time was that she yearned for it. Yearned for her family to see her and love all of her, not just the little prescribed role that she'd been assigned twenty-odd years ago, that actually bore no resemblance to her current life and state of being whatsoever.

She thought she was the one who was across all the hopelessly ingrained, knee-jerk bullshit of her family. And here she was, being exactly the same.

Still, it was done now. She might as well play along. And there *is* something nice about being seen as emotionally astute, about her opinions mattering. It makes her desperately uncomfortable to be the salivating puppy, but she's going to enjoy being fed treats for a little while just the same.

"What was Celia like growing up, Beth? She's just so...cold, sometimes. Like I try and try and try to shower her with love, and it's like she doesn't even feel it."

Albert has a lot of questions. Which of course is reasonable: he wants to know his wife better, he wants to get them back on track. But Bethany knows he also wants to know her better, and Adele better, and that Albert is so invested in being woke, and kind, and the sort of person everyone confides in that he has forgotten how to actually be those things. All that matters to Albert is appearances. He's been waffling on about being a custodian for people's well-being and his approach to the responsibilities and joys in his work, caring for people, greatly inflating his own importance. Yes, yes, your GP is probably your first stop when something is wrong. But then you move on to a psychologist or social worker or psychotherapist or gynaecologist or surgeon and *they're* the ones who support you, who listen to you for hours in some cases, who know and understand you and actually make the difference to you.

Bethany gets the feeling he tells these stories to convince even himself of his own critical importance. If her GP came across in this manner, it would make her skin crawl, and she would definitely not be confiding any secrets in someone who brought so much of themselves into the room. How could he truly listen to his patients when his ego was sitting in the corner, like an elephant, eating popcorn?

But she also doesn't think he was always like this.

"Were you close to your sister?" he asks, not waiting for her to reply to his previous question, innocence shining from his bright blue eyes.

"I don't know that I'd call it close," Bethany muses, staring off into the distance. The ocean is green today, choppy and restless. The sun is shining brightly, but there's a cold wind. It was too cold to walk the headlands track this morning. Bethany loves this weather: crisp, sunny, with winter just around the corner. "Celia liked to win. She liked to win with boys, she liked to win board games, she liked to be the most liked. She was always fun to be around, but I'm not sure I trusted her very much." This is true, but not the whole truth. Bethany was too lost in her own world to be close to her sister. The dreamy label didn't come from nowhere. But in retrospect, Bethany thinks she also was quite rightly escaping. She didn't feel safe in her family, so she made safer places for herself. Everyone always thought Celia was so clever, but Bethany thinks she herself was a bloody genius. She absented herself from her family in a way that gave her pleasure and gave them no pain, and no cause to interrogate her. And she's still reaping the rewards, after all these years.

Dreamy Bethany, don't bother trying to get her to help with A, B, or C.

Don't expect Bethany to get anything done.

She was a goddamn genius, and nobody knew it. It was infuriating.

Now, Bethany watches Albert through narrowed eyes, but he doesn't notice. He's fussing over a cheese board. Soon he'll present it to her, his eyes shining with enthusiasm, desperate to please her. To take care of her.

To be noticed for how thoughtful and kind he was.

"What about you? Were you close to your sister?" she asks Albert. Mallory had moved away recently. Bethany had thought she and Albert were close, and Celia seemed fond of the woman, though Bethany hadn't taken to her on the couple of times they'd met.

"Yes, I love her dearly. I looked up to her so much growing up. Although, my father never encouraged us to spend much time together." Albert looks grim, and Bethany's interest is piqued.

"Why not?" she asks, watching him carefully. It's hard to pick fact from fiction with Albert.

"He didn't like me joining in her games. Too girly for a boy," he says, a trace of bitterness in his voice. Then his features smooth out again, ever the sanguine host. "And you've met Mal, right? She's a force of nature. No way would I convince her to join in my games. It was Barbie dolls, or nothing. And I loved her so much I'd have done anything she asked." He grins at Bethany, self-deprecating, the loving little brother. Even prepared to play with dolls to be near his big sister.

Bethany wants more of what's underneath, though. The history to that terse look.

That bitterness.

The trick with Albert is to let him believe he was playing you. You had to let him feel superior. She had to stay doe-eyed, admiring. When he felt sure of your admiration, his tongue loosened a little bit.

Bethany has met men like Albert before. In truth, she knows far too many people like Albert. Her fascination is perhaps stronger than her sense of self-preservation. *Why can't he just be authentic? He probably is an interesting person. He's well-off, well-liked, has led an interesting life. Why must he shove it down your throat and insist on moulding every single person's perception of him? Was it low self-esteem? Was it more insidious? Was he trying to manipulate her, to get something from her?*

She doesn't remember him being like this, at the start. She was sure, in fact, that she had quite liked Albert, at one time. Had she misjudged him, or had he changed? Living with Celia certainly couldn't be easy. Celia liked getting her own way, and was certainly adept at manipulating situations. *Perhaps Albert was just trying to keep up, trying to stay relevant, and loved?*

Or maybe, back then, she, Bethany, just wasn't paying as much attention.

She giggles in collusion with him. "What would you have done, if your father wasn't interfering?"

Albert looks out to the ocean, too.

He's prepping for dinner. Adele is coming over, and Celia will be home from the gallery any moment. It's supposed to be a laid-back family dinner, but Bethany has an ulterior motive, and she gets a bit of a rush from doing things that no one would expect of her. The way her family view her offers her the perfect place to hide.

You snooze, you lose, suckers, Bethany thinks, grinning to herself. She thinks this is her best idea yet, though occasionally has moments of doubt. She doesn't want anyone to get hurt, and there is still a bit of ditzy Bethany (*not ditzy,* she corrects herself, rejecting the family narrative, replacing it with the correct one: *suffering from a medical condition which affects concentration, dammit!*) lurking around inside her. *What if she missed something?*

Focus, Bethany, focus, she thinks, turning her attention back to Albert.

Celia is trying to make things up with Adele after that disastrous lunch. Family get-togethers aren't usually a walk in the park with her family, but that one was worse than most. Harrison broke the vase (*did Celia really say it was worth four thousand dollars? There was something slightly obscene about that. Bethany knew Celia and Albert were rich, she knew Celia liked expensive things, she knew Albert bent over backwards to give Celia everything she wanted. It wasn't like it was a surprise, but she still feels this shock of discomfort whenever she thinks about it*) and Adele, who usually rushes to fix everything, every little bump in the road, had been almost taunting her with her failure to offer to pay, or even clean it up. Adele hadn't even brought her usual selection of cheeses, which Bethany felt the lack of very dearly indeed. (If one had to put up with family get-togethers, one at least should get some damn nice cheese.) No one had enjoyed themselves, and Adele had not called anyone in the family ever since.

Adele was the *fixer*. If there was a catastrophe, Adele would sweep in and sort everything out. She'd call the right people, smooth over the ruffled feathers, intuit solutions to problems the rest of them hadn't even fully appreciated existed yet.

It felt very odd and very empty to have Adele just...vanish like that. To be there, but not there. To have vacated her role.

It doesn't occur to Bethany that she is insisting Adele stay in her lane in the very same way she resents her family when they insist she stay in hers.

Anyway, they are all getting together tonight, which Bethany doesn't think about in words, but feels somewhere inside as a hope that it meant Adele was coming back to them, back to her usual kind and thoughtful self. Back to her role, so they can all carry on in much the same way they always have. Dissatisfied, but without any surprises.

And with nice cheese.

"Art, probably." Bethany is pulled back to the present. There's something wistful in Albert's voice, and she thinks he is telling her the truth, for once.

"No way," she says, genuinely interested. "Like painting, yourself, or running a gallery, like Celia?"

"Painting, sculpture," he says, turning back to her, his eyes resting on her appraisingly. The veneer is back, the way he frames everything in the way that is expected of him.

Bethany wonders, if less was expected of him, if things would have been different.

"But my father would never have allowed it," he says, expressionless. "And I became a doctor, which is lucky, don't you think?"

Bethany wonders which part he thinks is lucky. The money? His beautiful house on top of a cliff, overlooking the ocean? The social status?

The women, who let him pry, let his fingers creep into their secrets and maybe into their pants?

Or is it something more sinister? Is it that, like Bethany, Albert is lucky because he always has such a perfect place to hide?

18

AFTER

Thursday

December 2021

After Adele has cleaned herself up (looking hopefully at the bin like it might actually be feasible to rescue the paper, but deciding against it; if only she'd had some nice muesli for breakfast like she normally did, instead of pancakes and yoghurt and stewed plums!) she sits opposite Peter at their dining table.

It has seen a lot of drama, this table.

Adele had first told Peter about her purging here. He'd been as unfazed as he was about most things in their lives. Calm, steady as a rock.

"Do you want to tell me about it?" he'd said, and Adele was surprised to find that yes, yes, she did want to tell him about it.

"People always think it's to lose weight," she'd said. That always annoyed her. It was so simplistic. It didn't get at the roots, the dark swirling messiness underneath. The desire to be invisible. Yes, it was about being small, because that was what we were taught, wasn't it? Be thin, don't take up too much space, don't be too loud, don't be too demanding! But it was also about your sense of self. Did you deserve to take up space? Were you allowed to have needs, to demand things? And if you were to be thin, and smart, and successful, and selfless, and kind, and look after everyone around you, how were you expected to cope? There wasn't enough time to do all those things, there wasn't enough headspace and enough energy! Mental load, they call it now. The endless ticker running through your mind, about what needs to happen and by when, the laundry, the meals, the kids' appointments, who needs a supportive phone call, all of it, endless. When the drip, drip, drip of expectations and pressure got too much, when you were about to burst with all of it, what did people *think* would happen? You burst, goddammit.

Out of your mouth.

Other people burst in different ways, but Adele threw up, and then she felt better. For a while.

Or did she? Did she just feel too confused, too light-headed to register all the distress for a little while? *Maybe it was never about feeling better, maybe it was about drowning one bad feeling out with another.* This notion shocks Adele, and momentarily derails her train of thought.

But still. How did she get to that place when she was only ten years old? What on earth was dripping on her so relentlessly, making life so unbearable, when she was just a little girl?

"It's just like drinking, really, isn't it?" She'd asked Peter then, without really expecting him to reply, or to understand.

"When you can't cope, when you don't know what to do with the bad feelings, it's an escape, a refuge. A way of absenting yourself." He'd said this without the disgust, or fear, or deep discomfort that appeared on everyone's faces if the topic was ever raised (and Adele did her very best to make sure that it was never raised, ever), and she'd looked at him in surprise.

"Yes," she'd said, and then she didn't feel the need to talk about it anymore. He got it. That was enough.

She never circled back to how it started. She was so tired of it all by then. She had wanted to talk about it, and then she hadn't needed to, anymore.

Anyway, she hardly ever did it now. It surprised her when she did. That day on the cliffs, when they'd found the body. What was that about? She can't even remember now. Something had unsettled her. Mostly, now, though, if she was unsettled, she'd pull out her yoga mat and settle in with the bad feelings. *They'll pass,* she'll say to herself, and stretch and balance and almost enjoy how it forces her to take some time to just sit with her body. This lovely body, it did so well for her, really. It strode around the headlands, it grew and birthed a beautiful boy, it survived her relentless abuse of it for all those years, and it still functions so wonderfully well! Forty-five years old, and not a crook hip or bung knee in sight. What a trooper this body was.

What a star.

Now, she and Peter stare at their mobile phones. They have both tried to call Harrison, but he's not picking up. Adele even called Tom, but Harrison wasn't with him, either.

"Um, well this is awkward, Tom, but I believe there is a... love interest. Harrison has not told us about this, so I don't want to share secrets or pry, but we really do need to get on to Harrison, something quite urgent has come up. So if you have a contact number for...this person, that would be very helpful?" Her voice had lilted upwards hopefully at the end there in a question. She was trying to say to Tom, you don't have to betray any confidences! Don't even tell us anything at all!

But Tom didn't have a number. He'd been so sweet, and Adele thought once again how lovely it was that Harrison had such a wonderful best mate. They'd been thick as thieves since primary school.

"Everyone needs a best friend like Tom," she says now, as she hangs up. Peter nods thoughtfully.

"You don't think..." she starts to say, her voice trailing off. But no. Jocelyn would have recognised Tom, she's sure.

"Do you think we should call the police? There's at least two notes. We don't know what the other one said. Maybe it *was* threatening Harry. It doesn't seem like it's worth risking, does it? Waiting and seeing?"

Adele feels agitated.

Last week, everything was going perfectly well.

And now, there was a body on the cliffs, their son was gay but not telling them (*maybe he was just experimenting? Oh God, was she being homophobic again?! Of course she doesn't care if Harrison is gay, but she wants him to be safe, and happy, and how could you not worry when dozens of men had been thrown to their deaths just up the road for this very very thing?*), she kept thinking there was a man lurking on the cliffs, and someone was leaving threatening notes on her door.

And she was vomiting again.

"Yes. Yes, I think it's probably best," Peter says, and Adele's heart plummets to her groin, because she had hoped Peter would say, "No, let's wait, no, it's not so bad," and Adele would have believed him, and been comforted. She does not want Peter to be worried because then she needs to be worried, too. And she wonders if that is perhaps not the best dynamic to have in a marriage. One party, offloading responsibility onto another.

Isn't that just a different kind of ticker, a different mental load? She and Peter might have shared the obvious tasks of the mental load out equally—they'd written it down, even! She does the shopping, Peter cleans the house, etcetera—but they had never accounted for this particular matter.

Who carries the worry?

Who decides what is to be feared?

Adele always turns toward Peter to see how worried she should be. And Peter is always so calm, so rational, so thoughtful, she is almost always soothed.

But not today. Peter doesn't look very happy about calling the police. He seems distracted, and uncertain, and it fills Adele with more fear than notes nailed to her door, even.

What is Peter so worried about?

And suddenly it occurs to Adele that they only *think* they know what secrets these notes are referring to, but really, in her family, there are more skeletons in the closet than a gay child.

Has someone found out something else that someone else in this house would rather they didn't know?

Adele's heart starts to thump, and her stomach starts to flip-flop, and suddenly she wants to throw up again, very much indeed.

Because she's never asked about it. She's not quite sure of what she saw. But that night Celia disappeared, she thinks she remembers—she'd nipped out to vomit in the toilet block she always used, she wasn't coping after the night with Albert, her brain wasn't working properly, she was like an overzealous energiser bunny, bouncing off the walls—but she is almost certain that she saw her husband, shadowy and elusive, slipping along in front of her on her way home, and in their front door.

19

AFTER

Thursday

December 2021

Melissa eases into the chair opposite Adele gingerly.

Peter let her in as he was leaving. He'd given her a brief rundown on the phone, asking her to come and keep Adele company for a while.

"Are you sure you don't need me at the police station?" Adele wants to be there for Peter, but is also relieved that he'd suggested she stay at home. She feels weightless, like she might float away, like she certainly can't cope with all of this, and certainly not all at once. She needs to deal with one problem at a time. Her focus is scattered across all these problems to the extent that she can't give any of them the attention they deserve.

"No, you stay here. I've asked Melissa to come around."

"That's not necessary," Adele had said, her voice sharper then she intended. She's not a child. She doesn't need babysitting.

"Isn't it?" Peter had countered, his face sterner then she had expected.

"I know you're purging again," he'd said, his face softening, his voice mild. "I think some support while I'm out might be a good idea. And when I get back we can talk about that a little more." And Adele had slouched back in her chair, ashamed. For everything she understood about this particular coping mechanism, there was no escaping the deep sense of shame and horror that accompanied it. It would be far more socially acceptable to be drunk.

She can't meet Peter's eyes.

Melissa was a good choice. She's never avoided the hard conversations, but she won't seek them out. How this progresses is entirely in Adele's control. Just the way she likes it.

Adele thinks, for the nine millionth time, how lucky she is that Peter knows her so well. She feels so seen, which is exactly the antidote to not coping, to purging, to her family. If you're not coping, you talk about it. You find a way forward. You learn to understand yourself. You learn what triggers you.

Unless you're a Stonwald. If you're a Stonwald, you sweep it under the rug, you never talk about it, you suffer in silence, and you don't make a fuss.

Is that what went wrong? Adele wonders. She *was* a sensitive child. She was so sensitive, and everything hurt her so deeply, and she was never allowed to talk about it. You didn't talk about feelings. You shut up and buckled down and coped. You did more than cope. You *succeeded.* You certainly never addressed conflict and you never let your problems get in the way of success. Her father may not have said more than three sentences in one day any day of her life, but Adele certainly knew when he was pleased and when he was not. You slapped that smile on your face and you kept your feelings to yourself.

They all did that. Jocelyn, Adele, Celia, Bethany. Adele can't remember seeing a true, spontaneous, non-positive emotion in her family, ever. Sadness or anger or upset—they might as well not have existed. Until she met Peter, Adele certainly never realised it was normal to feel them and perfectly reasonable to express them, too.

But all those repressed feelings—they didn't spill out in purging in Bethany and Celia. *Why did she end up so dysfunctional and they, not?*

Melissa sits quietly. Then, unexpectedly, she says: "I never knew how to help. How to talk about it. I wish I'd said something. I'm sorry I didn't."

Adele stares at her friend blankly. She is so used to people studiously ignoring the distasteful ickiness of her purging, that she has tricked herself into thinking it truly is a secret that nobody but her and Peter know about. For a minute, she thinks Melissa must be talking about Celia, and how Adele coped, or didn't, after she disappeared.

"You're purging again, aren't you?" Melissa looks her in the eye steadily. When the silence stretches out more than she can bear, Melissa sighs and drops her eyes. "Is there anything I can do to help?" And it is so unexpected, and so normal, and so reasonable and kind (your friend is struggling, so you ask how you can help, how novel!), that Adele bursts into tears.

"Oh honey." Melissa starts to stand, but Adele waves her back down, reaching for tissues, blowing her nose loudly, only to start sobbing again. Loud, ugly tears. The lack of control feels shameful to her, too.

"I'm sorry, I don't know what's wrong with me," she manages to hiccup out between sobs. Melissa has seen her cry, but not like this. Her mouth hangs open, like she can't breathe, her cries sounding more like being strangled than being devastated. *She doesn't even know how to cry properly, dammit.*

"Nothing's wrong with you. You're upset. The body on the cliffs bringing back the trauma about Celia. Scary notes on your door. Worrying about Harry. Of course you're crying.

Adele." But Adele can't look back at her. She stares at the table, her pain almost silent, an open-mouthed, shuddering, silent scream, until it passes through her, and she feels calm.

They sit quietly for a while, Adele snuffling and blowing her nose.

"Do you remember when we were little, and Jingo was hit by the car?" Melissa says eventually, and Adele's head snaps up, surprised. Jingo was her cat, who was missing for two days before they found her remains down a laneway not far from their home.

"Dad sent me to my room 'for some privacy' when I started to cry," Adele says, bitterly.

Jocelyn had organised a burial, tight-lipped and silent. Afterward, she had said, "Let's not talk about Jingo. It makes everyone too sad." But she'd been looking at Adele, and her message was very clear: *these feelings are not welcome here.* So Melissa was the only person Adele had cried to, and talked about Jingo to, for weeks afterward.

And Celia. Celia had been surprisingly gentle and kind, for a while.

Once, when Adele had slipped, when her feelings had gotten away from her, she had become a little teary watching a television commercial with a cat in it. And Jocelyn had slapped her hands down either side of her thighs on the couch with a sharp movement, and a dull thump, saying, "Aren't you over that yet?" It's Adele's family story, the one she trots out to any new therapist in order to sum up, as succinctly as possible, what she feels is wrong with her: at ten years old, she wasn't allowed to cry about her dead cat. No wonder she never learned how to cope with any bigger, more challenging feelings.

"Yeah, your parents kind of sucked with healthy emotions. But that's not what I'm talking about. I tried to tell you, but you were so upset. And then I kind of forgot..." Melissa's voice trailed off. She looks uncertain, and Adele's tears have dried; she's curious. "What?" she says.

"We were so young. What were we, twelve? Thirteen?" Adele had always thought she was ten, but it was all such a miserable blur, maybe Melissa was right. "I can't be sure I remember it right," Melissa continues. "But after you found her. It was Celia that found her, wasn't it? And a few days before. Maybe the day she went missing. I can't remember. But I saw Celia and Albert. He was older. But I knew him from school. And I'd seen them on that street with Jingo. And at the time I thought she must have been hit just after that. And it wasn't till later..." Melissa's words trip over each other, her sentences half-formed, and Adele has no idea what she's talking about.

"For God's sake, Mel! What?!"

"They were fighting. They looked like they were pulling Jingo apart. Jingo was yowling and clawing. And they looked so guilty when they saw me. And I always wondered afterward, was Albert hurting the cat? Was Celia trying to rescue her? There was something so weird about it. But I was just a kid, I couldn't make any sense of it. And it was only a few seconds, a snapshot. It was only later,,,well this DV stuff, the appointment. Do you think it's true? They say that people who are cruel to animals rarely stop there..." Melissa's voice trails off again, and Adele is staring at her in alarm.

But she's not alarmed about the thought of Albert hurting her cat.

She's remembering something else, something she'd forgotten her entire life until this very moment, and she shoves her chair back violently from the table, gasping, "I'm going to be sick," and flies just in time to the sink, heaving up the almost nonexistent contents of her stomach against her will, for the second time that day.

20

March 2006 (one week before Celia disappeared)

Albert chuckles with glee out of all proportion to the joke Adele had made, through slurring words, and Bethany frets nervously at her sleeve.

Something has gone very, very wrong.

Waving Albert aside, she squats next to Adele and peers into her eyes. "Dell?" she asks, then again, louder. "*Dell?*"

Adele's eyes are vacant though, and she's starting to slouch forward, like she's drunk way more than the single glass of expensive Merlot Bethany had given her.

Fuck.

Bethany needs to think quickly. She's completely tuned Albert out. Whatever he is saying in the background doesn't make it through the pounding in her ears. He'll notice the switch; how unimportant he was in that moment. But Bethany doesn't have room in her brain to indulge Albert and deal with Adele.

Fuck, fuck, fuck.

Adele being inebriated was not part of the plan. But

Bethany doesn't have time to work out what has gone wrong. She knows she's not good at multitasking. That's one of the strategies she's worked on with her OT, in fact. Itemising, prioritising. Not trying to do two things at once, or she becomes overwhelmed and gets neither of them done.

She needs to help Adele to bed before she makes a fool of herself, before Albert notices how out of it she is. That's task number one.

Bethany tugs one of Adele's arms around her shoulders and tries to pull her up. "Come on, honey. You've had a bit too much already, I think. Let's have a little rest. I'll lie with you till you get back on your feet." Adele feels surprisingly heavy, and Bethany reluctantly looks back at Albert.

"Can you help me? Let's put her on the spare bed for a bit. I think she's had too much. She probably hasn't eaten enough today." Bethany thinks back darkly to the eating disorder days. All the fuss around Adele, all the appointments. She doesn't like involving Albert, but she doesn't have any choice.

Albert gets up wordlessly and puts his arm around Adele's waist from the other side. Her head lolls forward and Bethany feels a spike of panic.

"Jesus," says Albert, peering at Bethany from behind Adele. Bethany steadfastly ignores his gaze. She concentrates on getting Adele lying down as fast as possible. By the time they get to the door of the spare room, they're basically dragging her.

By the side of the bed, Bethany tries to gently lie Adele back, but she flops backward, too heavy for Bethany to catch her and slow her fall. Breathing heavily, Bethany pulls her legs up onto the bed, whispering softly in Adele's ear. "We're just going to pop you down for a little nap, Dell. I'll be right outside. You can have a little rest and I'll come and get you for dinner."

She's not sure if she's saying it for Adele's benefit, or

Albert's. She certainly doesn't think Adele is getting up for dinner. But she needs everyone to believe that she will be.

Albert watches her from the doorway, a strange expression on his face. Bethany studiously avoids his eyes. Their camaraderie from earlier has vanished. But Albert has had at least two glasses of wine too, and if anything was playing on his mind, he seems to shrug it off. He heads back to the lounge room, and Bethany frantically sends off some text messages.

Shit, shit, shit, shit, shit.

She has fucked it all up, and the fallout could be spectacular.

Her heart thrumming in her chest, Bethany goes back to join Albert, waving Adele's drunkenness off with a little bit of disgust.

She needs to get Albert back on her side.

She needs him to think they are a team.

Task number two.

She'll have to throw Adele under the bus a little bit, but she doesn't think she has a choice. Not if they're all going to get out of this unscathed.

"I think she's throwing up again," she says, breezily. "Don't judge her. It fucks with your electrolytes—you'd know, of course." Flattery. Always with the flattery. "She should know better than to drink, though." Here Bethany frowns, annoyed. The fun younger sister, annoyed at Adele for ruining their party.

If only she knew how much more was ruined.

Albert pounces on this inside information, like Bethany knew he would. There's a satisfied glint in his eye. He turns on his charm, his most caring voice. "Oh, I didn't know," he says. "Celia never told me." A hint of resentment, if you were listening, that such a tasty family titbit had been withheld; framed, as always, within the notion that Albert only wants to help. He doesn't want *gossip!* Oh no. He just wants to use his considerable knowledge and expertise to *help* them. Bethany's skin crawls a little bit, but she forces her smile to stay fixed on her pretty face, expansive, oblivious to the dynamics in this house.

"Oh, it was all a long time ago," she says, and that much was true. She doesn't think Adele is throwing up again. In fact, she's certain that she's not. Adele seems content, for the most part. If you take out her family of origin, Bethany thinks Adele would consider her life pretty perfect. She and Peter seem blissfully happy, and Bethany thinks that Adele is a good mother. Motherhood suits her. She's warm, and engaged, and attentive. Harrison seems to be thriving.

No, Adele isn't overly affected by the alcohol because she's been purging.

She's overly affected because somehow, Adele has drunk the drugs that Bethany put in Albert's glass.

And Adele is going to be out of it all night, instead of Albert.

And Bethany's plan is about to go stupendously balls up.

21

Thursday

December 2021

Peter watches his wife through half-closed eyes.

She's alone, and he wonders what happened to Melissa. He's not worried though. Even a little bit of time with a friend would have helped Adele. Sometimes all she needs is time.

He wonders why she can't see it herself. It's like a storm in a teacup—that saying sums it up perfectly. When Adele is distressed, it's as though the world is ending. She hasn't learnt, after all these years, that the storm passes faster than she expects, and she copes. She's stronger than she thinks she is. All she really needs from Peter is a steadying presence through the storm.

Still, there's something gratifying about her adoration of him. Peter knows that Adele really would cope just fine on her own, but it's charming to be so loved, so needed. Sometimes he has to remind himself not to bask too much in her belief that she copes because she has him. It makes him feel safe, that he will never ever be redundant, but you don't love somebody by celebrating their dependence on you.

"Where's Melissa?" he asks his wife now, and she turns to him, looking pale.

"I remembered something," she says. "And then I threw up. By accident. Again."

She's shivering, and Peter feels uneasy.

"You look cold. You can't be feeling great, have you kept anything down today? Can I make you something? Toast? A cup of tea?"

Adele shakes her head vehemently. "It'll come back up," she says, fretting at the sleeve of her jumper.

Peter goes into the lounge and comes back with a throw rug from the sofa. He wraps it around Adele's shoulders and squeezes them lightly.

"What did—" she starts to ask at the same time that Peter starts to tell her: "The police said—"

They pause for a moment, then Peter goes on: "They said there's not much to go on without an actual threat, like we expected. They suggested obvious things like finding out from Harry what the other note said, and why he destroyed it. Like, have there been more? Has something else happened? They also suggested security cameras, so we can catch the person if they leave another. Apparently there are very easily concealed ones you can have these days, so I'll do some research tonight and pick something up tomorrow. But of course, the priority is finding Harry. Shall we try Tom again?"

Peter moves next to Adele, and makes the call, but Tom has no more information than earlier. He gives them the numbers of a couple of the other basketball boys, ones Harry spends less time with and whose numbers Peter and Adele don't have; they've tried all the main group. Peter is about to call them, when he remembers what Adele said earlier.

"What did you remember that made you throw up?" he asks, his voice carefully neutral, his eyes busy on his phone.

Adele looks startled.

"Oh God, it sounds so silly. But the memory of it was so powerful, the feelings really shocked me. I don't know where I've buried it all these years. But Melissa was telling me about Celia and Albert fighting over Jingo around the time she died. She thought maybe Albert was being cruel to the cat and Celia was trying to rescue her. But I remembered—I remembered this thing when we were little. Celia and I both got kittens at the same time. And Celia cut her kitten's whiskers off. And Mum told her that was not okay, that they needed their whiskers, that it could be dangerous for them to not have whiskers. And right after that, like the same day, I found Celia with Jingo, cutting her whiskers off. And the look on her face."

Adele stares off into the distance, frowning, thinking. She shivers again, her eyes finding Peter's. "It was...kind of...mad. Like my cat couldn't have something her cat didn't have. Like she wanted my cat to suffer, too. But more than that, she wanted me to see it. She wanted me to know that she was making my cat suffer. And when I told Mum, Celia said she did them both at the same time, before she knew it was bad for them, and she looked so sorry and sad and repentant. But she smirked at me when Mum wasn't looking. And Mum didn't care enough about exactly when Celia had done it and that was the end of it, but that wasn't the awful thing, that Celia got away with it. It was...there was something so...evil about it. So deliberate. And I saw for the first time how dishonest Celia could be and it was shocking, you know? Like she was this whole other person. I had this image in my mind of her being loveable, and someone to look up to and aspire to be like, and I thought so highly of her, and the look on her face was so...awful. I don't know how to describe it. And I must have found it so distressing that I just blocked it out. It was like this weird memory came out of nowhere and whacked me over the head. But that's not the worst part."

Adele has been talking so fast, she's breathless. She stops, checking Peter is with her, that he understands her, and is reassured by his calm, attentive face. She goes on: "I just suddenly had this thought. I don't know where it came from. But Celia's cat had disappeared a few weeks before Jingo died. And I just had this horrible feeling that Melissa got it back to front. What if Celia was trying to hurt the cat, and *Albert* was trying to rescue it? Because her cat was lost, so mine needed to be lost, too? What if Celia actually threw Jingo in front of a car? Oh my God, it's crazy, isn't it? I'm going mad." Adele leans forward, banging her forehead lightly against the table, as though trying to gently dislodge the thoughts.

Eventually she rests there, and her breathing slows. She talks into the tabletop, repeats her own words, softly. "I'm going mad, aren't I?"

Peter stares at his wife, his face blank. He thinks absolutely that if anyone was hurting Adele's cat, it would have been Celia. But he can't quite believe Adele has finally noticed this, and even further, is considering the possibility that perhaps Albert is not the one in the picture whom the pointy stick should be levelled at, all the time.

"That's awful," he says, after a beat. "And absolutely possible. I can see how you might think that, yes." He doesn't want to overdo it, doesn't want to show Adele the relief he is feeling, that she might finally see that her sister wasn't the angel Adele seems to remember, this perfect sister that she needed to agitate for justice for. It's been a blind spot that has endlessly frustrated him. At the start, because Adele was so accommodating of Celia's endless demands; and later, because she used up so much energy fighting for Celia's memory, when he thought that energy would have been much better spent on *their* family, their son.

Especially since, he was fairly sure Celia did something to Harrison that day he broke the vase.

Harrison always denied it, but he was three. He didn't have enough language, enough grasp of expressing subtle, nuanced things. He probably repressed it. He was so shaken that day, so teary and clingy for days afterward, and Peter had seen the look on Celia's face after the vase was broken. You might expect some anger, some sadness, some regret about a valuable item being broken. But you don't expect to see *hatred* when a three-year-old makes a mistake.

Peter had been coming back in from the car, with some toys for Harrison that he'd forgotten. He was fumbling at the door, rearranging all the things in his hands to get the door knob, cursing and dropping things. Crouched down there, Celia hadn't noticed him.

But he had noticed her, through the large window pane next to the door, an intricate blue stained-glass flower suspended between Peter and his son. And he had noticed the sheer terror on Harrison's face, right before Celia had grabbed him by the arm, twisting it viciously, and frog-marched him toward the back door. She leaned down ominously close to him, her mouth right next to his ear. And Peter had dropped everything that he'd just fumbled to pick up, rushing to open the door and get to his son, but by the time he got inside, Harrison was already with his mother, and Peter was not entirely sure what had happened or what he had seen. Celia was tense, but measured. Too measured for it to seem possible that she had just hurt a child. Harrison had smiled uncertainly at Adele and ran off around the yard, looking rattled but not terrified, and Peter was unsure. *Had the stained glass warped what he had seen? Would this scene be possible if Celia had just hurt*

Harrison? Did he get it wrong? He was so confused that he said nothing, and regretted it.

So yes, he had always thought there was something a little off about Celia, and he didn't mind at all if Adele was starting to see it, too.

22

Friday

December 2021

Bethany knocks on the door gingerly.

She really doesn't want to see her sister, but it would be odd if she didn't. She's in Sydney so rarely—she had moved to Perth a few years after Celia disappeared—and to be in town right when Celia's name is in the media again and to *not* visit would look peculiar. But she is so tired. She doesn't want to be thrust back in to Adele ranting about Celia and Albert, and Bethany having to try to calm her down.

She would really rather forget every single thing about Celia and Albert and that entire week when Celia disappeared.

She knocks firmly on Adele's door, nevertheless. Her shoulders slump in anticipation of the onslaught.

Adele doesn't look pleased to see her, though. She looks about as pleased as Bethany feels. Which is not what Bethany expects. Usually, Adele would love a captive audience with whom to espouse her theories with, or to.

"Is it too early...?" Bethany asks, and Adele looks confused.

Bethany thinks that her sister looks awful. Blotchy skin, bags under her eyes, clothes that one would only ever wear if you weren't expecting to see anyone any time soon, or maybe ever.

Bethany, on the other hand, looks great. She's wearing a designer dress that looks elegant and simple but which cost her nearly two thousand dollars. Her hair is newly done, the highlights subtle enough that they look like a natural side effect of a seaside summer, not five hundred dollars' worth of chemical alterations. Her skin is smooth and tan, her lips plump.

"Harrison didn't come home." Adele stares at Bethany blankly, as though that explains everything, and now Bethany looks confused.

"He's just finished exams, right? A party probably got a little too rowdy and he's sleeping it off somewhere. We all did it, don't you remember?"

Adele does not remember any such thing. Her sisters, yes. But she, Adele, would never have caused her parents more than three seconds worry throughout the entirety of her childhood.

"He has a few more exams. He wouldn't be partying yet. He's very sensible. He's gay. Might be gay. We don't know. Maybe someone hurt him." And here Adele starts to cry. Bethany doesn't know it, but Adele hasn't slept at all. She and Peter took to driving around the streets at some point in the night, the history of the headlands like a grasping, clawing presence in the darkness. They walked around the headlands, and Adele feels guilty for considering the memorial glum and seedy. Now, she sees it in a different, panicked light.

How did any family ever sleep again, when their loved ones were lost, and never found?

The sound of the crashing waves had shaken and rattled something loose in her. She'd cried out to Peter that they needed to leave, unable to bear the sensation, the feelings that rose up in her and threatened to engulf her. Then immediately after the words left her mouth and they'd turned back toward the car, she'd cried out in the opposite vein; that they needed to stay. Peter had looked as fearful and uncertain as she felt, and that had unmoored Adele, as well.

If Peter was lost, then she was beyond that. Peter was her found, her home, her steadiness. If he was uncertain, she had nowhere to head toward, let alone land.

They'd clung to each other in the dark, a new and treacherous wedge between them. And it occurred to Adele that Peter could calm her in a storm, he didn't even have to say a word, he could soothe her with a look, or even just his presence. He was unruffled and un-shockable. But being her anchor was different to how he managed parental fears. Such as, where had their son disappeared to, the very day he was seen kissing a man in public, after at least two threatening messages were found at their house, the only day he hadn't come home in seventeen years?

Now, Bethany takes Adele by the arm and leads her back into her own home, sitting her at the table and putting the kettle on. Her instinct is to make a nice cup of tea, shush Adele's fears, and give her the sunny pep talk that she always gave when things were tricky in their family. But she finds that she doesn't really have the stomach for it. She thought she'd need to have a quick chat about the body found on the cliffs, present a relieved and hopeful front that it wasn't Celia, that Celia may yet be found, and then trot back over to Perth, which was really just a great amount of distance to keep between her and her family at all times.

"Right," she says, letting the roll of the boiling water fade, cups of tea left unmade.

This is *not* more of the same.

This is her sister, with a real problem, and Bethany surprises herself, by wanting to find a real solution. She puts aside the niggling notion that she needs to book her return flight to Perth before she gets sucked in to any more Celia drama. She settles in to her chair and occupies it fully, her eyes clear and sharp, her full attention on her sister.

"So we need to find Harrison. Tell me everything, and then let's work out how I can help." And Adele does, not even noticing that Bethany is being practical, down-to-earth, attentive, and the very opposite of dreamy.

23

Friday

December 2021

Albert Armstrong sits in his sunroom, sipping his whiskey absentmindedly.

He'd need to be careful or he'd be drunk, soon. One shouldn't sip whiskey absentmindedly. One should savour it, attend to it, relish in it. Especially when it cost four hundred dollars for the bottle.

What would Celia say? he wonders. She never let him buy whiskey. "It's such a cliche," she'd said, and to be honest, he never really minded. He was so desperate for Celia to love him. He would have done anything she had said.

He was desperate, and a fool.

He doesn't think about her so often, anymore. But now there was the body, and the alleged appointment with the family violence service, and police knocking on his door again, after all these years.

How had it all gone so badly wrong? He had loved Celia. He was attentive, he bought her whatever she wanted (he bought her an entire art gallery!), he was interested in her, he always wanted to hear how her day was, he was kind and thoughtful. Well, except that one incident with Adele. Okay two, two incidents. Two incidents where he was a royal prick and he deserved anything that was thrown at him. But he still can't make heads nor tails of what happened between him and his wife. He did everything he was supposed to do! Why did he not get the life that he thought he had been promised?

There was of course the gay problem, but that would never have gotten in the way of him being a good husband, a good father. He can't believe he had been so stupid. In his mind, he and Dan never even had sex, so it seemed only fair that he paid less. Dan hadn't been keen on that though, stammering that clients paid for his time, and what happened during that time was agreed upon by both parties, and Albert had felt annoyed. Three hundred dollars for a chat and a quick handjob! And he was *giving* the handjob! It was ludicrous, and Albert told himself that it was only fair that he gave him fake notes. He pretended to agree, and the stupid kid didn't even check!

He glossed over to himself the question of why he was carrying fake notes to a meeting with a sex worker in the first place.

Anyway, Celia didn't even ask him! He could have told her that he was curious, that he'd always been curious, but that he decided just to have a chat and leave it at that. But like everything, he could see the cogs turning in her mind, her working out how she could use that information to her advantage. He had the distinct sense that Celia tackled life like a competitive board game. It was all about how she could win, not anything about the journey, or connecting with people, or kindness or integrity.

Albert shivers, with his whiskey.

He thinks perhaps he got a little too caught up in Celia's games.

He had had good intentions when they got married, hadn't he?

What had happened between their wedding day, and Celia vanishing?

That moment at the dinner table, Celia mocking him about Dan, that was the moment he really saw what Celia was capable of and it was terrifying. He had hated her so blindly in that moment. He felt powerless, and stupid, and like all his efforts were in vain.

Why did Celia hate him so much?

The more she'd been cold, the more she'd seemed manipulative and unkind, the harder he'd tried to be agreeable and thoughtful. But his idea of what "normal" was in a relationship had been warped by Celia, he can see that now. It had become all about how she would perceive things, not about how things actually were. And he'd found himself trying to outsmart her, trying to play her games, trying to manipulate things so that he looked appealing and loveable. Or maybe he'd just tried to manipulate things so that Celia would never consider leaving him. He can't even understand it now. He shudders to think back on it.

He'd gotten on with his life. He'd avoided relationships. He'd found a way to live with it, to be productive, to ignore Adele's ridiculous claims and pretend none of it ever happened. It was not a skill set he'd recommend to his patients, but his father's teachings had come in handy, after all. Knuckle down and get on with it. Don't dwell on the bad stuff.

Like the deeply regrettable time he punched Celia, though God knows it would have taken a saint not to hit her in that moment. Because all of his doubts, all of his worries, came to a head right then. He and Celia both knew that what she was doing was not working out how to address a problem in their marriage, but how to use that problem to elevate herself and get what she wanted, regardless of the cost to Albert. In that moment, Albert saw his wife clearly for the first time.

Celia truly, absolutely, utterly did not care for anyone except herself. And she would go further than any sane person to get what she wanted. He saw danger signs for the first time. Previously, he'd felt petulant. He did all the things he was supposed to do. He didn't think about kissing boys. He married the pretty girl and worked hard and bought her everything she wanted.

Where was the respect? Where was the love?

He thought he wasn't getting what he deserved. But that night, for the first time, he realised it might be worse than that.

But that wasn't even the ghastliest part.

In that moment, in his response, his blind rage, his helpless, trapped, petulant and vengeful lashing out, he saw himself clearly for the first time, too. How far he'd drifted from his own principles. How far from acting with integrity he was. How it had happened so incrementally that he hadn't even noticed. And how there must have been something inside *him* that allowed it to happen.

So, no, he didn't dwell on that.

He had told himself that now that Celia was gone, things could go back to normal. He could be himself again. Wiser, more cautious. More upstanding.

He could move on from the bad stuff.

And he could most definitely not ever, ever think about what happened out there on the cliffs that night.

One bad egg shouldn't spoil the case. Was that the saying? Albert can't quite remember.

All he knows is that Celia went down, and good people shouldn't be dragged down with her.

But no one would understand. No one would believe him. Except maybe Adele. That's why Albert is sitting here, in the dusky evening light, sipping his whiskey. He's trying to build up the courage to call Adele. *It's been fifteen years, for God's sake! Surely they could have a conversation now?*

Or maybe that was the point. Maybe they never could. Maybe they were both so changed, or so blinkered, or just so damn confused about what had happened, that it was not possible to make sense of it. To talk it through like a normal problem between normal people and find some resolution.

Perhaps some dark secrets are best never finding their way into the light.

24

After

Friday

December 2021

Adele wakes up with a start.

She must have dozed off.

How can you possibly sleep? She starts to berate herself. *Your son is missing! Someone is threatening...someone!*

She feels a familiar agitation in her blood, in her veins, in her mind. It's like there are so many thoughts, and they are so uncomfortable, that her thinking short-circuits. She feels like a caged tiger, pacing the fence line, her thoughts whittled down just to: *walk; escape; walk; escape.* Without even thinking about it, she starts to stockpile food stuffs in her mind. There's the caramel ice cream that Harrison likes—a full tub! There'd be biscuits too, bulky cheerful chocolate chip ones—

Adele takes some deep breaths. What is *wrong* with her? Her son is missing. She needs to focus. Purging isn't going to help her! Purging is an escape, and if she sometimes needs to escape her own mind, her own reality, that is one thing...but when Harrison might need her, it suddenly seems selfish, and awful, and dizzyingly stupid.

She looks around for Peter, hoping he might have some news, some answers, a return to comfort for her, but as she cranes her neck and peers around, she sees a face staring at her through the window, and lets out a blood-curdling shriek.

Peter appears by her side as though he was magical, capable of teleporting, and is staring down at her in alarm, and all Adele can do is point at the window, her heart thumping.

"A man," she gasps, staggering to her feet. For herself, perhaps, she might have cowered in fear, but for Harrison, she is propelled to the front door, flinging it open with Peter right behind her.

"Who's there?" she shouts into the darkness. It can't be later than 7 p.m., but the blackness is absolute out beyond where the house lights throw their golden arc into her lush garden.

It is completely quiet on their street. In the distance, there's the usual traffic noises from the main road, and the low sound of the Barkleys' television next door. But no sound of activity in the garden, or even footsteps retreating in the gloom.

Adele is breathing heavily. Peter strides out into the garden, and Adele can hear him walking the perimeter of their block. He's switched on the torch app on his phone, and she can see great sweeping arcs of white light as he peers into every corner.

When he comes back to the front door, he shrugs. He looks concerned, but Adele isn't quite sure if it's concern about a man in their garden, or concern about his wife losing her mind.

"Are you sure?" he asks, looking at her carefully. "Could it have been our own reflections in the glass?"

Adele shivers. She can't say she exactly trusts her own mind one hundred percent at present. Especially with the purging. You've lost control of your mind a little bit already by the time you get to purging. And afterwards, well. There's that fuzzy, weightless feeling she loved so much, which is exactly one hundred percent useless when you're trying to focus and be as sharp as a tack.

She will stop purging. She *will*.

She must.

And then she remembers with a start. The trigger. For a while, it was all her therapist banged on about. *Know your triggers. What are your triggers? What triggered it this time? What happened? What was the trigger?* A deeper understanding is all well and good, but you also need to know what triggers you into that state. So you can be prepared. So you can have a plan in place, something to do, something as familiar and well-known as purging, so that when you were triggered, you could set in motion your plan, and try to keep yourself safe.

You have to try different things, her therapist had urged her. *You can't just try a hot bath one night and declare it a failure, and never try anything else. What else soothes you? A walk? A run? A chat with a good friend? Painting? Writing? Have a tool box of twenty, thirty, fifty things you can try when you feel the need to purge! If one fails, try the next one. Then the next. Then the twenty after that.*

Well, it turned out having a good life soothed Adele. A good life with a family that she chose. A husband who listened to her, really saw her, who wanted to know about all of her feelings, not just the ones her parents deemed acceptable. Someone who loved all of her, not just the surface, pretty, palatable parts.

That had soothed her for twenty-odd years.

And Celia. Well, Celia was a trigger. She had worked out that much. Feeling undervalued by Celia. Feeling used, or ever-so-subtly devalued. But more than that, Adele thinks, remembering Jingo's whiskers, perhaps what triggered her was the deep sense, beyond language, beyond comprehension, that sometimes Celia triggered her deliberately. For no reason other than enjoying her own sense of power. Of watching Adele flail.

She's never before been able to pin it down, put words to it, but the shock of the whiskers memory has shifted something in her memories more broadly. And for the first time she thinks, *Celia wasn't just thoughtless.*

She wasn't just selfish.

Celia was awful.

Celia enjoyed watching other people fall.

And this week, after all this time, what had happened this week that had set her off, after twelve years of not one single incident of purging?

It feels like a failure. She knows it is ridiculous, that she is not back to square one, she doesn't need to start again. It's just a relapse, and honestly, wasn't it a miracle she hadn't had a relapse in all this time? She didn't have to start again. She had all the tools she needed, all the skills within her to defeat this again, just like she'd done before.

She just feels untethered because everything that had happened this week was too much.

And then Adele remembers, how could she forget, what is *wrong* with her at the moment? Her mind is not working at all. Her brain is not her friend.

She'd received a text message, out of the blue, from an unknown number, and she'd deleted it immediately, because she knew, she just knew it was Albert, and she couldn't cope, couldn't cope with any of it, couldn't bear to think about it all for one more single minute.

Can we talk about Celia?

And she'd deleted it at once, and gone storming off for her power walk around the cliffs, and had thrown up for the first time in over a decade.

25

BEFORE

March 2006 (one week before Celia disappeared)

Bethany hesitates at the threshold of Albert and Celia's house, then steps out into the night.

She's thinking quickly, trying to get everything in order before Celia gets home.

She'd already texted Celia to tell her that everyone had drunk too much and dinner was a shambles, that she'd put Adele to bed in the spare room. And she'd been about to go home herself, she'd said good night to Albert, made excuses about rescheduling when Adele felt better. But then she'd lingered in the kitchen, trying to work out a way to salvage her plan. And, feeling guilty, she'd gone to check on Adele just one more time.

It can't have been more than five or ten minutes later. Did Albert think she had left? Apparently so, because she heard grunts and moans coming from the bed. Hesitating at the door, she was torn between outrage and self-preservation.

She'd stood there for a moment, watching through a crack in the door.

It was too late, she reasoned. Albert was already having sex with Adele. What could she do? She could go in and cause a fuss, but what could she say? She couldn't accuse Albert of having sex with a drugged woman without outing herself. So what did a few more minutes matter? She could take advantage of Albert's post-coital stupor to get the information she came for. So it wasn't all in vain.

Later, she finds it hard to forgive herself for this.

She could certainly have walked in there and accused Albert of raping a barely conscious woman, who couldn't consent.

The thought haunts her. Not just because she didn't help her sister. But because it showed something to her about herself that she really, really didn't want to see.

Self-interested.

Selfish.

She'd known this about herself, of course. She just never imagined how far she could push that envelope. That she could be selfish to the point of letting people that she cared about be harmed. She'd always told herself that she didn't *hurt* people. That she knew where to draw the line.

That evening, she learnt that that was not true.

She'd stepped away from the door, listening, all her senses zinging. She heard Albert breathing deeply, then snoring. She reasoned she had a few minutes. At least three or four. Surely, on some level, he'd know something wasn't right and wake up, not just sleep beside his sister-in-law the entire night?

Stepping as lightly as she could, she opened Albert's study door. The filing cabinet was locked, but the key was in the lock, and the files were arranged in perfect alphabetical order.

Her heart thumping so loudly she thinks she won't even hear if Albert gets up, she starts flipping through the labels.

Bank accounts.

Birth certificates.

Cat (Bethany stopped momentarily. Celia and Albert didn't have a cat).

House stuff.

ID.

Bingo. Bethany eased the documents out of the plastic sleeve. *Oh, joy and hallelujah!* There were certified copies of all of them. *Who was so organised?* Bethany wondered. It couldn't possibly be Celia. But she silently thanked whoever it was, and slipped one copy of a passport, a driver's license, and a birth certificate into her satchel.

She hesitated, and then took a copy of their bank accounts, all listed neatly, with names, BSBs, account numbers, and login details.

So easy.

Then she remembers Albert's grunting and huffing, and her heart stops in her chest.

Not so easy for Adele.

She won't remember though, thinks Bethany. She's heard Celia make fun of Albert's penis size before. She'd cringed away from her sister, something too intimate, too cruel about the off-hand way Celia mocked the man she was supposed to love, and Celia had noticed, brushed it off. "Just joking!" she'd said lightly, as she always did when she noticed she'd gone too far. But now Bethany lunges for that memory. She hopes against hope Adele isn't sore. That she never knows what went on in that room tonight. That she manages to forget it, which she sometimes seems to do.

A memory tugs at Bethany—Celia, dressed for a party, sequins shimmering on her luscious navy dress. Bethany moving up the hall, wanting to ask Adele something. She was four years younger than Celia, maybe fourteen at the time, so it was probably something of no interest to eighteen-year-old

Celia whatsoever. Already, Bethany was wary of her eldest sister. So when she heard Celia's low voice coming from Adele's bedroom, she had hesitated in the hall.

"Don't feel bad," Celia is saying, her voice soothing, honey and milk dripping from every syllable. "I can help you make new friends. There's no point hanging around with people who don't like you."

Adele had made a strange, strangled sound, and Celia had swept out into the hall, abruptly, it seemed to Bethany, when Adele was clearly distressed behind her. Celia had stopped when she saw Bethany. Her eyes had rested on her youngest sister, thoughtfully, and then she had carried on without a word. Bethany had thought she would come back, that she was off finding a solution to soothe Adele, but whatever the interaction was, apparently it was finished, as far as Celia was concerned.

Adele had rushed past Bethany into the bathroom, and Bethany had rolled her eyes. She didn't understand how fragile Adele was, and she resented the drama around her eating disorder, how thin-lipped Jocelyn became, when she was thin-lipped and emotionally withdrawn anyway. *Why did Adele have to make things worse?*

Still, she waited for Adele in her room, legs dangling off Adele's bed. She was supposed to tell her mother if Adele was purging, but she never did. Her irritation with her sister never extended far enough to get her into trouble. And any purging was met with disappointment, anger even. It was definitely trouble. Even as a child, Bethany could see that her mother's response was the opposite of helpful.

Adele returned, not long after, her eyes red and vacant.

"What did she say?" Bethany asked, curious, and Adele starts to cry again.

"Melissa told her they're sick of me hanging around, and

they don't even like me, and I should find some new friends." Adele sniffles. "Celia said she'd help me, though."

Bethany stares at her.

"Well, I'd rather know the truth!" Adele shouts at her, suddenly defiant. As though she and Celia are a team, and Celia has just done her a favour, and Adele needs to defend her, and bind herself even closer to Celia, which to Bethany seems like the definition of insanity. What is *wrong* with her sisters?

"You know she's just making it up to get you worked up, right, Dell? There is no way in a million years that Melissa said that to Celia." And Bethany had had to convince Adele, reminding her of events that occurred so recently that it is bizarre to her that Adele could forget them, could place more credit on Celia's version of events than what Adele's own reality told her. Melissa had just invited Adele to go up to the Gold Coast with her family for the Easter holidays. They spent Saturdays together, wandering around the beaches and the headlands, aimless, chattering endlessly.

"She might have changed her mind," Adele protests, still clinging to Celia's version of events like they're the only version worth attending to.

It was the first time that Bethany truly thought that both her sisters were batshit crazy, and she sidles out of Adele's room as soon as she feels confident that Adele is settled. She can't wait to finish school, and get the hell away from all this drama.

But then, a few days later, Adele repeats virtually the same conversation with her.

"We talked about this." Bethany is impatient. But Adele's face is blank. She doesn't seem to know what Bethany is talking about. So she repeats her arguments. She watches Adele slowly come around, for the second time.

Her friendship with Melissa is solid. Her family has bought Adele the tickets to Queensland. Celia is just being Celia, making stuff up. That's what Celia does. It's awful, but she's not going to change.

"We talked about this," Bethany repeats, disbelieving that Adele can have forgotten, thinking that Adele might be looking for attention, or else truly be deranged. "Do you really not remember?"

The memory had stuck with Bethany, of Adele being so easily swayed by Celia, so under her spell.

And also—so able to completely forget an entire conversation, as though she were never even there at all. *Was Adele so adept at burying hard things, or did the purging scramble her brain?* Bethany will wonder the same thing many times over the next ten years.

Either way—probably Adele will never know what went on in that bedroom tonight.

But Bethany knows, and she feels awful.

But not so awful that it puts a stop to her plans.

As she steps out into the night, she types the block number code into her phone, then Albert's number, and starts calling Albert's phone, which she'd put on the hatstand in the hallway close enough to the spare room to hopefully be easily heard. She needs Albert to wake up, and feel ashamed, and get the hell away from her sister, before Celia gets home.

She dials, again and again and again, until a gravelly, confused voice answers the phone.

Then she hangs up and hurries away.

And hopes everyone can forget the horror of this night from start to finish.

But she got what she came for.

That was something, at least.

She just hopes that Albert is smart enough to pretend that what just happened, never happened. And that no one would mention it to anyone, ever.

A drunken mistake.

No need to hurt anyone. Not Peter, not Celia, and most especially not Adele.

For once, she thinks her family's approach might be the best one.

Shut up, be silent, don't make a fuss, and forget all the bad things as quickly as you can.

26

AFTER

Friday
December 2021

John Stonwald watches his daughter with interest.

He knows his daughters think he shows no interest in their lives (Adele roped him in to a family session with her therapist once, and she'd said exactly that, and he had stayed silent and showed no interest in either the therapist's opinion, Adele's accusation, or the surreptitious way the rest of the family exchanged glances and said exactly nothing in his defence) but he is actually acutely wondrous that he produced such strange creatures and that, more than that, they keep coming back to visit.

They would never guess it in a million years, but he once went to his own therapist to talk about the disconnect between how he feels about his family and their perception of how he feels about his family. And the therapist had given him some ideas about talking to his children about the things that mattered to them, and they all sounded completely ridiculous and wishy-washy and made him deeply uncomfortable and embarrassed. He never went back, and he continued to care for his children in exactly the way he had been taught growing up: with a stiff upper lip, hiding his feelings, providing all the things a family needed (failing to notice that emotional support might indeed be right up there with a roof over their head and dinner on the table) and expecting they would understand that to be a declaration of his love, and need nothing more.

Bethany has made herself right at home.

"I can't stay long," she says, as she unpacks vials and vials of goodness knows what in the bathroom, calling out to them both through the open door. "I'm going back to Adele's to help. She fell asleep on the couch, so I thought I'd give her some space and drop my stuff off here. I don't know when I'll be leaving."

She emerges moments later, smiling brightly.

"Now, tell me about this man you saw Harrison kissing, Mum. Every single thing you can remember."

"Do you think this is a good idea, darling?" Jocelyn glances nervously at John. She imagines her youngest daughter going door-to-door, asking inappropriate questions and supplying inappropriate details about their family to the entire neighbourhood. *Do they really need to shout from the rooftops that Harrison is gay?*

She thinks of something else, which she grabs hold of with relief. "He might not be ready to tell people. You can't just go around asking everyone about the man he was kissing."

Something catches on Bethany's face, and Jocelyn feels satisfied. *Didn't think of that did you, darling?* She feels a little bit smug, that she's the progressive one, the one thinking about such things, forgetting that just a moment before she was actually reaching around with blind desperation for some reason to not reveal to their neighbours this particular fact about her grandson.

Bethany, for her part, is squashing down her frustration.

Does her mother really think she's so incompetent, so thoughtless, that she'd be careless with her nephew's private information?

Yes, she does. Of course she does.

"I won't betray any secrets, Mum. It just might help us to work out where Harrison is." She doesn't mention the threatening notes. She doesn't think her parents will cope, and their way of not coping will be to make the rest of the family feel bad about having any feelings about the situation whatsoever.

"Well, I couldn't see much anyway," Jocelyn says, irritated. "Tall guy, very camp looking, dark hair. I didn't see his face. He looked older, though. He looked like a man. Not a boy. Not a teenager. That's all I can tell you."

Bethany is disappointed. Someone older than Harrison could be anyone. She can't narrow it down by his school friends. Still, she has ways and means. It's a start.

"Good," she says, bright. Enthusiastic. A woman with a hairbrained plan that her parents think she has no idea how to execute, even if it were a good idea.

Ditzy.

"Thanks. Now, is your Wi-Fi password still the same?"

27

Before

March 2006 (the night Celia disappeared)

The woman hurries along the cliff top.

It's late. The sky is a murky black, tiny pinheads of stars invisible through the gloom and city smog.

The moon, though, is luminous.

She's later than she meant to be.

Her step quickens.

They were supposed to meet at 10 p.m., but she wanted to be early, to make sure everything goes exactly as she envisioned. She doesn't like being late. Her clothes are slowing her down, though. Bulky and masculine, she's even padded out the shoulders, and she isn't as quick and nimble as her small frame usually allows. Her arms feel weird, like she has to hold them out farther from her body than she usually would.

She has it all planned out, but she didn't account for this awkwardness. *Is it telling? Does it give her away?*

Anyway, it's too late now.

There was nothing to be done about her height, but she's

hoping in the dark and the shadows nothing else is quite as it seems, either.

Despite the layers of clothes and her fast pace and her careful planning, she shivers.

There's something creepy about this path in the dark.

Far, far below, she can hear the waves crashing into the rocks. The sound is ominous.

There's still no rail between her and the cliffs in some places, despite numerous complaints to the council.

Not for the first time, she thinks how easy it would be fall.

To die.

To push someone.

She wondered, once, if pushing Albert might be the simplest way to get the life she wanted. But she's too small. She didn't think she'd have the strength.

Still. Here, in the dark, dressed like a gay man, she feels suddenly vulnerable.

It's just the hormones, she tells herself again, the feelings uncomfortable and unusual. She always feels like the strong one, the one calling the shots.

She breaks into a run. She wants to get this part over with. Move on to the life of luxury she's set up for herself.

Not be out here in the dark, spooking at shadows like a child afraid of monsters.

Maybe monsters are real, though.

That thought makes her relax, and smile to herself.

If anyone on the cliffs tonight is a monster, it's probably her.

She lets out a sharp huff of laugh, and slows back down.

It's nearly over.

Up ahead, a figure emerges from the shadows.

He's not where he's supposed to be. He's too close. Celia stops suddenly, pebbles scattering underfoot.

They were supposed to meet at the seat at the tip of Marks Park, looking out at the ocean. Her plan, perfectly thought-out, was to get close enough to be seen, in Albert's distinctive aubergine coat (she worried it would be too dark to see it, but the moon was glorious, and the coat as ridiculous and attention-seeking as Albert himself; if someone had to remember one thing about who they saw on the cliffs tonight, they'd remember the coat: full length, purplish, ludicrous, with furry trim at the cuffs. She actually can't believe she had never noticed her husband's effeminate side before).

Not for the first time, Celia thinks perhaps this plan is madness. But she's too far along now.

Too far along the mad plan; too far along in the pregnancy. Any day now, Albert is going to notice her stomach getting rounder, the nausea that is stretching out over the whole day.

He'll never let her go once he knows she has a child coming.

He'll never let the child go.

For all the trying and planning and thinking about it, Celia had never considered how the prospect of a child might interrupt her approach to life. And for a brief moment, she had wavered.

A good man.

Albert was a good man.

He'd be a better man if she didn't find ways to subtly goad him. He'd be a good dad.

For a while there, she thought about starting again.

Then she'd fallen on the side of things she always fell on: self-interest.

Albert should have had more backbone. He might have been happier. He might not have annoyed her this much. He might have been worth staying with.

It wasn't her fault he was such a sook.

No, she needed to do this last thing. She can't bear the thought of a life with him. Parenting a child with him.

It's a bit much though, really, and something churns uneasily inside her. She wishes she hadn't done it. But she can't undo it now. Too many things have been set in motion. Plus, it's kind of a masterpiece.

She had thought it would be so entertaining, that she would feel so clever. But all she feels is a little bit hollow.

Is this what a conscience feels like?

She's never felt bad before. Not one single pang. *Is it the baby growing inside her? Does motherhood make you want to be a better version of yourself?*

Will it last?

No, she realised, in a session with Evan. *Guess not.*

Evan saw more than she let on. She'd caught Celia out in a lie and they'd stared at each other, because it was a lie like all the others: pointless. Just because. Just to see what she could get away with. It was so stupid. She'd been trying to lay the groundwork so that Evan would tell the police that Albert sounded like a sociopath. That *he* was the one who told the endless, pointless lies. She'd hinted at violence, at emotional control. She'd told stories of his cruelty. And it was the bloody excellent one about the melanoma that undid her! She'd told it exactly right, exactly how she'd imagined, but she'd become complacent, she wasn't paying attention. It was after her pitch-perfect delivery: her confusion, her wondering about people who take some purposeless, inexplicable pleasure in another person's distress. Her self-doubt—had she confused the messages? Was it her fault? She needed Evan to be able to join the dots when the police came knocking, after she vanished. She'd squirrelled away enough money to get started, in a bank account in Bethany's name. They all looked so alike, it had been far easier than even Celia had hoped for.

Bethany would never even notice. She was so damn hopeless and vague. Celia doubted she'd even noticed her driver's license was missing from her wallet for a few days.

She'd made sure her mother had Evan's details, too, so

could tell the police: *she was seeing a therapist! Can you talk to them? They might help us to find her!*

Everything was lining up just right.

But then she'd decided, why should she leave?

At first, a little cottage somewhere new, just her and the baby, sounded so idyllic. An adventure! But the more she thought about it, the more she wanted Albert to leave, not her. She liked her house. She liked her gallery. She wanted her life exactly as it was, without Albert in it. And she knew, with a baby on the way, that was never, ever going to happen. Albert would be cramping her style for as long as this child existed.

And she decided: she had to leave, or the baby did. And that decision was far easier than she imagined. She would probably be a terrible mother, anyway. She thought back to Jocelyn's birthday lunch, Harrison breaking her very expensive vase. And yes, yes, she'd probably be nicer to her own kid, but when he'd turned to her, wide-eyed, scared, her hatred and rage had bubbled over so readily. It was so close to the surface—closer even than she herself had realised. She saw this little boy, all alone, no parents anywhere nearby...and what she saw was an opportunity, so rare these days. To be alone with someone else's child. And she'd lent down close to him, let her eyes burn into his, twisted his arm, and whispered, "I'll gut you like a rabbit if you don't get the fuck out of my sight this minute, you revolting little shit."

So no, she wasn't really very sensitive to children. She didn't like them very much. She didn't really want them around, hers or anybody else's. She'd booked the appointment to terminate this little leech inside her, sucking the nutrients out of her, making her sick, making her feel pangs of regret about things she'd never thought twice about before, and she felt much better.

Still, she needed Albert to be in the spotlight, on the back

foot, ready to negotiate. So she just changed her plans a
little bit.

She'd invested so much in Evan. Months of plotting and
planning and thinking about the best answers, the best
responses, the very right and correct things to say. Not to
mention all the time and money, sitting in that fluffy little
office, full of cushions.

She'd added another detail, on a whim, just to entertain
herself, just to see how far she could push all these stupid,
stupid people in the world. She didn't even need it! Evan
believed her. She'd already proved she was smarter than her. It
was very meta, talking to her about people who take pleasure
in other people's distress. And Evan wasn't distressed, but she
would be, professionally, if she knew how much Celia had run
rings around her. She *should* be distressed. And Celia's stupid
ego had ruined it. She'd just thrown in, "There was a weird
message, too. When he was telling the patient, something
pinged on his phone. And I shouldn't check it, I know it's not
okay! I know this isn't how to resolve issues in a marriage! But it
was thanking Albert for something, with weird suggestive
emojis, and talking about being underpaid and kind of
implying they needed to be paid or there would be
embarrassing consequences. And then it had some banking
details. That's weird, right?"

And Evan had looked at her carefully, saying, "Didn't you
say Albert took his phone into the study to call the patient?"

And she still might have got away with it, made something
up, something feasible, because people don't want to believe
they're being lied to, they want to believe the best in people,
they want to believe what you carefully lay out in front of them.
But she missed her chance, because she could feel the flash of
irritation and the knowledge of being caught out in a lie flash
across her face. It was so fast, most people would have missed
it. Bethany and Jocelyn and John would have missed it. But not

her therapist. Not her therapist who was trained to look at not just what she said, but her body language, her non-verbal cues. And Celia could fool her when she was on guard, when she was playing her role, but not when she knew exactly what Evan would have seen on her face.

When this was your gig, you know when you've been caught out.

So she and Evan had stared at each other. "Oh, it must have been later," she'd said, breezily, her composure completely recovered. Celia didn't blink, and she didn't look away. *I dare you to say it,* her eyes said, and Evan didn't say it. But Celia could see the cogs turning in her mind. She knows that, for one split second, the truth was written on her face so clearly she might as well have spelled it out to Evan in dictation.

Celia knew Evan wouldn't be telling the police any concerns about Albert when news of her disappearance surfaced.

Never mind. She made an appointment with a family violence service, carefully giving her birth date, and a mobile number just one digit different to her real one. *Surely that would get Albert questioned, at least.*

Initially, she'd planned to siphon off enough money to leave, with Albert in the spotlight for her murder. But now, she planned to do the same thing, but return when Albert had had a while to sweat. She just needed the waters to be muddied enough for her to get away, have the termination, have Albert under a lot of pressure (violence! Gayness! Sex workers!), then swan back in, making her demands. When he was vulnerable, and weak. And likely to comply.

The house. She wants the house, and she wants the gallery.

She must remember to get her money back out of the account she opened in Bethany's name, too. But that could wait until after they'd settled the separation and the finances.

She doesn't think about how hurt Albert will be, how much he will miss her. For a brief, impossible moment, she had wanted to start again, to try to be better, somewhere new, where all her past misdeeds could be forgotten. But...*why?* This option was much more agreeable. And it was kind of fascinating to see if she could pull it off. Have the entire neighbourhood believe that Albert was violent, and slept with sex workers.

She had quizzed Dan, that morning, of course. And he had admitted that Albert had only wanted to talk, "*and a little touching,*" he'd said, not meeting her eyes, uncomfortable. But they'd never actually had intercourse. Celia, apparently, had grasped that the fee was the fee, regardless of what activities they got up to, much quicker than Albert had. But where other wives would have seen devastation, Celia had seen an opportunity.

She had taken Dan's number (he had shared it reluctantly) and pondered her next move.

She might be going insane. *Was this the baby, too? Hormones, clouding her judgement?* She could always get what she wanted without going to such spectacular, risky lengths. With all this drama, she was no longer going to be able to hide. Albert and Evan will know who she really is. But who would believe them? Evan is bound by doctor-patient confidentiality, and Albert will have the distasteful accusations of using sex workers and being violent hanging over his head.

No, no one will believe him. Celia will be pretty much as safe as she always is.

People see what they want to see. And she is a master of curating a pretty picture for them.

So here she is. Dressed in Albert's clothes. She's asked Dan to meet "Albert," using Albert's phone. He had said no, at first, but "Albert" had been so genuinely remorseful in his correspondence. He'd sent extra money. He'd expressed that he misunderstood what the payment was for. She made Albert sound like a lovely, thoughtful man, capable of growth.

She'd cackled to herself at the thought, and deleted all the messages from Albert's phone.

She's told her sisters, too, though she omitted the gender of the sex workers. She doesn't really know why. There was something distasteful about it, something that reflected badly on *her*, perhaps. She shed a few tears to them, let them hold her, rub her back.

Her sisters will be there for her, once Albert is out of the picture, and out of the house.

She's arranged for Dan to meet Albert for a walk and a chat only (he's still so nervous and unsure, you see). She's paid him in advance. A twenty-minute walk on the headlands, all arranged on Albert's phone. A photo sent, of Albert in his aubergine jacket, so Dan would easily recognise him in the distance and in the dark. *I'll be wearing this jacket,* the text had read.

If Dan wondered why a nervous man would choose to organise a gay rendezvous on the cliffs where so many of his peers had met a violent end, he doesn't raise it.

It doesn't occur to Celia that Dan might be nervous. That he, too, would be aware of all the people who had died here, and might also have a backup person, a backup plan.

Celia just needs Dan to see someone who looks like Albert on the cliffs, someone wearing Albert's jacket. She intends to get close to their meeting place, then turn around. Look as though "Albert" got cold feet. She's banking on Dan at least having enough insight not to pursue someone who is hurrying away. He's been paid. He should, she hopes, shrug it off, maybe send a text, but what is Albert going to do about that? He'll just think his escort texted the wrong client. He's not going to mention it to anyone.

Then she's catching a taxi to a nice little Airbnb (also under Bethany's name, she'd asked to borrow her computer and it automatically logged her in, then she'd carefully deleted the confirmation emails from Bethany's account, although she supposes there will be "thank you for your stay" ones she'll need to attend to) for a few days to have a termination, and watch the shitshow that unfolds. Celia missing. Dan being there at just the right time. Hopefully, if he is not too dumb, which Celia knows she can't bank on, he'll recognise her name in the media, and go talk to the police, describing Albert, that they were supposed to meet. That Albert was definitely on the headlands right when Celia disappeared on her walk around them without a trace (she's texted both her sisters from her own phone just now to say she's taking a walk on the headlands to "clear her head about the stuff with Albert," and sent a picture of the waves in the moonlight, so there is absolutely no doubt when and where she was last definitely alive).

Even if Dan doesn't report anything, there's still the odd late-night runner about. The headlands attract beautiful people, conscious of their bodies, lean and tanned and alluring. They will run, even in the dark.

Someone will remember this aubergine coat.

Just to be sure, when she leaves, she'll throw it near the cliffs and run over to the Junction, don a dark beanie and scarf, and catch a taxi to her Airbnb. Hope she is forgettable to the taxi driver: masculine, gruff, a shadow in the back seat.

She just needs the upper hand. She needs to get Albert on the back foot.

She had always thought she'd get the life she deserved by marrying a rich man and being looked after, but now she wants all the trimmings without the man, and she thinks she has master-minded a way to get it.

It was dizzy-making, it was so grand.

But Dan is not at the right meeting place. He's too close, he's not going to sight "Albert" from a distance, he's about to accost her, and realise who she is!

For a moment, Celia feels a rush of blind rage. If Dan was

close enough, she might shove him off the bloody cliff she is so angry. *Can no one be trusted to follow simple instructions? How is she supposed to plan something meticulously if stupid people keep doing stupid things, and ruining her plans?*

But the figure stepping out of the shadows isn't Dan.

It's Adele.

28

AFTER

Friday

December 2021

Dan Pontini has a problem.

He has ignored the problem for as long as he is able, but now he has a crushing sense of guilt and wrongdoing and absolutely no skills whatsoever to work out a way forward that will get him in as little trouble as possible.

He wishes Jonno were here to help. Jonno helped him out of more than his fair share of pickles, and always with such a knockout sense of humour, too.

Life was better when you had a Jonno to rely on.

He should have moved away. Jonno had told him that's what you do when you want to start over. Go where no one will recognise you, and there's no chance of your past coming back to haunt you. But that's easier said than done, when all your friends and all your routines—the daily rituals that kept a person sane, everyone knows that, life isn't just about the good parts and the nice beer and the fancy French food and kissing hot boys—were built in this place. Starting again sounded horrible. Once, it might have sounded exciting, but he is thirty-two years old and that feels exactly old enough to have earnt a happy, quiet life, without anything more exciting than a new boyfriend to entertain you for the rest of your days.

To be fair, he only felt guilty because he might be exposed. He hadn't felt guilty all this time and what did that say about him? What sort of person is so blasé and so uninterested in the sanctity of human life? Maybe he doesn't even deserve to be happy. Maybe he doesn't deserve love, and security, and a family—but he stops these thoughts. *Unhelpful thinking patterns. Check the evidence.*

What is really the case here?

He saw something he wasn't supposed to see, but in itself it wasn't so unusual. He didn't see anything *illegal*.

He's fallen in love with someone that he shouldn't.

And someone is threatening to expose him. Maybe.

What could he have even done differently?

Not fallen in love with a seventeen-year-old. That certainly would have been better. He wouldn't have even remembered Celia Armstrong if he hadn't inadvertently seen a picture of her, large as life, in his boyfriend's house. But would that have helped, really? It didn't change what he saw on the cliffs that night. It's not like he could erase that moment, that memory. He just wouldn't have been *reminded* of it. He might have carried on forever and never have thought about it again.

Certainly, he was too old for Harrison. But he wasn't some creepy pervert! All his other boyfriends had been perfectly age-appropriate. Some even older than him! He still can't quite explain what had happened at that party. Harrison had looked older, and by the time he realised he was definitely way too young indeed, it was too late, he was already smitten. They had talked until the sun came up, and kissed, and laughed, and Dan really very much wished Harrison was twenty-seven, not seventeen.

But no. That was not the main problem.

The main problem was that he had seen bloody Celia Armstrong fighting with her husband on the cliffs fifteen years ago, and because there was something unpleasant about his dealings with Celia and Albert, something not quite right about the whole thing, and because there was no way in the world he was going to go talk to the police and admit he was a sex worker and that's how he recognised both Celia and Albert, he had told exactly no one about it, even when Celia's disappearance blew up all over the news.

He had only been seventeen. It wasn't even legal for him to be working as a sex worker. He'd had no idea what to do, and like probably hundreds of uncertain, scared seventeen-year-olds before him when faced with a difficult situation which they were ill-prepared to cope with, without good role models (his parents sucked, if you must know, and they have had no contact with their shameful little gay son whatsoever, ever since the day he came out to them at fourteen and they kicked him out of the house) he buried his head in the sand and pretended none of it had happened, and hoped it would all go away and if he didn't mention her to anyone, he would never have to see or hear about Celia, ever again.

And that part, at least, had gone roughly to plan.

Until now.

Now, she was in a frame in his boyfriend's living room, she was a speculative by-line on the news, and she was, large as life in his memory, asking weird and inappropriate questions about male sex workers, before arguing with her husband on top of a cliff, then disappearing and never being seen or heard of by anyone, ever again.

The first time he'd mentioned it to Harrison, Harrison had brushed it aside, and Dan had let him. It was only their third date—a slightly awkward movie night at Harrison's house, when his parents were out—and Dan was grappling with so many difficult feelings, it was a relief to be able to put that one aside.

There was the age gap, for a start, and whether he needed to call the whole thing off.

Then the uncomfortable feelings about Celia, and not doing the right thing back then. But also, interwoven deeply with that, was his work history, which was long forgotten, most of the time, but always a source of anxiety in a new relationship.

But then just yesterday, Harrison had dropped by, and Dan had tried to ask about Celia again—*that woman in the photo, was she ever found?* But Harrison had dumped his bag on the floor, shoved a piece of paper at Dan, and burst into tears.

Only a loser would date a sex worker, poofter.

That was what had led to their first row: some idiot had left it pinned to Harrison's front door. Twice, apparently. And Harrison had been outraged, *why would someone say such a thing, do they just hate him and Dan because they're gay, what did it even mean?* It was Harrison's first experience of homophobia and it was so shocking to him that it broke Dan's heart.

Although, it was some kind of miracle he'd made it to seventeen unscathed by it.

Still, homophobia aside, Dan had to sit Harrison down and tell him, "Actually, when I was your age, I worked as a sex worker for men," and Harrison had nearly lost his mind.

If it was anyone else he'd told, anyone older with enough life experience to know better, Dan would have kicked them to the curb. He was too old and too tired to have to unpack another person's big feelings about his past, their whorephobia and hatred. It was just a job, for God's sake. And yes, if his parents hadn't kicked him out, perhaps it wasn't a job he would have chosen for himself, fourteen and homeless and having an identity crisis. But it was a job that had saved him, in many ways, and he's sick of people and all their bloody stupid preconceptions about it. He'd learnt a great deal about himself, about holding a boundary, about love and trust and friendship and community. He'd found Jonno, the best friend (father figure, he supposes, really) a man could ask for, even if it didn't last for all that long.

But still. Even as he brings out the familiar lines, tells himself these exact, reassuring, soothing things, the thought of someone knowing about his past and using it against him brings with it a wave of shame, swift and sharp and unmistakable.

Dan misses Jonno, still. After all this time. The best way to eradicate shame about sex work was to hang out with bloody awesome sex workers, and remember he was valid, just like them.

Jonno also would have given good advice about Harrison, who was so young (too young, yes, yes, Dan knows). Everything was so new to Harrison, it was a world he'd never even thought about. Being gay was huge enough; thinking about paid sex was too much, and Dan's feelings shifted slightly from infatuated lover to protective gay mentor, which was probably a better fit. Things changed between them, in that conversation; Dan doesn't think they can change them back, and his heart is breaking a little bit. But he's too old for Harrison. It was for the best.

So he sat Harrison down and explained the work to him as best as he could.

Not failing to notice that he had patiently explained similar things to bloody Celia, fifteen years before. She had been so strange that morning when they'd gone to chase up the money Albert owed him. At first, self-righteous. Denying it could be true. But then, when she accepted that it was, in fact, true, she flipped so quickly. She didn't cry or seem hurt or upset or even angry. She had seemed strangely curious.

Calculating.

She asked a lot of questions, so many questions that it was he and Jonno who ended up uncomfortable, desperate to get off her porch.

There was something unsettling about Celia, her cool, appraising gaze.

The way she shifted to charm, and warmth, when she should have been blindsided, and sad, or at least full of rage.

After the talk with Harrison about Dan's past, Harrison had taken off in the dark, angry and volatile. Dan had sent a text message, inviting him to talk about it whenever he was ready, but had respected his desire for space. He thought Harrison would come back when and if he was ready to talk. He thought he probably just needed to walk off some steam.

But now he was worried. Harrison never replied or returned, and then at the cafe today, Tom had dropped by and asked after Harrison, told Dan that Harrison's parents were worried, that he'd never gone home last night; that they were asking after Harrison's love interest, and that he, Tom, wasn't sure if it was okay to pass his details on, but maybe Dan could get in touch with them if it was appropriate?

Dan didn't explain what had happened to Tom. He did ask if Tom was worried, and he'd hesitated.

"He's never not gone home before," he said eventually. "I would think he'd call me if something was wrong, but..." His voice trails off, and Dan had nodded.

It was only one night, and Dan tried to settle the uneasiness spreading inside him. But it was hard not to think about all the people that had disappeared around them, all the lives lost, all the violence and fear and hatred and bigotry.

And between what he knows about Harrison and Celia, he wonders if it might be time to have a talk to Peter and Adele.

29

Friday

December 2021

Adele stares at her reflection in the mirror, and wonders if Celia would look like the woman staring back at her if she was alive, and forty-seven years old.

She and Celia shared the same blue eyes, the same wide forehead and petite nose. Somehow in Celia the features had combined to convey something to be aspired to: the beauty ideal. Perhaps it was all the money she spent on her hair, perfect blonde highlights to complement her pretty face (Adele had tried to copy them for a while, but at some point over the last fifteen years, she had shed the idea that Celia was the "right" version, the correct way to do things, even down to her hair, which was longer now, and an inconspicuous, unremarkable brown).

She is certain Celia would not look as tired as she does. Celia would have paid for all the creams and massages and treatments that would maintain a fresh youthfulness, if she'd stayed married to the local doctor and had not vanished into thin air. Even if she hadn't gone so far as Botox, her lifestyle itself would have minimised the impact of worry lines and tired eyes. Even with children, Celia would have availed herself of nannies and au pairs and anything she could afford to ease the burden, the relentlessness of caring for small people.

No, she and Celia would not look even the tiniest bit alike anymore.

She washes her hands, and goes back out to the dining table, where Bethany is organising things. Even Peter seems to have handed the reins to her without so much as a moment's hesitation. For the first time in their lives, they both, concurrently, have no idea what to do. Bethany's presence is a welcome relief. She's making lists, calling basketball mothers and fathers, calling cafes where the boys like to hang out, even talking to the police about what they should do next. She tells them she's found some leads on social media, and is busy taking notes and messaging people.

Adele feels too exhausted to even be surprised.

As they're sitting helplessly, watching her, though, someone knocks timidly on the front door, and Bethany leaps to her feet. A few moments later, she appears back in the doorway, looking uncertain and confused.

A nervous, friendly face pops around the door behind her, and with a bravado that he definitely doesn't feel, Dan Pontini says: "Hi, Adele and Peter! I'm Dan. I'm a friend of Harrison's. I wondered if I could have a little chat?"

Bethany, Peter, and Adele all stare at him, their thoughts too slow, but in the moment before anyone he speaks, he rushes on, nervous: "I'm sorry we had to meet like this, but I can probably answer some of your questions about the notes on your front door. And it's way too late, it's very definitely not okay that it's so late...but I might, maybe, possibly, know something about Celia, too."

And all the worry, all the swirling thoughts and murky

blackness inside her head, all the purging and all the nervous, unintended vomiting, all converge in one great overwhelming shitstorm in her psyche, and Adele slides off the chair so quietly, without making a sound, that it takes everyone a moment to notice that she has fainted away.

When Adele comes to a few minutes later, she's lying on the couch with Peter gently stroking her brow. Bethany and Dan are hovering in the background.

Everything comes to Adele through a fog, a mist of confused perceptions.

She sees Peter, on the headlands, hurrying away into the night.

She sees Albert, hurrying toward her.

She sees Celia, her eyes hard, her jeering face, telling Adele something, something awful, and she can't quite remember, she doesn't *want* to remember.

Dan's voice comes down to her as though from high above, and she lets her eyes droop, she doesn't want to participate, she doesn't even want to hear about the notes on the door. She feels like she is on a giant truck, one of those freight trains that carry produce right across Australia, the vast emptiness of the desert endless in front of them, nothing in their way, nothing to slow them down, roaring through the night, unstoppable, at speeds you wouldn't dream of travelling at any other time.

And they're going to crash.

Adele doesn't want to crash.

"...someone knows...sex work...notes...old..."

"Albert...I left...fighting..."

"Are you sure it was Albert?" Peter's voice cuts through Adele's stupor. "How can you be sure?"

"I can't," Dan falters. "I wasn't close. I didn't see his face. But he was wearing that beautiful jacket, he'd sent a picture of it. It was so unique. And I know I should have come forward. I should have said something. But I wasn't close, I didn't hear anything, and I...didn't want to admit to the police how I knew either of them. I was just a kid! It was the wrong thing to do, I know that now. But at the time I felt like the world was against me. My parents, the police, shitty clients. I didn't want to out Albert, and even though he was a jerk that first time, he seemed decent after that, and it's a terrible look for a sex worker, talking to the police about clients! I got a strange text from him, and I couldn't work out how it fit together. It was like he didn't actually have any idea we were supposed to meet, or maybe he was covering his tracks, I don't know."

Dan's voice is getting higher and higher, his words falling over each other in his haste to get them out. It was like he'd held them in for so long that after one sentence spilled out, he needed to get the rest out yesterday to calm himself down. Adele, Peter, and Bethany can barely keep up.

"I'd just texted to say I was waiting, and I got this weird message back, like 'what are you talking about' sort of thing. And I didn't want him to turn on me. It all just seemed messed up and confusing. And I was doing a lot of ecstasy at the time, if you must know. I didn't trust my memory, I didn't trust myself to remember things right. And my best friend disappeared that week. He was like my mentor. He always talked about taking off to a new city, starting again, putting sex work behind him. A fresh start. It happens all the time in that industry. People cut all ties when they're ready to move on. But I took it pretty hard. He just cut off all contact, disappeared. I felt abandoned all over again. I didn't know what to do and I didn't have Jonno around to ask. He probably would have told me just to tell the police I was out for a run, saw them, had never seen them before in my life. I thought of that, later, but it was too late. It was just easier to pretend it never happened. I told myself it wasn't my business, and honestly I buried it so far away I forgot about it until I saw the picture of Celia over there."

It was a small print of Celia, laughing on Adele's wedding day. There had been a bigger one, a shrine to Celia, almost, hanging in the hallway. But one day Adele had taken it down, and put it in the study with all the other piles of things, and Peter hadn't mentioned it, and the house had felt lighter, for a time.

Adele sits up slowly.

"I missed what you said at the start," she says to Dan. "The notes on the door."

"We had a fight. About my past. Someone had left a note. Two notes. He'd torn the first one up." Dan repeats the phrase, embarrassed, staring at his feet. "It was such a shock to him. The note. My past. I think he just wanted to walk it off. Blow off some steam." But even as he says it he can feel the fear creeping into his voice. Not that there's been any violence on the cliffs for years. But a gay teenage boy, humiliated and angry, alone in the dark? Fear stirs deep in his bones, even as he offers Harrison's parents platitudes.

It seems too much, having these conversations with Harrison's parents.

"But Tom came to tell me you called. He wasn't sure if he should give you my details, so he suggested I call you. Harrison was upset. I understood. I thought he needed some space. But Tom said he didn't come home and he wasn't answering anyone's calls, and it's all connected, isn't it? Celia, and my past, and Harrison being upset. I just wanted to do the right thing. I don't know if coming here is it."

Dan looks younger than his age, uncertain and hapless, and Adele's heart softens.

"I had thought with the body on the cliffs, it was time to come forward. Own up. Confess. But then the body wasn't her, and..." Dan squints at Peter. He looks confused, and uneasy, shifting from one foot to another, glancing between Adele and Peter, then back to Bethany.

"The thing is," he says, shifting again, looking like a drowning puppy, not sure which way to head for help, to get out of the strong currents and the cold, cold water that is trying to suck him down into depths he might never resurface from.

Was coming here a stupid idea?

He had wanted to do the right thing by Harrison's family. If he had information that might help them, it was his duty to come forward, he can see that now. He was also worried about Harrison, and had felt some overpowering urge to confess, finally, to someone, what he had seen. A cleansing of his conscience, maybe. But it seems foolish now, preposterous even. Because he didn't really have any idea what went on that night, he had no firm evidence of anything, and because now, in this house, he is almost certain that he saw Peter that night, too.

Dan was hurrying away, and almost ran into someone. And it was only memorable because he'd gone over that night in his mind again and again, agonising, trying to decide if he should tell someone, ultimately deciding that it all felt off, and that he didn't want to get mixed up in it. But here, now, staring at the wedding photo over the fireplace, he feels a jolt of recognition. He noticed it before, but didn't *really* notice it, had no reason to really look, with Harrison hurrying him out of the house before his parents arrived home.

Peter doesn't look that different. He has the same physique, the same strong jawline and short, thick hair.

He takes a deep breath. He thinks he should shut up and go home, but it's like the stop has been forced out of a hole in a tank—now that he's starting talking, spilling everything, words gushing out of him, he can't seem to rein them back in, make himself stop. "I think I saw you that night, too, Peter. As I was hurrying away from the headlands, you were hurrying toward them. We passed right by each other on the path. It was you, wasn't it, Peter?"

And Dan, Peter, Bethany, and Adele all stare at each other, and nobody says anything at all.

"If you can't trust your memory about seeing Albert, how can you possibly trust it about seeing Peter?" Adele starts to say, her voice sharp, confusion and fear creeping toward her, crawling over her, sinking their nasty little teeth into her.

And just when she thinks she can't take it anymore, can't take one more single thought in her head, a face appears at the window, and there's a firm, invasive banging on the door.

And when Peter flings it open, there, on her doorstep, after fifteen years, is Albert Armstrong, with a grim expression on his face, and a bottle of red wine.

30

AFTER

Friday

December 2021

"It's not a good time, Albert!" Adele shrieks, and everyone turns to stare at her, her voice cutting through the silence, shattering something between them all. A conspiracy to stay quiet, perhaps.

That night is coming back to her.

The darkness.

The coldness.

The fear.

Peter is standing at the door, confused, wary. And Albert says, clearly, firmly: "I need to talk to Adele, and I need to do it alone."

"We need to find Harrison," Adele says, her voice high and shrill, panic washing over her, everything so far out of control she doesn't know how to exist in this moment. She wants to shut it all down. Pause it, go back, start again. None of this is acceptable. None of it is calm, and methodical, and soothing.

It's all falling apart, and Adele starts to cry. Peter comes and stands protectively close to her.

"It's really not a good time," he says, grim. He's trying to make sense of Dan's revelations, and also whether anyone would and should trust his memories, after all this time.

Of all the times for Albert to drop in, why on earth did it have to be right now?

"So no one has any idea where he might have gone?" he asks Dan, businesslike.

"No," Dan says uncertainly. He feels vulnerable, and exposed, and his heart hurts, and is that really the same Albert *right there, looking through him as though he doesn't exist?*

"There was another note," Adele says. "*I know your secret.*"

She doesn't know what she thinks about this man in her lounge room. Dan is too old, she's shocked and faintly disgusted about his past, but she has a grudging respect for him for showing up at her house like this. Only a good egg would put concern about Harrison in front of protecting his own secrets. But right now, she just wants to find her son. She wants to know if the person leaving messages might hurt him. She needs to not be hearing anything about Celia, who seems irrelevant and somehow painful, intruding into this house while her son is missing. It makes no sense, but what she feels is resentment—that bloody Celia, once again, is taking up all the space and dominating everything, as though she is the most important person in the world. All her fears and anger about her sister being missing have retreated with such velocity she almost has whiplash.

Who cares what happened to Celia fifteen years ago, when Harrison is missing right now?

Dan looks confused. "Well, it's not Harrison's secret, is it? Isn't it *my* secret?" And then everyone looks confused, until Bethany slowly lowers herself onto the couch opposite Adele.

"Maybe there's more than one secret," she says.
And then everyone looks suddenly afraid.

31

After

Friday

December 2021

Dan is staring at Albert in confusion, but Albert does not give him a second glance.

Dan supposes he doesn't look anything like he did in his promotional photos fifteen years ago, and Albert himself is hard to recognise, too. He's greyer, and much heavier. Dan wouldn't have recognised him if he'd passed him on the street. It was only this context, this family, the unusual name, that made him realise Albert's identity.

"I'm going to go driving and look for him," Peter says, scooping his keys from the key bowl, a determined look on his face. "Adele?"

Adele starts to rise, but Bethany puts a hand on her arm. "She just fainted, Peter! She needs to stay here. I'll stay with her. Dan?" Dan looks uncertain, but stands awkwardly near Peter. "Sure, I'll come. I know some spots to look."

Peter looks uncertainly at Albert.

"I'm going to stay here," he says grimly. "I need to talk to Adele."

"She has more important things to think about right now, Albert," Bethany snaps, an old, familiar anger rising in her. Albert and his self-centredness. Albert thinking what he had to say was the most important, most riveting item on the agenda at all times.

She remembers all the things Celia told her over the years, all the things she'd seen, and is about to tell Albert exactly where he can stick his precious needs. But then she remembers with a start that Celia hadn't always been honest with her. Not about a lot of things, including Albert.

Which parts were a fabrication and which parts were the truth?

She has a sensation like being a wet dog, wanting to shake herself, shake all the confusion and dank wetness away.

Task One, she thinks to herself. *Find Harrison.*

Task Two, maybe: tell the truth.

"I've waited for fifteen years. I'm sick of waiting. I want to talk, now." His gaze is steady, resting on Adele, determined. Peter and Bethany may as well not have been in the room.

Peter starts to protest, but Adele put her hand up, waved her acquiescence. What could it hurt, after everything else that had happened? She can't bring herself to care. She feels so weak, so spaced out.

Harrison is probably just licking his wounds somewhere. Peter will find him. Peter will bring him home.

What were the chances? His first boyfriend was a sex worker who knew Celia and Albert?

And Albert really was gay? What a pity they were estranged. Maybe a gay uncle would have been a great support for Harrison.

Unless he was a murderer. Is that why Celia left? Is that why he killed her? She found out he was meeting Dan?

Dan and Albert.

Dan and Albert.

Adele's thoughts feel sluggish. Something feels elusive, just out of her grasp. But it was all too complicated. She wants to lie down. But she also wants to get some answers, close some doors, and here is one, right in front of her. She might as well close it while she waits.

"Wait here," she instructs Beth. Then she indicates Albert should follow her into the sitting room, not glancing back.

But Peter steps in front of Albert.

"No," he says. "Unless you have something to say that will help us find Harrison, it can wait, Albert. Go home."

There's a flash of something on Albert's face, a momentary swell of anger, at being thwarted, or told what to do, but it passes quickly, and he looks attentive and caring and ready to acquiesce. But Adele intervenes.

"It's okay, Peter. Go with Dan. He said he knows some places to look. I'll just go crazy sitting here waiting. Albert can tell me...whatever it is. Beth is right here. *Go,*" she urges, and Peter looks torn, glancing from his wife, to Dan, and back again.

"No," Peter says, again, and Adele looks impatient.

"*Please,* Peter. Find Harrison."

Peter looks deeply unhappy. He glances at Bethany, his face a question, and she nods at him, like a promise. She would look after Adele.

Peter and Dan sweep out the front door. It shuts firmly behind them.

Adele and Albert retreat to the sitting room.

For a moment, there is the sound of movement through the living room, as someone moves about and pulls wineglasses from the cupboard. Then there is stillness, and Bethany finds herself holding her breath.

32

After

Friday

December 2021

It's like history repeating, Adele thinks to herself with a shiver. *Her, with Albert, alone. With wine.*

She leaves her drink untouched on the table. Even though she knows, what could Albert try, with Bethany just in the next room?

He'd managed before, though, hadn't he?

In what context does Albert think they could sit and casually sip wine together?

She's about to tell him he has precisely three minutes to explain himself, when he speaks.

"What were you doing out there, the night Celia disappeared?"

And it comes to her, that night, like a slap across the face.

She starts to feel weightless, like the chair she's sitting on can't keep her connected to the earth.

She hadn't intended to confront Albert, she remembers

now. She'd been so unsettled, so miserable, so full of guilt, that she'd gone out in the dark to walk and purge.

She hadn't purged in years. She felt ashamed and distressed and like her brain wasn't working, let alone her body. Everything she'd built with Peter, every obstacle she'd gotten past, seemed undone in that moment.

Then she saw Albert, hurrying along the path on the cliff edge, as she came out of the public toilets.

She hadn't even thought about it. In her unhinged, post-purging state, she had just hurried to intercept him, cutting across the park rather than following him along the path.

"I didn't consent!" she wanted to say.

"Did you drug me?" she wanted to ask.

She darted across the little expanse of green grass as fast as she could, and came out at the tip of the headlands, the furthest point poking out into the ocean, just in time, Albert approaching from below.

She stepped out, strong, fierce, into his path.

And instead, she saw her sister.

Adele closes her eyes. Takes deeps breaths. Tries to steady herself.

"What were *you* doing out there?" she whispers.

"I saw Celia putting on my coat and hat. She was dressed so strangely. You know how fussy she always was about her appearance. And I'd seen her on my phone a couple of times. I thought she was up to something. It's hard to explain."

Here Albert starts, glancing over his shoulder at the door behind him, toward the room where he'd just stood metres from Dan. He turns back to Adele thoughtfully, but seems to make a decision, and carries on.

"A few things had happened. A few lies. I was starting to

think I was married to someone completely different to who I thought I was married to. I thought she was trying to set me up, but I couldn't work out what on earth it was. Someone texted me, to say they were waiting at the spot, and I had no idea what they were talking about. So I followed her. I was just going to watch. See what happened. It was cold that night, do you remember? And I was in such a rush, Celia had taken my winter coat, I just threw hers on at the door. Some ridiculous flimsy pink thing. It did not a thing to keep me warm. And it made me realise afterward, when she never came back, when the police came...when *you* came, with your accusations, that anyone who came forward saying they saw me or Celia on the cliffs, well they might have thought I was Celia, and she was me. And the latter, I think, was the point. That was her plan. She wanted to look like me. I'm still not entirely sure why."

Albert stares off into the distance, glancing over his shoulder again, perplexed.

He's different, Adele realises. He's less worried about what she thinks, how he presents. He's more thoughtful, more measured. He seems unknowable.

Fifteen years might change a person, she supposes.

"I saw Peter." Albert's eyes rest on Adele. There's regret in them. Pain. "I thought perhaps he had come for me. That you'd told him...what happened."

"What *did* happen, Albert? Because I only had a glass of wine. I was so out of it. Did you drug me?"

As Adele says this, she closes her eyes. She can't bear it. She can't bear to know, or to not know. She wants to be absolved, to blame someone. It's like choking; she didn't realise how much it still weighed on her, huge and restless and unresolved. Like there's not enough air to sustain her in the entire world.

Was knowing better, or worse?

"No," Albert says, his eyes resting on her. "But I was a fool. I went to check on you and thought you were inviting me, making eyes at me. I'd been drinking, too, remember? I didn't usually drink much. The wine had affected me more than I'd expected. And I was so lonely. Celia was so...cold. I didn't realise at the time how much I was longing for some connection. I was so desperate for connection I mistook you watching me like that as an invitation. You were just staring at me, lying on the bed, arms flung wide. I can see how I confused it, honestly. Lying on a bed, your pose, God, it..." Albert stops, putting his head in his hands, shaking himself. He takes a deep breath, tries again: "It's no excuse, I know that. The next day, I knew something was wrong. With a clearer head, I recognised something was off about it. Like, you were staring at me because you were so out of it, or something. I wondered if you were on medication that interacted with the wine, or something. Bethany said something to me that night that you were purging again. I didn't know. I thought maybe you weren't well. But I was so ashamed. I was mortified. I wanted you all to like me. I always felt that you were laughing at me, while I was trying so hard to be a good part of the family." Albert looks wistful, and Adele feels a pang of something uncomfortable. Her usual role, tugging at her, beckoning her to fall into line.

Poor Albert, she finds herself thinking, and shakes herself.

So sensitive.

Oh God, oh God.

The words slam in to her, and she doesn't want to remember, she doesn't, she can't bear it, she will make it stop. *Just the night of the rape,* she tells herself, hanging on to just that day, fighting to not letting any other thoughts in, or out.

"And then you were so angry, when Celia never came home. And I thought it was about the sex."

I wasn't purging, Adele thinks through the fog, holding on to one true thing, one thing she knows for sure. *Not until after that night. That night was the trigger, that time. That relapse.*

Why had Bethany told Albert that?

Memories scratch and claw at her, holding something aloft, just out of her reach, and she wants to understand, but she also doesn't. She feels like she can't breathe. She tries to keep her face calm, neutral, tries to squash her panic down.

Bethany is ten metres away.

She is safe.

"I've been wanting to talk to you, you know. You never replied to my text. And then they found the body, and I thought it would just bring back all the anger, all the blame, and it felt like I'd missed my chance. I had been thinking, it's been fifteen years! Surely we could talk now? And then they found the body, and it all came back to me, and I thought...maybe, after that brought it all back, stirred it all back up, you might need another fifteen years."

"Why are you here then?" Adele asks, her voice faint.

But she doesn't need to hear the answer.

She already knows.

33

March 2006 (the night Celia disappeared)

"Albert." Adele steps out onto the path, bold, forceful. And then squints at Celia in confusion. "Cee?"

Celia throws her hands up in exasperation. "I can't stop, Adele. I have things to do, people to see."

"Why are you dressed in Albert's clothes?" Adele looks genuinely confused, and a little disconcerted.

"Why are you trying to intercept Albert in the dark on the headlands?" Celia counters. She doesn't actually care about the answer, but knows that the best way to deflect questions you don't want to answer is to ask someone something that insinuates something uncomfortable right back.

Adele thinks as quickly as she can, but everything seems foggy. Her brain isn't working properly. She has that light-headed, fuzzy-around-the-edges feeling she gets after purging. Her legs feel weak.

"I wasn't. I was just walking and thinking. And then I saw you and thought it was Albert. I don't know what I thought."

"Right," says Celia. She looks impatient.

"Are you done walking now? It's late. You should get home. To Harrison. And Peter." There's something mocking in Celia's tone, and Adele is flustered.

"Yes," she says. She should get home. She *should* get home.

Now that it's Celia in front of her, she's lost her nerve, anyway. Could she really ask Albert if he drugged her? It seems unlikely. It seems so aggressive, so forceful. So unlike Adele.

Don't make waves.

Don't make anyone upset.

Keep everyone happy, at all costs.

But her brain whirs and stumbles.

"What are you doing meeting people out here, at this time of night? It's...kind of creepy, don't you think? You should go, too."

"Didn't you get my text? I'm just walking and thinking. About the sex workers."

Celia's eyes rest on Adele, weighing something up in her mind.

But she seems to come to some resolution.

Adele can't think clearly. She thinks about Celia's story about the sex workers on her doorstep, her fear and outrage, her thinking that she might leave Albert. Something doesn't seem quite right, now, on the headlands, with Celia wearing Albert's coat, and Adele can't quite put her finger on it, what feels wrong. Somewhere, deep in her bones, she feels that Celia is tricking her, laughing at her, and a memory floats by unbidden: she is seven years old. Celia is telling Jocelyn that the boy up the road took her schoolbag and pushed her over. She is detailed in her story. What he said before and after. The colour of his shoes as Celia stared at them, scared, her face in the dirt.

Adele was unable to speak. Earlier that day, she'd watched Celia throw her schoolbag off the cliffs, leaning far out over the perimeter wall, gleeful as the bag soared through the air, then disappointed when it snagged on a rock, and never hit the water. She'd turned around, and seen Adele watching, and stalked back past her. And kicked her on her way past.

Later, she'd hugged Adele, said sorry, told her that Adele was her favourite sister, and offered her a little toy pony, and Adele had been so thrilled. So much so that as she watched her sister lying to their mother in the kitchen, she couldn't make her mouth work to say the words. She felt afraid, though she couldn't say why. And Celia had glanced at her, conspiratorially, and Adele had loved being included with Celia. Loved being part of Celia's golden team.

Then as Celia walked back out of the kitchen, she'd flicked Adele with her forefinger, hard, and smiled.

That was the thing with Celia—you never knew which version of her you were going to get. And Adele lived for the moments where she felt loved and understood. Celia was the only one in her family who ever made her feel that way. Chosen. Valuable.

She brushed over the rest, told herself Celia was just in a bad mood. Such was the force of her attachment to this sister who could—and routinely did—wound her. Celia always gave her just enough love to keep her hanging on for more. To keep forgiving her.

Celia had gotten the new Barbie schoolbag that Jocelyn had previously refused to buy her—"You already have a schoolbag!" —and was satisfied, and kind, for a few weeks after that. It was the kindness that was the problem. It was so warm, and so good, and so much fun, that when the other things surfaced, Adele started to doubt herself. It didn't seem possible that the two truths could coexist. Which meant that Adele must be misinterpreting one of them.

The bag incident unsettled her. It wasn't the lie that confused her so, it was the detail around it. And poor little Robert up the road, Jocelyn had marched down there and accosted his mother, and to this day still frowns when the Petersons are mentioned, remembering that nasty little boy who hurt her daughter, and never admitted or apologised for what he had done.

"Were there really sex workers on your doorstep?" she asks her sister now, her voice faint.

"Of course. I wouldn't tell lies, now would I, Adele?" Celia smiles, mockingly, a secretive, knowing look in her eye as she twirls Albert's coat flamboyantly, as though she has a secret that she's dying for Adele to know, and something scratches at Adele, more memories from years ago, and Adele doesn't want them, she doesn't want to remember, she fights and shoves against the memories with every bit of strength she can muster. She will not remember. She does not want to know.

But then there's Celia, in the gallery, in a beautiful black dress, that same look in her eye, asking Adele to file a police report about a missing piece, a tiny watercolour of the headlands by a well-known local artist. "It was right here before lunch. I was just adjusting the height of the hooks to bring it in line with the other three," Celia had said. "Someone must have literally picked it up off the counter while I was up the ladder."

The police had been very interested in the security cameras, but they hadn't restarted after a power failure that morning.

"Convenient," the more junior officer had said, staring at Adele, and she had felt frazzled and naughty, and had had a crippling fear that she'd find the watercolour tucked in her wardrobe a month or a year or a decade later, Celia's mocking smile haunting her dreams for weeks afterward.

"I didn't tell you the whole story though. I didn't tell you they were *male*. Oh, I knew it was part of him," Celia goes on, cheerful now, proud of her cleverness. "I knew it was something he dreamt of. I found his porn subscriptions, I knew exactly what he looked at on the internet." She doesn't mention that, in fact, she only found these in her investigations after Dan and Jonno's visit, and they were so insignificant and infrequently visited they were hardly worth mentioning. "He's always so bloody cheesy. Trying so hard, wanting people to like him. It makes me sick. I just want to make him go away. Settle our divorce. Leave me the gallery and the house. So I've just made a little date for him, out here. Nice young man. Just a bit of fun, really."

Celia smiles at Adele mockingly again. "Anyway, I saw you with him. I came home earlier than you expected, didn't I? You and Albert, pumping away in my spare bed." Her smile vanishes. "That bed is probably worth more than your shitty little house," she hisses, her face close to Adele's, something violent flickering in her eyes.

Adele staggers backwards, leaning against the rock face, her breathing ragged. She can see the slow build of water on the string of moss hanging down in long wet braids off the rocks, gathering volume, building to a rich, full droplet before dripping to the path at her feet. She stares at the drips, unable to lift her eyes, unable to meet Celia's gaze, as though if she stares hard enough at something else, what's in front of her won't be real, it won't all be true.

"Just kidding," Celia says now, smiling slightly. She didn't actually see anything between Adele and Albert, but she did change the sheets in the spare room and wonder. Albert, Adele, and Bethany were all very odd after that dinner, and Celia is well-practiced at using guesswork to find out useful truths. She watches her sister now, carefully. "You were dead to the world when I got home. I came in and watched you, for a while." There's something menacing about the way she says this, her eyes boring into Adele, dark and expressionless. Adele shudders.

"But why? Why don't you just leave?"

"Because I like watching stupid people suffer," Celia replies, her voice flat. Then she cocks her head: "Have you vomited today, Adele? You look a little puffy around the eyes. A little puffy around the waist, too. Are you pregnant again? No more little monsters in my house, please. Did Harrison ever tell you what I said to him at that lunch? He actually peed his pants, you didn't notice that, did you? You didn't change him till much later. And every time I looked into his eyes, I could make him pee himself a little more. Whenever you pissed me off, that's exactly what I'd do."

Adele drags her eyes back to Celia in horror. Celia smiles again, as though she's offering up any story of her daily routine, not the story of how she terrorised a child.

But then her expression softens and she shrugs. Adele can almost feel Celia reaching out to her, pulling her in, offering her a space in her warm orbit. The flip was so stark. Adele can't believe she's never noticed it before. "Which is why, dear sister, I have a little favour to ask." She leaves the silence hanging, and appraises Adele with interest.

Was it always like this? Adele thinks through her fog. *How did she forget? How did she live like this?* It wasn't like Celia had never shown Adele her true colours before. *Why did Adele keep burying things, insisting on the binding ties of family? Trying harder and harder to find the warm spots, like she had any control over Celia's behaviour whatsoever? Like if she was just a better sister, more attentive, more acquiescent, the result would be different, and she would be more loved?*

She sees Celia tearing up Bethany's project on Mount Everest, then diligently helping Bethany try to find it for the next hour, making comforting noises and offering to help rewrite it. Confused, she'd gone to the bin outside, smoothed one of the pages out, not comprehending. *Was she going mad?* And Celia appeared beside her, ephemeral, telling her, sounding so reasonable, how Bethany's teacher had asked her to help Bethany, that the standard of her work was so low, and this was a way to help Bethany score better without having to embarrass her about how bad the project was. How Celia would help her write a better one, and everyone would win.

But then Celia had vanished, and it was Adele who helped Bethany, confused and unsettled.

Earlier, Adele had exclaimed over Bethany's original project, the hand-drawn mountains and hikers, their expressions so delicate and detailed, their hope and awe and determination. She had thought it was brilliant, had been proud of Bethany's skill, but now she doubted her own judgement. That was how convincing Celia was.

Then other times, she remembers being sick, and Celia bringing her cold face washers, stroking her brow, her expression soft and loving, and it's too much for Adele, she can't make any sense of any of it, is it possible that both things could be true—that Celia was a good sister, and also a monster? The ground feels like it is moving underneath her, churning and bucking, she wants the memories to stop, she does not want to remember, she needs to get away from here, get home, to Peter and safety and Harrison and love, but memories are cascading over her, and she feels like she is drowning, and the truth isn't setting her free, the truth is going to kill her.

Why does she not want to remember? Is it because she wants to preserve the lie of her sisterhood, or because she cannot fathom or face the wilful forgetting that has sustained it?

Why did she hide from herself who Celia was?

How can she trust herself, when she has lied to herself so consistently for decades?

It's like something opening up inside her—what is rising to the surface, into her line of vision, is not so much the duplicity and evil of her sister, but how Adele abandoned herself in order to be close to her. She clung on to the puny offers of toy ponies and occasional hugs and whispered secrets, and wilfully buried the rest, for what? Because that shitty little sliver of love was all she ever got, in her emotionally stunted family?

"So, all I need is for you to corroborate my story. Just confirm you saw me out here on the cliffs tonight, that Albert sees male sex workers. He really did punch me, the prick. Just don't mention I was wearing his coat, will you? Better yet, you could mention that you saw Albert out here, too." Celia smiles lazily, something heavy in her eyes, a satisfaction, her plan coming together even more convincingly than she had thought, but a coldness, too. She tilts her head, watching Adele. She looks almost disinterested.

Through her confusion, something starts to drag at Adele, pulling her down, like drowning. She wants to give in to it, to go under, to let the dark water suck at her hungrily, drag her away. To do what she always does.

Please her sister.

But for the first time, something starts to rise up, too.

"No," she says.

Adele might not like Albert, but she's not going to lie about him.

She's not going to do Celia's bidding, try to win her favour, scurry about like her little minion anymore either.

At least not tonight.

Somewhere, deep down, Adele feels that pull as the pull of history, the pull of how things are always done. She knows, in her bones, that whatever her intentions, she might not be able to fight it. Tonight, maybe, but tomorrow? And every night that comes after? Celia has some power over her that she can't quite fathom, can't quite put her finger on.

Is it possible to see this pattern and still not be able to escape it?

Maybe not. But tonight she can. Tonight, she feels as though she has the strength. Tonight, she's suspended in this moment where she can see how Celia manipulates her, and why she, Adele, lets it happen.

Tonight she can be true to herself. She can say no. No more.

She can say we are not sisters. We are not normal, we are not happy, and I divorce you, sister.

I divorce thee, I divorce thee, I divorce thee, she chants nonsensically to herself.

She can't think straight. She *has* thrown up, and her brain is fizzing and fuzzing at the edges. She feels like she might fall over, might pass out. When did she last eat? What is she even doing up here? She feels so unsteady, so unsettled she might slip, she could die out here, and no one would ever know. No one would ever know her sister was trying to manipulate her, her sister was awful, her sister was not who she pretended to be.

No one would ever know that Adele saw it, finally. That she put her foot down. That she said, *Not tonight.*

"Excuse me?" Celia raises one quizzical eyebrow. It hadn't occurred to her that Adele might say no. That is not how their family works. Celia clicks her fingers, Adele jumps through her hoops. Then Celia rewards her with a treat, like you might a dog.

Love, attention.

Adele can see traces of it, swirling just out of reach, her mind trying to grasp on to it, but it was so elusive.

"Well, it would be a shame for Peter to find out about last week, wouldn't it, Adele? Peter, he thinks so highly of you. He thinks you're so perfect, God knows why. How fun to describe to him Albert on top of you, groaning and thrusting. There are so many details I could supply. You moaning my husband's name. Your orgasm, it was so noisy, wasn't it? Are you noisy with Peter, Adele? Does he make you scream like my husband did?" And Adele understands that Celia is not describing sharing a secret, but rather, sharing a lie; showing her that she, Celia, could do anything. That her power to hurt Adele was boundless.

Adele's blood is pounding in her ears, she can't think, she's got to think, everything is narrowing down to blackness, like she's going to pass out. This is not how her life ends, this is not how her future goes, this is not *fair*. She's never been able to think around Celia, never been able to defend herself, never been able to stand up to her. She's told *herself* a lie about who Celia is to protect *herself*, not to protect Celia. Because she has needed to believe someone in her family loved her—it was too painful to consider the alternative. Her father was too absent, Bethany was never paying enough attention, Jocelyn wouldn't allow her to feel anything—somehow she'd managed to choose the one person who was actually the least likely to love her and make her feel good.

Deep, deep down, she remembers all the taunts, all the manipulations, all the ways Celia erased her and used her, and the wind and the waves and her thoughts are screaming in her ears, and she doesn't even know how she got there, but she has Albert's fluffy coat lapels in her hands, she's shoving her sister and screaming, off the path, on to the rocky ledge, the spray from the surf drifting up all this way, and Celia is still laughing at her, still mocking her, her voice coming down to Adele from far, far away.

34

Saturday

December 2021

Bethany stares out over the water.

There's a couple of men down there in the water, hollering and whooping. She squints at them uneasily, a child walking past voicing her own fears to his father: "Do they know what they're doing?"

The tide is rising, the water sucking and crashing over the rocks, and even as she watches one of the men bombs into a waterhole, a small shallow indent in the rocks, not even consistently visible amongst the churning water. As the next wave crashes over him, he's swept ten metres to the side, for a moment only his feet visible in the crisp evening air. It looks cartoonish, it seems so unlikely a position for the human form to take; so unlikely that he'll reappear.

After a moment he pops back up, though, laughing and shouting. *He must be drunk,* Bethany thinks. *That, or not a local.* No local would face down the peril of those waves amongst the rocks. Sometimes, staring out to sea, it looks like giant sink holes exist there, sucking and slurping hungrily for something above, huge black holes amidst the rocks, going down metres and metres into the depths of the earth. But it's just a trick of the waves, the way the water moves over the uneven surface, the way the rocks catch the shadows. Another wave, and Bethany can see that it's just rocks.

The second man follows the first, bombing into the barely existent hole, and is swept violently sideways into his friend. They both get up, staggering and laughing. There's something offensive about them, their loudness, their lack of thoughtfulness. That perhaps everyone watching is feeling needless worry; that someone might have to come and rescue them.

That their families might mourn them if they died.

The beach would be closed while authorities investigated. A sombre mood would descend upon the headlands, again. For the twentieth, or thirtieth time.

It's outrageously selfish, and Bethany feels a swell of hatred for these men. She's torn between calling for help, and leaving the moronic creatures to their fate.

Her walk feels interfered with, lessened. Her calm communion with the sea.

The water is what Bethany misses most about Sydney. It's beautiful, but wild. For such a wealthy area, the water won't be tamed. It's a constant menace, swirling around the consciousness of anyone near it. The noise alone is overwhelming.

Out further to her left, there's a long, higgledy row of surfers, little black dots, rising and falling with the swell, biding their time till the next right wave. Sometimes they drift closer to the rocks and the cliffs, and Bethany feels a similar worry, a similar rage. Walking the coastal track, looking out over them—feeling this constant push and pull between breathlessness at the wild beauty, and worry for the puny humans who dare to get amongst it—feels like home, and also not.

Bethany smooths her expensive jacket. She wonders why her family never ask her about her finances. She doesn't try to hide it, and it would certainly make her wonder, if the roles were reversed. How does someone who can never stay in the one job (*so dreamy,* she thinks, sarcastically, to herself) manage to afford designer clothes? Sure, her parents are comfortable, they bought in the right place at the right time, and Peter and Adele haven't done too badly either, though their house was a "renovator's delight" and very modest, even after all the work they'd done on it. But Bethany, she lived in a tiny flat in Perth, and really shouldn't be flaunting clothes worth more than her humble wage should really allow for.

She has a story at the ready, should they ask. She's had it ready for years. But they never ask.

It's always been a blessing, and a curse.

Now, she turns her thoughts back to Harrison. Adele is beside herself. Bethany herself thinks her sister is overreacting. A seventeen-year-old, who's nearly finished school, who has a new, older gay lover he's had his first fight with? He's just forgotten himself momentarily, Bethany would bet her life on it.

Of course, given the context, she understands Adele's terror —she, Bethany, is right now walking the track where all the murders happened, just a few blocks from Adele's house. Adele is getting notes pinned to her door, and thinks she's seen someone watching her on the cliffs. And she and Adele know, better than anyone, that family members can disappear around here and never be heard from again.

So Bethany will do her very best to help Adele, and find Harrison as a matter of urgency. It's the least she can do.

Bethany thinks back to the previous night, her stomach churning uneasily. It's early, and all she's had is coffee—a mistake, again. But they'd stayed up so late, and she felt so exhausted. Reaching for coffee was like reaching for sanity, this morning. Something to keep her afloat, just.

Adele and Albert had talked in low voices for a little while after Peter and Dan left. Eventually, Bethany had relaxed. She'd continued scrolling social media. She had a few leads. People were so careless with their online data. She could put up a cute photo with a cute name and befriend almost anyone. Then she had access to so many photos, so many contacts, even where people were at any given moment. It was lunacy. She herself would never be so cavalier with her personal information. She didn't even have a real Facebook account. Just fake ones, that she used now and then. For very particular purposes.

Still, from what she had gleaned, the circles Harrison moved in were progressive, inclusive. She hadn't found anyone she was concerned about, who might harbour ill will toward a young gay man. *What a pity everyone wasn't like that, thirty years ago.*

Fifty.

One hundred.

And then Bethany had heard a sudden, piercing wail. High-pitched, terrified. Gurgling, almost, like someone was being strangled. She'd flown into the room in horror, arms raised, ready to grab Albert, or a weapon, or something. In retrospect she would have been unprepared and useless. She didn't even think to grab a knife. Like her sisters, she was slight. Blonde and pretty. She had used it in her favour for decades.

But being small, blonde, and pretty wouldn't help if you needed to help your sister fend off an attacker.

But Adele was shaking her head, as though she was trying to dislodge something. No one was strangling her. When she stopped wailing and shaking, she just stared at Albert, eyes pleading. *For what?* Bethany wonders.

"I can't believe you forgot," he'd said, softly, his eyes on Adele, not leaving her face.

And Adele had stared at him, her face a rolling mess of fear and terror, her eyes transfixed, and Bethany had shouted then: "What? What is it?" *Was he talking about the sex? Dear God, why would he bring that up at this moment?*

But before anyone can say anything else, before she can get to the bottom of her sister's terror, Peter bursts into the room, his face tight, fearful. He's waving something in his fist, and his voice, when it comes, is breathless: "We got another note."

If you dig for secrets in dark places, you'd better not have anything to hide.

"I didn't see it when we left. But I might not have noticed as I pulled the door shut." Peter suddenly jerks back, horrified. "I touched it. Shit." He stares at it, spread on the table, crumpled from where he'd initially grabbed it off the door in anger. "We just came back for my phone. I forgot it. I realised I should have it with me."

Adele is momentarily roused out of her stupor. She stares at the note, fear etched deeply on her face.

"Peter." She says, then louder: "Peter." He looks at her more closely then, and sees something in her face. And Bethany has no idea what's going on, can't make heads nor tails of it, but when she tries to ask Adele and Albert what was going on, they just look at each other, a long, intense look, a shared understanding. And then Adele is rising, saying, "We need to go to the police. We need them to help with Harrison. We'll file the missing persons now."

For a moment, Adele squeezes Bethany's hands. "Later," she says, her face pained, on the verge of panic. "I'll tell you later."

And they'd traipsed off to the police station, and Bethany had stayed up late, searching for clues online, getting lost down rabbit holes, waiting for Adele and Peter to come home. Albert had excused himself. Dan said he'd keep looking for Harrison, and had exchanged numbers with Bethany, getting Adele and Peter's numbers off her, too.

Bethany waited and waited. Dan had texted "no luck" close to midnight, and she must have fallen asleep on the table after that. She'd woken with a kinked neck close to 5 a.m., and not wanting to wake anyone, gone for a walk to clear her head, grabbing a coffee from the little cafe where she'd heard the old couple talking about the GoFundMe.

Now, it's after seven, and she's eager to hear what the police had to say.

As Bethany turns around and hurries back the way she came, her eyes automatically search for the foolish young men in the water. She can't see them, and she doesn't know if they walked out, or if they drowned.

35

Before

March 2006 (the night Celia disappeared)

Out on the headlands, Peter trails behind his wife.

He sees her go into the public toilets, and reappear ten minutes later.

Efficient, he thinks to himself, and then shakes the thought away. *Can one attach any positive word to an eating disorder? Is it okay to think, "At least she's quick"?*

He's left Harrison alone, though, so he's acutely conscious of the time.

He just wants to make sure she gets home okay. He knows she loses herself, loses time after purging. And the headlands still seem tinged with menace to him after dark. He'll just check she's heading home and seems okay, then he'll dash back to Harrison, he tells himself, uneasiness settling in the pit of his stomach.

In the distance, the waves crash, relentless, pummelling the rocks.

Unexpectedly, he sees Adele darting across the grass away from the toilets. He hangs back in the shadows, embarrassed to be following her. Guilty that he has left their son unattended. The house is locked, and Harrison is asleep, but still. Adele would be upset, uncomprehending. *Who leaves a child alone in the house?*

Who *should* he worry more about, though? His wife or his child? Both seem helpless tonight, in need of extra care and attention. Adele wasn't herself, she seemed agitated and afraid. Somehow he knew she'd return to purging tonight. He wonders why, why now? And thinks it's probably bloody Celia, stirring the pot. Causing trouble.

Peter doesn't like Celia, but it's hard to explain to people. She's charming, people love her. She turns her smile on you and you're bathed in her special, golden light. She manipulates Adele, but lots of people use their charm to get what they want, don't they? She's so subtle. Other people don't notice.

There was the incident with Harrison, of course, but that incident seems so slippery, so unlikely, so uncorroborated by anyone else that he still feels unsure of what exactly he saw through the blurry blue glass. *Could he have been mistaken? Even a manipulative person wouldn't hurt a child, would they?*

Now, Peter walks along the edge of the park. Something moves behind him, and he shifts uneasily. There's still something so creepy about this place in the dark. Up ahead, he can hear voices. He recognises Adele's voice, distressed, and the low, syrupy voice of Celia. And he's just about to intervene, risk Adele's wrath that he left their child alone, take her hand and take her away from Celia, away from what makes her feel bad, away from purging, if he can, when he hears Celia say something that stops him in his tracks.

36

BEFORE

March 2006 (the night Celia disappeared)

At the tops of the cliffs, Adele can barely hear her sister.

The foaming water below them throws up a fine mist, settling on them both uncomfortably, the roar of the wind and the waves making Adele feel exposed, alone, untouchable.

Her sister will not win this time.

"Oh, Adele," Celia is saying, her voice sounding so tiny to Adele, so distant. Celia is not even worried, so sure she has control of her sister and the situation, like she always does. "Don't be so emotional. You always were the sensitive one. You're not going to hurt me, and you're not going to hurt Peter by letting this dirty little secret get out. Think, Adele, think. How are you going to fix this? Are you going to tell one little lie for me, or are you going to ruin your marriage? Are you going to suffer the burden of the lie, or let Peter suffer? You know what you're going to do, Adele. We both know. You're the kind one. You'll eat yourself alive before you cause anyone else to suffer. Go on now. Tell me you'll do it. Then go off and have a little vomit to make yourself feel more in control.

"But you've never been in control, little sister. You can't be in control when you're trying to please everyone. You're too invested in being the fixer. The good one. You're the *kind* one, Adele."

Celia's eyes have not left Adele's face. And Adele's thoughts are thundering in her ears.

The fixer.

The good one.

The kind one.

"*Am I, sister? Am I?*" Adele shouts, trying to drown out the sound of the waves, and the thunderous, murderous chorus of voices and memories in her head.

And she pushed.

37

Saturday

December 2021

Peter wakes before his wife, and is surprised that they fell asleep at all.

He watches Adele now, in the hazy light of dawn.

He glances at the clock—6:45 a.m. Adele is restless in her sleep, her mouth working around words he cannot hear. She grips the doona tightly in one fist, pulling it up and then pushing it away.

Peter turns away and stares out the window, letting the happenings of last night wash over him. The note on the door (*there are so many secrets. To which one did these notes refer?*); Adele's vulnerable, sagging face. The way Albert melted away.

Peter had helped Adele to the car. She seemed weak, and was murmuring to herself, making no sense. Little snippets of conversation, directed at nobody. "He was there...there were no...they weren't there..."

He'd barely pulled out of their garage when he heard the whisper:

"I killed her. I did."

Peter had gone very still.

"What's that now?" he'd whispered back, gently easing the car into the gutter, putting it in park, leaving the engine running. His movements were very slow, as though he didn't want to startle Adele, as though she was a flighty newborn foal, wild and skittish and long-legged, about to dance and gallop out of his reach.

Adele had turned to him, her eyes wide. "I remembered. Oh Peter. Oh God. That night. I was on the cliffs." She goes to say more but the words don't come. Great, wracking sobs coming instead.

Minutes pass. Adele's cries are so loud Peter almost expects someone to knock on the windows, demand an explanation. Wonder what he is doing to this woman in his car. He has one hand on hers, gently stroking her wrist. Thinking quickly.

He'd thought a lot about Celia and Adele's exchange that night, over the years. Who could blame Adele? He certainly didn't. Her wild crusade to blame Albert was ludicrous, and for a while, Peter was terrified about her mental state. Had she lost her mind? What would become of her? But gradually she settled. She came back to him. She came back to Harrison. She stopped purging and started living. She seemed, at last, to be at peace. And Peter, he thought it was behind them. He hoped she never remembered that she had been on the cliffs that night. *Did that make him a bad husband?*

It was Celia's confession about Harrison that did it. Her mocking demonstration that she could lie about Adele sleeping with Albert was bad enough, but making his little boy wet himself filled Peter with so much rage he would have stepped out there and pushed her himself.

So no, he doesn't need to forgive her. That was not the pressing question. He doesn't even think whether she will be able to forgive herself is the question. The pressing question was: *If she knew what* he *did,* would she *forgive* him?

Gradually her breathing had settled, and Adele had turned to him. He was sitting in the driver's seat, and he'd reached awkwardly across the console to try to comfort her.

"It was me on the cliffs," she had whispered. "I pushed her. I fought with her and I pushed her. I pushed her in." She had closed her eyes, trying to squeeze out the memories, not wanting to replay them ever again.

Once was enough.

"And Albert was there. Albert saw me. He was less than ten metres away. He must have seen. And he never said anything. He never turned me in. Why did he never turn me in? After everything I accused him of. Why did he not tell the truth? That it was me?" She turned pleading eyes to her husband. "I forgot. I can't believe I forgot. How could you forget a thing like that?" And Peter can almost see the replay behind her eyes, the memory she allowed herself to not know for fifteen years, and he can see the pain breaking out of her like a wrecking ball, smashing her open from the inside out.

She had collapsed forward, out of his embrace, folding in half, her forehead against the dashboard, and sobbed and sobbed and sobbed.

Now, Peter stares at the ceiling, the corners of his mouth turned down, a small frown line across his brow.

They had filed a missing persons report, but they had both been quiet at the police station. How could they explain the notes? All they'd shared was that they assumed they were about Harrison's sexuality, and they feared for his safety. That Adele had thought a man was watching her on the headlands. With all the bad publicity resurfacing about the crimes and how they had been handled, the police had been reassuringly attentive. No crime had been committed, but they were going to circulate a picture of Harrison and ask all their patrolling officers to keep an eye out. They were going to send foot patrols around the headlands to establish an additional presence, especially after dark. And they promised to keep in touch with any updates.

They'd been mostly silent on the drive home. Peter was kicking himself for not setting up the little security camera he'd bought, but there just hadn't seemed to be enough time.

Briefly, Peter had wondered aloud whether Albert could be leaving the notes on the front door. "I didn't see it on my way out. But I was upset, and in a rush. Albert could have put it there before he knocked, for all we know."

"But why would he?" Adele had whispered. "He's kept my secret for all these years. Why would he taunt me with it now? He seemed to want to make peace, not cause trouble."

And Peter had kept silent, because it seemed so familiar. Except instead of trusting the logic of Celia's behaviour, Adele was trusting Albert's.

He also kept silent because he thought that Albert had his own reasons to keep that secret, and they had nothing to do with protecting Adele.

But he couldn't untangle it now. Adele was so fragile. Peter was surprised she could function at the police station at all. They'd sat in the car talking for a long time before proceeding, agreeing that they wouldn't speak of the evening's revelations to the police at this time. Celia was one problem; Harrison was another, more important one.

Peter had probed gently: *what had Albert said?*

"He didn't need to say anything," she had replied, dully. "I remembered. It all came rushing back."

Not all of it, Peter thinks. *It didn't all come back.*

"Let's find Harrison. Then let's deal with the rest of it," he'd said, decisively, and Adele had sagged against him as he helped her into bed, relieved that he was taking control, steering her in the right direction. She had searched his face, looking for damnation, or forgiveness, maybe. Peter couldn't tell, and it didn't even matter.

He doesn't need to forgive Adele, and he doesn't have the slightest inclination to damn her.

Because if she'd kept a secret about what happened on the cliffs that night, well, so had he.

38

AFTER

Saturday

December 2021

Jasper Montana whizzes along in the crisp morning air. Occasionally he'll tilt madly to the side and slam on the brakes of his old BMX and try to do a wheelie, but he hasn't perfected it yet, and more often than not he stacks his bike and loses the pile of papers in his basket.

The paper round is his favourite part of the day. He's only just turned thirteen, and his mum still doesn't let him go anywhere else by himself. But these few blocks around their house and the corner newsagent feel like his private domain. It's his first job, and the power of the cash and the freedom combine to make his heart sing as he speeds along the familiar roads, tossing the paper as close to the front door as he can, stopping to pat the neighbourhood dogs and cats, feeling like a king. He's practising whistling, because he thinks hurling papers while he whistles would be cool.

He turns up the narrow road behind the coastal track, the part of his round that he likes the most, but finds the most tricky. Expensive houses line the coast, but access to them is either slow or lacks precision. High fences keep out the riffraff, and also mean he can't see where he's aiming his newspapers. Sometimes a loud splash makes him jump and pedal away at high speed, pondering the dilemma that high fences might also *attract* the riffraff, because trying to keep someone out kind of implies that there's good stuff to protect within those walls.

Today though, his papers land with a satisfying thunk and without any splashes. He's definitely not operating at high speed, but he's getting far more precise.

He knows from listening to the hushed whispers of his parents that Albert Armstrong lives along here.

"Why do you have to go to the police?" he'd asked his mother, confused, earlier that week, and had been given a halting explanation: that perhaps she had some information that would help them in an investigation. And of course in his mind he had her handling stolen diamonds, or taking a call from a crime king, or solving a cold case that had been haunting the police for decades (which was in fact rather close to the truth). She'd been quite unforthcoming with the details though, but Jasper was a resourceful boy, and with a little bit of eavesdropping and an afternoon surfing the local news online, he had put two and two together, and was avidly following any updates on the Armstrongs, and whether his mother was helping to put a villain behind bars.

At the end of the block, he takes a sharp right, and covers another slow patch—apartment buildings, where he has to stop completely, poking the paper into the rows of mailboxes. He thinks he can do it by memory now, but after a mix-up last week and a stern chat from his boss, Trevor, he now checks them off against a printout in his pocket. Then he's off again, zipping back and forth along the streets, catching glimpses of the ocean between houses and apartment buildings, the sky getting lighter and lighter, streaks of pale pink above the glassy grey of the sea.

He likes to be home by 7 a.m., but there's really no time limit on his deliveries. "Before school," Trevor told him at the start, and sometimes he does sleep in, barely scraping in the school gates before the bell, but today he thinks he'll cruise in by quarter to, for sure.

On the last leg of his trip, he spins around the corner into a long street, the houses separate here, with big gardens and meandering cats. He tries to hit all ten front doors without stopping, but likes to start with a good skid, feeling like he could be in some kind of action movie, letting his bike fall to the bitumen and casually jumping over its spinning wheels, and sliding effortlessly into some high energy rap. No one ever pays him any attention, and Jasper feels like he could be anyone out here. He's just finishing his air guitar solo in the middle of the road, right behind the big black van that's always parked outside number eight (monitoring spies, no doubt) and grabbing his bike back up, when he sees none other than Albert Armstrong stride purposefully up the path of number ten, push a bit of paper over a nail on the front door, then slip away over the garden fence, his hoodie pulled low around his face, and something decidedly sneaky about his posture.

39

BEFORE

March 2006 (the night Celia disappeared)

Peter melts into the bushes as Adele rushes toward him.

He sees her slam to a halt as another figure steps into her path, and he's about to rush forward, when the figure steps to the side, and Adele rushes on.

He only has a few minutes. He needs to beat her home. But as he turns to cut across the park, Albert Armstrong steps in front of him. And behind him, Celia rises like a phoenix from the cliffs. Even in the dark, Peter can see the rage and fury on her face.

"That bitch!" she splutters, staggering toward them. "She tried to kill me! She can't even fucking do that right, the weak, pathetic little slut." Celia collapses on the park bench, and for all her rage, Peter can see that she's shaking, doubled over, gasping for breath. Her hands are scratching at the empty air like she's still trying to claw at something. "Albert! Help me! We have to call the police!" Her voice is shrill, a tremor in it Peter has never heard before. She raises one shaking hand, pointing a finger at Peter. "You. You saw it! Attempted murder! She's a killer!"

"I saw it," Albert says. His voice is slow and thoughtful. He stares at his wife, a strange expression playing across his features in the moonlight. He looks both smaller and larger, the light playing tricks on Peter, Albert's pink, feminine jacket confusing his perceptions. Peter's heart is hammering in his chest. Everything is going very slowly.

Albert stares at his wife, then takes a long, pointed look at Peter.

"Go to your wife," he says, and his voice is both distant and commanding. Peter looks from Albert to Celia, a frown creasing his brow, and he hesitates.

"Now!" Albert barks at him, and then he is off, running, cutting across the park and planning his route to get ahead of Adele, who won't be as fast as he is in the dark, distressed.

"You saw nothing!" Albert's voice carries to him, light as a feather, an instruction, a promise, and his feet are flying over the grass and then over the tarmac, and he's never run so fast in his life, darting through backstreets and alleyways, turning his key in the front door, panting, panting, but Adele isn't there, and he drops to the floor in the lounge like he was doing push-ups, which is where she finds him thirty seconds later, and he wraps her in his arms, and shushes and shushes her, her distress bulky and mutating and almost alive.

The next day, he tries to talk to her about what he heard, but she becomes hysterical, nonsensical, her eyes both terrified and pleading, and he thinks he will leave it until she has recovered herself, until she is calmer. He doesn't want to distress her. He has always known how to soothe her, how to make her see things from a different perspective. But this is different. There's a pressure behind his eyes, a sense of urgency to work it out, to fix everything, and for the first time he doesn't know how.

So when it becomes clear, over the next few days, that Adele has no recollection of what happened on the cliffs that night, when she frets and worries about Celia's disappearance, he does not hesitate for even a single minute. He falls into step beside her, always reliable, always having her back.

He never mentions what happened on the cliffs that night to anyone, ever.

They will worry about it later.

If she remembers.

If Albert reminds her.

If Celia appears, screaming for blood.

He tells himself Celia is probably taking a break after a fight with Albert.

He leans in to what's easy. What will soothe Adele.

He doesn't quite comprehend it. But Celia is gone, and no one saw anything.

And for a short space of time, it seems like that is for the best.

40

Saturday

December 2021

Peter hears the front door open and close with a quiet click, and wonders if Bethany is going out. He feels bad that he didn't wake her when they got home last night, get her into a proper bed, but it was all too much. The tasks of daily life seem impossible right now.

Sighing, he swings his legs out of the bed. He glances at his wife again, and his heart feels heavy.

When he pads through to the kitchen, though, Bethany is sitting right where they'd left her, her face thoughtful.

She startles when he opens the fridge, having not heard his quiet patter into the room.

"What did the police say?" she asks, without preamble, and Peter catches her up quickly.

"Adele's not doing so great. Did you hear what happened with...?" Peter is not sure how much Bethany knows. Did Adele tell her what she remembered?

"No. Did she tell you? It sounded awful. Albert must have said something terrible to distress her like that?"

Peter hesitates. "Yes, but I'll let her talk to you about that. Did you just come in?" he asks, changing the subject. *What on earth are they going to say to Bethany?*

Celia was her sister, too. Peter might be able to forgive Adele, but Bethany might not. And would either of them forgive Peter? He saw Albert out there on the cliffs with Celia, but he never told the police, because if he told them about Albert, Albert would tell them about Adele, and it was all far too difficult and confusing and murky to make sense of.

Had Albert pushed her?

Had Peter left her to die?

"I went for a walk. And I've got a couple of leads I'm going to follow up." She stands quickly, a sweeping gesture collecting her phone and keys into her bag, and strides purposefully toward the door. "Call me if you need me, okay? Tell Dell, too." Then she's gone, and Peter starts making coffee.

Two nights. Harrison has been gone for two nights, and the past is catching up with them all.

Something nags at him, about Albert and Dan. Did they recognise each other? Was it too much of a coincidence?

Dan and Albert.

Dan and Harrison.

Celia dressed as Albert.

God. Why did Dan have to come forward now?

What would happen if everyone started to come clean about that night?

Peter sits heavily at the table and waits for Adele to wake up, to see what this day brings and how they will get through it.

41

BEFORE

March 2006 (the night Celia disappeared)

Albert watches Celia, his expression hard. Through her gasps, she looks back at him, and starts thinking fast.

Albert is clearly not of a mind to help her.

How much did he hear?

All of it?

"How can I fix it?" she says now, watching him carefully. She needs to understand where he's hurting, to know what her next move should be. How to placate him. How to win him back.

"You can't," Albert says, his gaze level. "I think I've been caught up in your games a bit too long, Celia."

"What games?" she says, innocent. That face. He believes her, every time. *Shouldn't you notice if someone is lying to you?*

Albert never notices. Celia is so sunny, so sweet. So beautiful. The other things seem so out-of-character. One-offs, that happen an awful lot of times.

"Don't bother," he says, tiredness creeping into his voice. "I heard you. Your plan. Divorce? And Harrison. Jesus."

He takes a step toward her, his movements slow, deliberate.

But still Celia isn't worried. She's used to winning, and she's used to being the most clever, the most cunning. She has no doubt that she can get things back on track. Even if she has to go back to being the happy little wife. It wasn't so bad, was it? She has a nice house, a nice job. Perhaps she overstretched. Perhaps she aimed too high.

"Oh, I was just teasing Adele, honey. You know how weird she gets after purging. Can't remember things. I just wanted to see if she'd remember something as wild as that. I bet you a hundred bucks she doesn't remember."

Albert knows it's ridiculous. Even that is despicable, but so badly does he want to believe Celia is on his side, and so endearing and loving is her expression, that he wants to believe her, even though he knows it is madness.

"You never told me she purges, actually," he says.

Another step.

Another.

Celia licks her lips.

Albert looks different. Harder. More distant. She grasps about, searching for the thing that will reach him, hook him back in.

He needs her love. He thrives on being loved. He needs to believe he is loveable.

"You can't think I was serious, Albert? Come on, that is crazy! I'm trying to have a baby with you! Would I go to all this trouble if I didn't want to be tied to you forever? And you know what? I just got news yesterday that we're pregnant! I didn't want to tell you till I was sure. I'm having a blood test tomorrow. In case the home test was wrong. I didn't want to get your hopes up. Can you believe it? A baby!" She turns her face up to him, adoring, in rapture.

Albert looks at her in wonder.

How did he never see who his wife was before?

"Why were you meeting that guy, dressed in my clothes?"

he asks her. He doesn't want to say Dan's name. He knows Celia will know who he means. "He texted me, said he was at the spot."

"He must have texted the wrong client, darling! You can't expect a hooker to be organised and on the ball, can you? It's just a coincidence. I just grabbed your coat cause it was warmer than mine. It's cold out here. You must be freezing. Would you like it back?" She goes to unbutton it, caring, conciliatory, youthful excitement on her face. "We can go home and do another test, you can see for yourself. You're going to be a dad!" Here she leans forward and squeezes his arm, her eyes shining, and Albert could nearly believe her, she's so convincing, so captivating. Love radiates out from her like honey.

Like a warm, sticky trap.

He's nearly above her now, his feet moving of their own accord, feeling like he is in a dream. He's seeing the same acts, the same moves, but he understands them differently now.

In the shadows, Jonno shifts uneasily.

He was just supposed to make sure Dan was safe, with that jerk who'd already screwed him around once. But Dan had melted away, and he'd heard shrieking from the cliffs, and bolted toward it.

Albert was there. So was Celia. *Is that why Dan had vanished? Had Celia followed Albert, caught him out? Is that what the shrieking was?* Jonno only recognised her because Albert called her by her name. She's certainly dressed in disguise, bulky masculine clothing. They're clearly having a marital dispute, and Jonno turns to leave. He doesn't want to hear whatever other foul things Celia will no doubt say about him and his peers. He'll go find Dan, check that he's okay.

Disorganised, he thinks darkly to himself.

Behind him, he hears Albert say, "I don't believe you." He doesn't know why he turns. He doesn't hear anything else. It's like a vacuum, black and empty and enormous, ominous in itself, its silence.

As though in slow motion, he sees Albert lunge toward Celia, grab her under the arms and pitch them both toward the cliffs.

He's moving before he even registers it. Hurling himself toward them on autopilot.

If he'd stopped to think about it, he might have chosen a different path.

He sees Albert lift Celia, who is flailing and writhing. She is so little. She looks so light.

He can't hear anything over the sound rushing in his ears, the crash of the waves as he gets closer. But he's too slow. He's too far away. One moment Celia is flinging herself about, and then she is gone, and Albert is panting, a satisfied little smile on his face.

Jonno is going too fast. He needs to stop, to backtrack, to not confront Albert. But as he tries to skid to a halt, to change his trajectory, Albert's eyes slowly rise, and lock onto his.

Jonno turns to run.

A meaty hand closes around his wrist.

"I don't think so," Albert says, and yanks him back.

42

AFTER

Saturday

December 2021

Albert Armstrong puts away his black marker and the neat stack of paper on his desk.

He throws away another pair of disposable gloves, deep in the trash. Not that anyone could make a case out of a man having disposable gloves in his trash can.

There won't be a need for any more notes.

He'd come so far these last few years. God.

And then he'd seen Harrison kissing Dan at a bus stop, and the world had ground to a halt.

He doesn't even know what rose up in him.

Resentment, that his nephew (who he didn't even know! He only knew his face because he'd been in the local paper several times, winning basketball tournaments, or topping his year in exams) was allowed to kiss men on the streets.

Rage, that Adele had been back to the police station as soon as those remains had been found, trotting out her stupid little theories, her stupid little lies.

A petty desire for revenge, because however he thinks about it, however much a little seed of truth tries to unfurl and correct him, he still blames that bloody whore-man for everything that went wrong on the cliffs that night. If Dan and Jonno had never hunted him down (*for two hundred dollars! How desperate and pathetic, to go to all that trouble for a mere two hundred dollars! To ruin a man's life, his reputation, for almost nothing!*) then Celia would never have come up with such a stupid ploy to get back at him, they would never have been on the cliffs that night, and maybe things would never have been *good,* but they would have been better than...what happened, right?

Still. He's given Celia a good run for her money. If only she could see him now.

He thinks Adele believed his story. Hell, he thinks she even felt sorry for him.

As if a doctor couldn't tell the difference between a drunk person and a drugged one.

Idiots. All idiots, he thinks.

Before the kissing incident, he'd reached out to Adele. He'd even tried to meet her when she walked the headlands. Like an accident, like he just ran into her, *whoops!*, even though they'd managed not to run into each other for fifteen years. But he saw her a couple of times, and changed his mind. Hid behind a tree once, like a goddamn stalker. He realised that any conversation they had about Celia needed to be done in private. And he resented how seeing Adele made him feel, anyway. All her blame, when she pushed Celia first! What kind of self-delusion allowed a person to not only forget that, but then blame someone else for it?

Last night, he'd heard them muttering about the notes, the lurker on the headlands, and he nearly apologised for the latter, confessed, but then decided not to mention that it was him.

Let them worry, he thought to himself.

He settles into his sunroom, and looks out over the ocean.

Adele was *grateful*. Grateful that he'd kept her secret. *Was it really possible that she'd forgotten? What a mess of a woman. What a sad little dilapidated excuse for a human being.* Eventually, he supposes, she'll realise that she had kept his, too. She and Peter would talk. But what could they say? No one was innocent, here. Adele tried to kill her sister. Peter had covered it up for years. If they tried to say that Celia was alive, and Albert was there, who would believe them? Very convenient thing for two people to simultaneously forget for fifteen years.

Especially when there was no body.

He'd held it close all these years. Ready to use it, when required. Of course, there was the pesky problem of Peter, too, but no one had seen anything. All you could do was join the dots. It was his word against Peter's. *Who pushed Celia? Who saw her last?*

Still, it wasn't a showdown he was willing to risk. He had bathed in the support of his community, played the grieving husband, and kept that card close to his chest.

After all, he'd been taught by the best about how to manipulate your audience.

Celia would be proud.

A familiar pain stabs at him when he thinks of Celia, though. Because for all her lies, all his conviction, there had been that phone call, a few days after she disappeared. A message left on her phone—recovered that night from where it had fallen near the bench—from a clinic down south, calling regarding her missed appointment. Did she wish to reschedule? He'd called the number, giving his credentials, a colleague's name, a concerned GP enquiring about Celia's appointment.

She'd like to reschedule, but is nervous about the procedure.

Can they send further information to her home address?

He'd had her Medicare number and all the details they

requested, and they had readily agreed. But they had also given him a website for her to visit "to speed up the process," they'd said. "Because obviously we like to do it as early as we can, and she's already nearly at thirteen weeks. Of course we can do it later, but if the patient is sure…"

At that point, Albert had found it hard to speak.

Anyway. He'd tried hard to put it all behind him. To pull himself back from the brink of whatever it was that Celia brought out in him. He'd spent time with his sister, he'd devoted himself to work. But sometimes, flashes of rage blindside him.

If only Dan hadn't come to his door.

If only Adele hadn't fought with Celia on the cliffs.

If only she hadn't given him the idea, in his state of pain and anger, that such an easy solution was desirable or even possible.

If only, if only, if only.

So when he saw Dan kissing Harrison at the bus stop, living life freely, without all this pain and rage and regret, it seemed so unfair, so lopsided, and also kind of harmless, to just make them feel it too.

A little bit of pain, and a little bit of rage.

And then, well it got a bit intoxicating. *What about Adele and Peter, too? Maybe they deserved a little misery as well.* And then he could feel the pull of something dark, something huge, which he might never pull himself out from under, and he'd had to give himself a very good talking to, and make himself put his texts and his sinister little messages (new ideas kept popping into his mind, once he started, it was disconcerting how much headspace it was suddenly taking up, how many nasty messages were so close to the surface in his mind) away once and for all.

So, it was finished now. Albert doesn't quite know what came over him. Everything he's worked for, everything he's put behind him, what on earth was he thinking? Today was too risky, it was daylight, he can't believe he could be so stupid. No one had ever doubted his story. No one except Adele. And he had risen even above that, showed his caring side, the understanding GP, *"of course she's looking for answers, of course she wants someone to blame, I don't begrudge her her grief, and I know one day she will look back on all of this and know, absolutely, that I am not to blame."*

Because she'll remember, he'd add, to himself, *the stupid little bitch.*

He worked very hard not to fling back in her face that it was her, she was the one who pushed Celia! Oh, it would have been golden. But to admit that was to admit he was on the cliffs, and then it all got very murky.

This was much better. This had worked out for him very well indeed.

Except for the baby.

Whenever he thinks of the baby, he howls like a monster trying to capture the moon.

43

March 2006 (the day after Celia disappeared)

A few suburbs away from the headlands, in her parents' house, Bethany drums her fingers on the table in irritation.

She's spent half her day yesterday comforting Celia and damning Albert, but now, Albert is saying that Celia never came home last night, and Bethany is pissed off.

Sure, sure, people can cheat. But Bethany knows that Celia lies. She lied when they were children and she lies now that they're adults. Bethany keeps enough distance between them for none of it to really matter. Celia is good fun, she throws good parties, and so long as you remembered with strict certainty that you could never trust her, not about anything, you could muddle through life with her just fine.

In this case, it does matter, though. Bethany would really like Celia to be lying.

For this not to be happening.

She has nearly, almost, pulled off her biggest scam yet—it makes all her previous ones look like child's play. The

GoFundMe is up to nearly two hundred and fifty thousand dollars, and Bethany is almost laughing all the way to the bank.

The bank that has a mysterious account in her name that she didn't set up.

Scams require so much planning, so much technical know-how. And her first few, well, they were pretty simple affairs. Selling things that didn't exist, getting deposits so small people wouldn't even bother reporting the loss or chasing it up (actually, she was surprised how often people did chase it up, but she just changed burner phones and email addresses, and the problem was solved).

And now, just as Bethany's about to cash in on her wondrous, clever honeypot, Celia has to go and ruin it. She had been talking about leaving Albert, exposing him for using sex workers, and the last thing Bethany needs is Celia and Albert to have a high-profile separation right now. She regrets using her sister's name (and photos for that matter, but there were such convenient ones of her in hospitals, Celia was always posting them on social media, complaining about all the procedures for IVF. That was what gave Bethany the idea in the first place, Celia looked so wan and pitiable, even Bethany—who was well aware how contrived things with Celia could be—was almost stirred to sympathy).

Bethany knows what Celia can be like when she's being spiteful. It wasn't likely, but she *might* go public about Albert to try to make him suffer. Pictures of a very healthy-looking Celia on the internet talking about her cheating husband might end up in front of the wrong person.

Someone who'd donated to the cause, say.

Someone who recognised her, and reached out to say, "*All this! On top of the cancer treatment!*" And then all hell would break loose. Because, of course, Celia knew nothing about her supposed cancer treatment and her GoFundMe, and even if

Bethany had covered her tracks well enough to not be able to be associated with it and prosecuted, she would certainly not be waltzing off into the sunset with a fat cheque.

One more week. She just needed one more week. Then the money would be transferred into an account that couldn't be traced back to Bethany, and whipped out of the country so fast it would be gone before anyone could protest. And anyway, who would? Bethany is fascinated by the people who donate to such fundraisers. There are no real vetting processes. How do they know the cause is real? By what mechanism can a donation truly make a person feel better about a tragedy? It seems so simplistic. Give a little money, then you don't have to do anything more time-consuming, more involved to help? You pat yourself on the back for being a good person, and never think about that particular problem again?

Bethany used her sister's identification, obtained at such high cost, to set up a bank account in Celia's name for the funds to be deposited in. It was so easy. Of course, it was only easy because she looked like her sister and had her ID, but she didn't even have to go into a branch! It was ludicrous. And then she just used one of her many fake Facebook accounts to spread the word, carefully targeting people outside of Sydney who would be unlikely to know Celia and approach her with their sympathy. America was surprisingly lucrative. Americans felt really bad about the little sick Australian woman.

Still, it was incredibly risky, and to be honest, Bethany had expected it would get shut down. She was careful to use emails and VPNs and photos that couldn't be traced back to her (anyone could have downloaded those photos off Celia's social media. Celia was a social media strumpet). She told herself it was an experiment, and never really let herself believe she might get away with it. She was careful to launch it and post comments at times when she knew Celia was at social events, so Celia could reasonably deny any knowledge of it if it all blew up. She didn't want her sister to get in trouble. She didn't want her to go to jail.

She just wanted a little piece of her life.

But now Celia is missing, and Bethany has no doubt that it is some stunt Celia has worked out to punish Albert. Bethany can't really believe Albert would hire sex workers. Celia is probably up to something (you recognise it more easily when you're up to something yourself) and it is at the worst possible time that Bethany can imagine.

And yet.

Bethany stares at the number she has written down.

$194,677.

That's how much money, she, Bethany, apparently has in her bank account—an account that is definitely in her name, but full of money that is definitely not hers.

It had caused much consternation when she'd gone to open a new account, only to be asked if she'd like to link it to her existing one.

"Remind me what that one is again?" she'd said, breezily, thinking she'd already used this bank for some other brief scam in the past, forgetting that she doesn't use her own name for scams, obviously, and then had nearly fallen over when they'd informed her of the details. And all she could think was, had Celia done to her exactly what she was now doing to Celia? Who else would know enough details to do this?

She'd updated the address from a post office box in western Sydney (nowhere near any of her sisters) to her own, and promptly emptied the account.

And waited.

Now, she thinks she understands. Celia was going to leave Albert and disappear.

An odd two-hundred thousand dollars wouldn't last someone like Celia very long, though. If that was Celia's plan, it wasn't a very good one. But Bethany doesn't have time to figure out Celia's strategy, her lack of genius in its execution (she was going to now have to ask for her money back, wasn't she? Bethany almost can't wait to hear how she tries to justify this one). She has to figure out what to do about the GoFundMe.

But all she can come up with, she realises, is that she has to wait.

See what Celia does, and what the fallout is.

She has a niggling sense of déjà vu, and for the first time, she thinks she might have had enough of Celia. She'd always let it go, thought there must be something very sad inside poor Celia, that the only way she knew how to feel better was to lie about things and have digs at other people (mainly Adele. Bethany had put her in her place a long, long time ago). She didn't *like* it, but she let it wash over her, irrelevant and unremarkable. Celia was Celia. You had to know how to handle her, that was all. Bethany had never even truly disliked her. Until now.

Now, it was *Bethany's* turn. Just once, Bethany would like to be the genius one. Bethany would like to be the one left laughing. Oh, she realises it's not okay. You shouldn't rip people off, you shouldn't take advantage of them. She will stop, she really will. This will be her last hurrah. She doesn't know why she feels so bitter and resentful toward the world. Perhaps it was that no one ever *helped* her, they all just labelled her ditzy and dreamy, no one even noticed she had a *diagnosable condition*, she had to figure it out for herself. She has this deep sense that the world let her down and laughed at her one too many times, and now she was laughing at the world. But it doesn't feel good. It feels bad, in fact.

She very definitely is going to get a proper job and be a better person.

As soon as this GoFundMe is finalised, one way or another,

she will knuckle down and do better. She will turn over a new leaf.

She will donate to charities to help children with problems and she will try harder to connect with her family.

She will make amends, dammit.

When she has this money, she'll have the time.

44

AFTER

Saturday

December 2021

Beth strides away from her sister's house purposefully.

She does have a few leads about Harrison.

But she has a lead about something else, too. And Harrison can wait another half an hour.

She swerves abruptly left, and hurries toward the beach. A plan is forming in her mind, and she feels the familiar stir of excitement, the tingling in her mind.

She really wants to know what Albert said to Adele to upset her so violently. She doesn't know if he will tell her. But it's worth a try.

Perhaps that will change her plans. But she doubts it. Once she has a good idea, she can get a bit tunnel-visioned. There's not a lot that will stand in her way. Certainly not the big, tumultuous feelings of her family.

She's been putting them aside for a long time.

But maybe this is a crazy plan. Is Albert dangerous? She

hesitates on the corner, flipping open her phone. Then she sends a photo and some text via SMS, locks her phone, and strides onward. And knocks firmly on Albert's door.

45

Saturday

December 2021

Peter is staring blankly at his computer. He's trying to set up the security camera, but his mind keeps drifting away to what-ifs and maybes.

He's startled out of his reverie though, by the front door opening, and slamming with a crash.

And there is Harrison.

Looking awful. Haggard, and angry, and ready to fight.

Bethany is standing behind him, one hand on his arm, gently pushing him into the room, something proud about her stance. But then she carefully puts her phone in her handbag, and says quietly, "I'll give you guys some space" and vanishes so unobtrusively Peter doesn't even notice that she's gone.

"Adele!" Peter's voice is too loud, too overeager, too something. "He's here! It's Harrison. *Adele!*" And he rushes toward Harrison, grabbing him roughly, crushing him to his chest, then stepping back to look at him.

"What?" says Harrison, aggressively, knowing perfectly well

that his parents would have been concerned, that he looks like hell, and that it's very possible that someone had left more notes on the front door, which, depending on their content, would have given his parents something close to a heart attack.

But he's also teetering on that fine line between childhood and adulthood, and what he really wants is to cry and howl and have his parents make everything all right, like they can do for you when you're little, and they can try when you're seventeen, but also you just have to face the fact that some of life's struggles are harder and more complex and more full of struggle than anyone can fix in that moment, and the realisation of it makes you a little bit angry and a little bit afraid.

Adele stumbles into the room, her hair a tangled mess, her eyes red and wild, and she lunges for her son, and grabs him to her, and lets out a strangled sob, and the rawness of her love and pain undo something in Harrison, and he wraps his arms around her gently, his stiff, angry stance melting back into boyhood, into kindness, and he whispers, "I'm so sorry, Mum. I'm sorry you were worried. I'm okay. It's all okay." And suddenly, the enormity and pain of the last few days feel less enormous, and less insurmountable. Harrison lets his mother lead him to the couch and smother him with love.

Later, when she asks him where he slept, he replies, "under the bridge," and Adele nearly faints again.

The thought of her beautiful boy sleeping under a bridge is nearly enough to kill her off completely.

"I wish you'd come to us," she says now, fussing over him, handing him a hot cup of coffee, touching his shoulder, checking his ribs, as though he might have faded away in thirty-six hours, as though she needs to check and X-ray and fatten every inch of him.

"Dan seems like a good chap," she ventures, watching her son under her lashes, trying not to stare. *How can she make him feel safe? How can she not let her upbringing spill over onto his? How can she make sure he knows he is loved, all of him, forever, no matter what?*

Memories of Celia are bubbling under the surface, and she knows she has to face them, soon, but she will not let her history poison her family. She will give Harrison what he needs. Celia can wait.

"But it's okay to be mad at him," she goes on. "It might not be reasonable. That's a big thing to share with someone you've only been dating a little while. And maybe he feels it was a long time ago, like it's not part of who he is now." She wants so badly to make everything okay, to make sure Harrison knows he can talk to her, and feel big things, and ask for what he needs, and the responsibility is crushing, how can she possibly get it right? When it took her thirty years to notice what her own sister did to her? How can she trust her judgement about anything, ever again?

Somehow, though, Harrison seems to be listening. His shoulders relax and edge downwards. He sips at his coffee, and lets Adele touch his arm, over and over again. He tucks his legs under him on the couch, leans back into it, and smiles at his mother. A small smile, but a smile.

Outside, Bethany hesitates. She's dying to tell Adele how she hunted Harrison down, how she followed a trail of comments on Facebook and a very unsavoury clip on TikTok, how she had asked the right people the right questions, but she knows that now is not the time. She doesn't actually need other people to know how clever she is. Being quietly cunning is sometimes its own reward.

Later, she'll drop back in, share a meal with them all, wave off Adele's thanks. Bask in time with her family, such as they are.

Right now though, she's going to book a ticket back to Perth, go back to her job as a locum at the local primary school, where she pays special attention to children that seem to be struggling. Parents love her; she notices things that other teachers have missed.

She always notices things that other people miss.

Inside, Adele and Peter and Harrison are folded into each other on the couch. Bethany smiles. She orders an Uber back to her parents' house, and in the car, she smooths out the crumpled note from the front door, and stares at it for a long time.

Later that night, Dan drops by, and stands in the kitchen awkwardly with Peter and Adele.

"I just made Harrison a coffee, do you want to take it to him?" Adele offers, handing him one for himself as well, and Dan pads down the hallway with two cups of coffee.

Harrison is lying on the bed. He opens bleary eyes when Dan comes in. For a moment he looks warm and cuddly and adorable, then his face hardens. Dan sits at the foot of the bed.

"Do you want to talk about it?"

Harrison glares at him. But he sits up and takes the coffee, blowing on it gently, his brows furrowed.

They sip in silence for a few minutes, and then Harrison asks: "Why did you stop?"

He doesn't meet Dan's eyes.

Dan considers the question carefully, as though he hadn't thought it a hundred times before.

"I got tired of the way it made me feel about men," he says, simply. "There are a lot of good men in the world. And a lot of good men who were my clients. But I saw a lot of awful ones, too, and I wanted to surround myself with good people, all the time. Even if it meant a different lifestyle, less lucrative work."

Dan is a barista and a handyman, and he definitely is not charging anyone hundreds of dollars an hour anymore.

He sits with Harrison, comfortable in his own skin. He knows that he might help Harrison see this differently, or he might not.

"Your folks have invited me to stay for dinner," he says, after a while. "Do you want me to?"

Harrison hesitates. When he speaks, his voice is small. "Are we just friends now?" Dan's heart lurches. Harrison looks every bit of seventeen.

"Yeah," he says. "I think that's about right, don't you?"

"Dinner's ready, boys," they hear faintly, from the kitchen and Dan drains his coffee and stands up, holding out a hand to Harrison, who stares at it for a long moment, and then takes it, and lets Dan help him to his feet.

46

Sunday

December 2021

Bethany stares at the note again.

Her parents dropped her at the airport that morning. Bethany had sat in the back seat, rubbing the note idly between her fingers as they drove.

"Did you ever think that Celia wasn't a very nice person?" she had asked, and they had glanced at each other uneasily.

"No," they'd said, in unison.

Now, the sun is setting, and Bethany stares at the note.

She's been so good, for all these years. She'd kept her promise to herself.

It was good to be home. She settles in to her reading chair in her modest apartment, funded by the money in the mysterious bank account that Celia had never come back to claim. She'd stopped buying designer clothes, though she still looked after, lovingly, all the ones she'd bought in the initial rush of joy she'd got from scamming.

"Be careful what you wish for," the note reads.

Bethany had seen it as she walked up the front path from her walk, and stopped in front of it, looking around.

She was sure it wasn't there when she left a couple of hours ago.

She was just sliding it off the nail when a small voice piped up behind her.

"Excuse me, Miss! Excuse me!"

She'd turned to find a small boy, with sandy hair and irreverent freckles, brandishing a newspaper. His little face was excited. He was trying hard to look serious, and important, and failing completely.

"I saw who put the note on your door, Miss! I was doing my paper round. I thought I better tell someone, with all the stuff on the news, and all."

Bethany steps toward him. "Oh yes?" she asks, carefully moving down the path, away from the door.

Somewhere where she might talk to this child quietly.

He's waving his phone around, conspiratorial, and so, so proud. "I took a picture, Miss! My mum was saying you need evidence. She's been talking to the police this week. She's been helping them."

"That is so helpful of you...?" She lets the silence hang, and he fills it happily.

"Jasper. I'm Jasper. And it was Albert Armstrong on your doorstop! His wife is missing. They're still looking."

"That's true, they are," Bethany says, her face warm. "And it is so clever of you to try to help, to know to get some evidence. Your mum is going to be so proud." She hesitates for a beat and then says, "Can you show me?" And Jasper unlocks his phone, zinging with the thrill of it. This was way more exciting than skids on his BMX. He had snuck up to the door to read the note, and it was disappointing, but still. It could mean something sinister, couldn't it?

Bethany peers at the phone he holds up to her. The photo is

perfectly shot, high resolution, capturing Albert as he swung his leg over the fence, his face curiously benign. The time stamp says 6:23 a.m.

"Do you think you could send me that photo, please Jasper? That would help me a lot," Bethany says. "Here, let me put the number in." She carefully types her number, and makes sure the photo sends. Then, after a pause, she deletes the message.

"Thank you so much for doing that. Do you think Albert saw you take the picture?" Bethany assumes not, or Jasper would likely not still be here, with his phone intact, jumping from foot to foot with excitement. But she just wants to check.

"No, Miss! I was—" Here Jasper stops abruptly and looks sheepish. "I was doing some air guitar behind that van over there. He didn't notice me. I was like a real spy."

Bethany smiles to herself. Jasper's joy is infectious.

"You sure were," she tells him. "But you know, he's part of my family. And I think he's just really upset about everything going on with Celia right now. So I wonder if you could do me a big favour?" Bethany thinks hard. Jasper is not going to be able to keep this story quiet, it's far too thrilling. "We're not going to tell the police about the note on the door. I'll have a quiet chat to Albert, and I'm sure he won't do anything like this again. So maybe you could tell your mum how smart and brave you were, but you can tell her I said we don't need to tell the police about this one, okay? But it's been such good practice for you. Who knows, maybe next time you'll break open a big case." Bethany smiles at Jasper, then a frown flits across her face. "Be careful, though, won't you, Jasper? Some people would be really angry about getting caught. And it's important to do the right thing if you see something bad happening. But it's *most* important to look after yourself, and keep yourself safe, okay?"

Jasper nods, still grinning and hopping from foot to foot. Bethany doubts he will remember her little pep talk.

"Well, thank you for the photo," she said. "I'll be heading off now. And well done, again, on being such a good spy."

Jasper grins widely at her, then jumps on his bike, and pedals frantically away.

Now, she pulls the note out, puts it in her filing cabinet with the others.

Fifty thousand dollars had seemed reasonable. Of course, there would be no repercussions for Albert for pinning obscure notes on someone's door. Trespassing, maybe. He could have laughed at her. But it would have left his loving, kind GP image in tatters. Raised new questions about Celia, again. Why would a GP taunt his gay, estranged nephew with homophobic notes on his door? No, it would be a very bad look. Bad for business. He had done the right thing, for both of them.

She doesn't feel bad. Albert can afford it.

The way he'd looked at her, though. *Did he know about drugging Adele? Did he know that it was meant for him?* His eyes were more thoughtful, more calculating than she remembered. He looked sharper. Like perhaps he'd wised up since then. If she fooled him easily fifteen years ago, she suspects she wouldn't be able to fool him now.

Still, she found Harrison. That was good, right? Her skills and her dedication had led her to him, under a bridge, shivering and dishevelled.

One good turn.

A big one.

There's some good karma right there, right?

She goes to her filing cabinet, and pulls out her collection of copies of licenses and identifications, ready to throw them in the bin.

Most of them are out of date, but that isn't a problem for Bethany.

Albert's is on the top, and she hesitates.

She doesn't even know what went on between Albert and

Adele. In all the chaos with finding Harrison, she'd forgotten to ask, and she's not even sure she really wants to know. Perhaps it's for the best if she keeps out of the messy business of her family.

Still. She stares at her file for a long moment, then idly flips through the ones at the top.

A blonde bob and perfect smile stare out at her; the new kindergarten teacher, who looks so sweet and sincere, but who yelled at little Aaron and sent him to sit in the corner for thirty minutes for sneezing on her in his first week of school. Bethany had found him crying, alone, at recess, and comforted him. Later, she'd found the teacher and raised the issue, and she had denied the incident ever happened.

Bethany had just had a little look in her personnel file. Just in case.

But no. She's going to be good now.

She's not quite ready to throw away her files, though.

She shuts the cabinet with a resounding clang, and walks back to her sunroom, sits back in her chair to watch the sun go down.

This was a good outcome.

This was better than even she had hoped for.

It was sheer luck, Jasper being there, taking a photo. What were the chances? She shouldn't look a gift horse in the mouth. It was done, the money has already hit her account, Harrison was safe, and she wouldn't mention Albert's petty, bitter little notes to anyone.

Everyone was winning.

Well, except Dan and Harrison, who had decided to just be friends. But Bethany thought Dan seemed like a good friend to have. Harrison could do worse.

"Keep away from them," Bethany had warned Albert. "I don't know what went on between you all, but it's not healthy. So here's the deal. You send me the money. You keep away from my family. And no one will ever know about the notes on the door. Okay?"

"I want you to delete it." Albert had stared at her, his eyes cold.

She'd shrugged. She'd already sent it to another phone. And she'd told Albert she'd taken it herself, carefully deleting Jasper's message, but saving his phone number, just in case.

She deleted the photo, and he'd smiled at her, something triumphant in his eyes.

"Quite the family, aren't you?" he'd said, but Bethany didn't care. She was already turning away, leaving him to his sad little resentments about young love. Imagining him harmless.

"You know your sister was out on the cliffs that night, right? You think a note is bad? Ask your sister what she did out there."

She'd turned back then, their eyes meeting.

"And how do you know that, Albert?" she'd said, and he'd faltered then.

She'd walked away.

Be careful what you wish for, she thinks to herself, now.

Aaron's wretched little face comes back to her, and she frowns.

Tomorrow, it's back to the classroom, back to the children, their delight in sharing with her, their trust, their joy in her attention, their easy openness.

She'll definitely embrace that tomorrow, with her whole heart.

Today, she has a little score to settle with someone.

She opens her laptop, and starts to type.

EPILOGUE

Six months later

Adele strides down the street, her new, cheerful red handbag swinging against her hip, the winter sun bright on her face.

She's on her way from therapy to meet her family for lunch at a fancy restaurant overlooking the harbour. Usually, she'd feel a swell of dread or worry. But today, she feels good.

Harrison is back from Melbourne for mid-year break, and he's brought his boyfriend with him for her and Peter to meet. Scott seems perfectly delightful, and has slotted into their house for the holidays with such ease Adele already feels like he's part of the family.

Jocelyn had fussed and worried over inviting him to family lunch (her friend's daughter is the head waitress, and it's not that she's *ashamed,* it's just, it's a new relationship, young love! And it's *awkward* to flaunt it, isn't it?). She'd nearly had a heart attack when Adele informed her she'd invited Dan as well. "Do you think that's...*wise,* darling? It's going to be so busy and noisy. Perhaps we'd be better off getting to know Scott at your house? And Dan's not *family,* is he? I thought we were having a *family* lunch?" And Adele had felt strangely unperturbed.

"I think it's perfect," she'd replied. "I want to celebrate Harrison's first semester at uni, and treat everyone to something nice. And Dan has been a lovely friend to him, and I want to celebrate that too. If it makes you uncomfortable, though, you're welcome to join us for dinner at home another day instead?"

Jocelyn's brow had creased, her lips making their familiar thin line, but to Adele's surprise, she didn't feel a rush to fix it. She could easily move on, and leave the discomfort with her mother to work out, or not.

Her therapist would be proud.

Now, her step quickens.

She's wearing a new pale pink wool-knit dress, and strides confidently.

She feels a little like an Italian mansion, with all the fine trimmings you'd expect on a mansion on the coast.

Adele is looking forward to seeing Beth, who's flown over from Perth for the occasion, and who's called her regularly ever since finding Harrison. It was Beth, in fact, who urged her to try therapy again, after that turbulent time, and who'd confided in her about how much some extra support had helped her with her own diagnosis.

Despite this, Beth has never brought up that night when Albert visited, and for a while Adele grappled with this—how much to tell her, what this new relationship between them required of her.

Eventually, she settled not on complete intimacy nor their historical lack of closeness, but somewhere grey, in the middle, that felt, surprisingly, just right.

Adele and Peter don't really talk about that night, either. Peter had told Adele that Celia was alive, screaming attempted murder, and that Albert was there. "You didn't kill her," he had said, holding her gaze. He doesn't say it, but he doesn't have to.

Let's leave the past alone now.

Adele could not find fault with Peter for rushing home, and giving up on getting her to remember. She knows better than anyone that she is a force to be reckoned with for forgetting what she doesn't want to know.

She's working on that in therapy, too. And purging, as well: she hasn't felt the urge to purge in a very long time.

At the restaurant, she sees her family before they see her. Harrison is glowing. Peter is sitting quietly with her father, as steady as a rock.

She kisses everyone, her father holding her a little longer than usual, whispering how pleased he is to be there, and she smiles at him in surprise, then slips in beside her sister, joins in the cheerful chatter. Dan is making Jocelyn laugh. Scott is looking slightly overwhelmed, but still beaming.

A little watercolour of the headlands is propped up next to the salt shaker, and catches Adele's eye. It's beautiful, and with alluring colours and sweeping strokes. Beth catches her looking at it, and shrugs. "Albert asked me to give it to Harrison. He's taken up painting. Perhaps he thinks it will be worth something one day. Or perhaps he knows it won't." She grins, and Adele startles.

"Why on earth were you talking to Albert?" she whispers, and for a moment Bethany gets a distant look in her eye, a familiar vacant dreaminess. Adele gets the sense that her sister is drifting away, somewhere that Adele can't reach her, and it feels like she's losing her, like she's out of reach, lost in her own world.

Then her eyes snap back, clear and sharp and meaningful. "I was just checking in on him, making sure he was keeping in line, not visiting you unexpectedly and causing any stress," she says, a little smile playing around the corners of her mouth, some secret satisfaction which Adele can't interpret. But Bethany goes on, as though Albert is meaningless: "I ordered cheese to share. Their biggest, most extravagant platter. Some olives and charcuterie, too." She leans in and gives Adele's shoulder a bump, her eyes dancing. "It's a family get-together, after all, and we must have cheese. It's my treat." And when Adele protests, saying lunch is on her, Beth can order whatever she likes, Beth waves her protests away breezily.

"No, darling. You always bring the cheese. Today it's my turn." She looks at her sister, and smiles, a joyful, playful smile, full of love. "I insist."

Adele smiles, surprised, and leans back in her chair.

She looks around the table at her family. For a moment, an image of Celia tries to rise up in her mind, tries to take her place at the table, and Adele sees her as a mythical creature, all flapping wings and flashing eyes, breathing fire. Demanding attention, demanding space.

Adele swats the image away, like she might a fly.

The cheese platter arrives, and she reaches for a cracker and scoops up some delicious, oozing brie with it, and pops it in her mouth appreciatively.

Then she turns back to Bethany, and the family chatter, and doesn't give her other sister another thought.

EXCERPT GOOD GIRL BAD

Praise for Good Girl Bad

"THIS DARK PSYCHOLOGICAL family drama isn't the same old plot. The basic structure involves good pacing and strong characters, making it a can't put it down thriller. You know it's good when you wake up in the middle of the night "for just one more chapter"." ★★★★★ Amazon review

"Wow! I couldn't read this one fast enough. Complex, well-written, and twisty! I thought I knew where it was going, but I didn't. Very well done, as usual. S.A. McEwen is on my auto-buy list!" ★★★★★ Amazon review

"A clever, twisted, magnetic read!!" ★★★★ Goodreads review

"Thought-provoking, compelling, complex." ★★★★★ Amazon review

"Intense, surprising and original." ★★★★ Goodreads review

"A master storyteller." ★★★★★ Amazon review

A perfect life, or a perfect lie?

Rebecca Giovanni has a beautiful life—a job she loves, a new husband who's a great deal better than the old one, and two charming daughters from her first marriage.

It's hard not to be smug about how well she's done for herself.

She trusts her new husband.

Then she wakes to find him and her sixteen-year-old daughter missing. Their dog is dead, and the front door is wide open.

No matter what the police insinuate, Rebecca cannot believe Leroy and Tabby went anywhere together willingly. She's doing a stellar job, but blended families always have their difficulties. And they'd never leave the house without their phones and wallets.

But where are they? What happened in the house that night?

Rebecca's younger daughter is acting strangely, and her ex-husband is hiding secrets of his own—like where he was that night, and the real reason that he left Rebecca.

And Rebecca can't help thinking about the last time she saw her husband, and heard him say something she'd rather forget...

———

Chapter 1

Monday

The house is silent.

Eerily so.

Rebecca Giovanni stands at the top of the small stairway to the kitchen. Below her, her sixteen-year-old daughter Tabitha's miniature poodle, Charlie, lies on his side. He could nearly be sleeping, except he never sleeps in the kitchen, on the cold tiles.

Rebecca can see that something is wrong, the position of his legs not quite right, his little head stretched back at an unusual angle, a rigidity about him sufficient information such that Rebecca does not go any closer; does not check.

Beyond him, the front door is wide open. A cold wind blows in from the street, through the leaves of the wisteria hanging lushly around the veranda, caressing Rebecca's forearms, swirling beyond her into the silent house.

The faint scent—her favorite flower—drifts past her toward the very back of the house, where her youngest daughter Genevieve is still sleeping. At fourteen, she is well and truly a teen when it comes to sleeping in. The house could fall apart around her and she would not so much as mumble a complaint. Rather, she'd roll over, tugging the doona around her ears, eyes resolutely shut against the intrusion.

It's spring—November—but still cold, and Rebecca shivers.

Leroy was not in their bed, and Tabitha was not in hers, either.

Rebecca's eyes roam around the kitchen.

She is not worried yet.

She notices Leroy's phone and wallet next to the fruit bowl; he has not gone far.

Tabby's phone, usually glued to her hand, is hanging precariously over the edge of the dining table. It looks like it should be falling, not balancing there.

But other than that, the house looks much the same as it always does when Rebecca gets up.

Rebecca is still not worried, despite the open front door, and despite the dead dog in her kitchen.

She's not worried yet.

But she will be.

Chapter 2

Six Months Earlier

Rebecca smooths her Armani skirt across her thighs, a tiny, self-contained movement that she uses as a break in conversation. It makes her look calm and certain; it soothes her when she needs to take a moment to think of what it is she wants to say.

It also reminds her of who she is: successful. Capable. In charge. The mother who wears Armani to parent-teacher interviews, her makeup flawless, all poise and perfection.

Rebecca doesn't speak rashly. She weighs her words, her cool blue eyes resting on the recipient appraisingly. In this case, the recipient is Tabitha's home room teacher, Ms. Paisley.

"I'm not sure what you're getting at?" she says eventually, her gaze unflinching.

Ms. Paisley is young. Much younger than Rebecca, with kind brown eyes, which are right now blinking too frequently.

Nerves? Rebecca wonders.

She is used to people being nervous around her. Being wowed by her, in fact.

"Well, it's my first year teaching Tabby, of course," Ms. Paisley responds, her words tumbling over each other in her haste to get them out. *It's probably your first year teaching, period,* Rebecca thinks to herself, patronizing, but she keeps herself in check. "So I've only known her for a few months, obviously. It's just, she's always been one of our top students, and certainly her work earlier in the year was of a consistently high quality. It's just the last month or so that things have started to slip a little. Work not handed in, or not much effort applied, that kind of thing." She nearly looks apologetic, but seems to be trying her best not to. Even as Rebecca watches, she pulls her shoulders back and sits up a little higher in her chair.

"I'll have a word with her. But she's been her usual self at home. I haven't noticed any changes." Here Rebecca stops.

Typical, she thinks. Just as she was taking ownership—"I" haven't noticed any changes—she spots Nate fighting his way around chairs and parents to reach them. Rebecca watches him silently. It's characteristic of her ex-husband to be late, and to look the opposite of calm and poised. Rebecca wonders if people think less of her because she was once married to him; if she's tainted by association.

"Sorry I'm late," he puffs as he comes to a halt beside them, casting about for a spare chair he can pull up. Spying one halfway across the room, he disappears again. Rebecca turns back to Ms. Paisley, who looks as though she's very happy to wait for Nate to return.

Does no one have a sense of time and urgency except me? Rebecca thinks. If the roles were reversed, she would plough ahead without the late ex-husband. She would say what needed to be said to whomever was present, and conclude the meeting decisively, precisely on time. Too bad, so sad if you were late and missed half of it.

She runs her hand over her skirt again, the soft black fabric feeling expensive and luxurious under her touch. It clings to her thighs elegantly, ever so slightly suggestively, the muscle underneath nicely defined by regular weight classes and running. She raises her eyes to Nate again, her expression patient to anyone who didn't know her well.

To Nate, the patience is feigned, or mocking.

Here we are, waiting for you, again.

He seems unfazed though. He plonks the chair down next to Rebecca, and beams at Ms. Paisley.

"How's my girl doing?" he says, and Rebecca has to stop herself from rolling her eyes.

"We're well past that, Nate," she says, cutting Ms. Paisley off, and summarizing the meeting so far, her demeanor crisp and business-like. She doesn't give Nate a chance to respond, but addresses Ms. Paisley again with the air of someone who is used to making all the decisions.

"So, I'll have a word with her. I'm sure it's nothing to worry about. Tabby has always been a hard worker. If necessary, I can always limit her phone time. That's always rather motivating for her."

Ms. Paisley looks surprised, and starts to open her mouth, but Rebecca cuts her off. "Did you have any questions, Nate?"

"Yes, actually," he says, though he knows full well that the question was rhetorical, designed to show Ms. Paisley that they were co-parenting cooperatively. Rebecca didn't really expect him to say yes—to the point that she was half rising from her chair, and stops mid-air.

She glances at Nate, something hard passing across her face fleetingly, then she smiles and sits back down. Poised and gracious.

"Well, obviously we'll talk to her," Nate goes on, glancing at Rebecca. "But have you noticed anything at school that might explain it? Any change in her friendship group? Any boys she's hanging out with, that might be breaking her heart?" Nate looks like he is joking, making light of it, but Rebecca can see that he's just not sure how appropriate it is to ask Tabby's home room teacher about her love life, so he's disguising it under a protective, jovial father spiel.

Joke, joke, joke.

Rebecca thinks Nate is wasting his time. *Her* time.

Of course Tabby isn't seeing anyone.

Rebecca actively discourages relationships—she thinks Tabby is far too young, and has more important things to do. Like excel at school and get into a good university. The truth is, though, that Rebecca would have no idea if Tabby was romantically involved with anyone; they don't have that kind of relationship. Her certainty is rooted entirely in confidence that Tabby would not defy her wishes. She's not worried by Ms.

Paisley's revelations. Tabby is strong-willed, and can be a little bit feisty, but she falls back into line when Rebecca flexes her parental rights.

For the briefest of moments, that reality is held up for her to examine, and the starkness of it feels uncomfortable, and nags at her. *Should she know her daughter better? Should her certainty be rooted in dialogue, not authority?* But she turns her thoughts back to the issue at hand.

"I very much doubt Tabby's been distracted by a boy," she says, somewhat pompously, and Ms. Paisley looks apologetic again.

"Well, actually, there has been a lot more socializing between the boys and girls this year, and I have noticed Tabby spending a lot of time with a particular young man, Trent Witherall. Has she mentioned him to you at all?"

Rebecca's demeanor shifts slightly, her posture stiffening, her jaw tensing. Nate glances at her uneasily.

"No, nothing," Rebecca says, her voice tight. She looks to Nate for confirmation, this time appearing genuinely interested in his response.

"She has mentioned Trent to me, yes," he says, directing his words to Ms. Paisley. "But she's never made it sound like they're dating, or that she likes him in particular. His name has just come up a few times when she's talking about her friends, what they're doing on the weekend. Do you think they're...seeing each other?" Nate is aware of something simmering in Rebecca next to him, and he keeps his eyes carefully on Ms. Paisley.

She, likewise, speaks back directly to Nate. "I would have thought so, yes," she says, but won't be drawn into why she thinks that. "I really think that's a conversation for you to have with your daughter, don't you think?" she hedges, and Nate wonders what she has seen.

Hand-holding?

Kissing?

Do kids kiss on school grounds these days? He can't even remember how you wooed girls back in his day. He can't imagine his broody eldest daughter being buffeted about by the strong feelings of young love.

But broodiness would be the perfect breeding ground for that intensity, that all-or-nothing consuming infatuation, wouldn't it?

Nate suddenly feels old and out of touch. Unlike Rebecca, he *has* noticed a change in his daughter. He would have said it had been much longer than this year though, and doubts very much it has anything to do with Trent Witherall. In fact, if his life depended on putting a date to it, he would have said it was a year or two ago that she started to become more withdrawn, more secretive. More broody.

About the time that Rebecca married that twerp, Leroy, in fact.

He steals a glance at his ex-wife. She is sitting very still, projecting that calm, reasonable, I-am-listening-to-you-deeply facade. He wonders if Ms. Paisley can see through it.

He wonders what sort of man *can't* see through it.

What sort of man would fall for it.

He did, sure. But he was so young.

You can't put an old head on young shoulders, his father used to tell him, and he understands the saying differently now.

But Leroy is his age. Forty-five, give or take a few years.

What was Leroy's excuse?

Or was he just as stupid as twenty-year-old Nate?

And if Leroy was just as stupid as a twenty-year-old, what might have gone on between him and Nate's sweet sixteen-year-old daughter, that might explain the changes in her mood?

Back at home, Rebecca dumps her handbag on the kitchen island with a loud thump.

She can hear chatter coming from the living room, the faint hum of the television, and she feels like storming up there and shutting it down, all of it. The television, the happy family time. Tabby has made her look stupid in front of her teacher, in front of Nate, but she's just glibly fooling around on a school night in front of the television without a care in the world.

"Tabby!" she shouts down the hallway, and there's a moment's silence, the voices quieting. Then the living room door opens and Leroy and Tabby both emerge, padding down the long hallway toward her. They look so easy, so relaxed, and she feels resentful that she has to be the one to bring things back to order, to interrupt their fun, to remind them of the real world.

But somebody has to do it.

But just as she opens her mouth to say something cross, something biting, Leroy jumps clownishly down the five steps into the kitchen and grabs her in a dance pose, swinging her around, one arm firmly around her waist. He grins at her impishly.

"Look out, Tabby, Becci looks a bit peeved! What is it? An F? An expulsion? You've learned that Tabby's quit math to do embroidery instead, and your dream of retiring on the back of your daughter's orthodontic practice has gone up in flames?"

He spins her around once more and then pushes her against the wall, kissing her right on the lips in front of Tabby, his eyes laughing.

They'll have sex tonight, she can tell from his kiss, the way he holds her against the wall.

Her tummy flutters.

"Slipping grades," she squeaks, as she tries to wriggle out of his grasp, but the tension has gone out of her.

Leroy gives her a final smooch, then releases her. As he turns to go back to the living room, to give her space to chat with Tabby, no doubt, she thinks she catches a small smile toward her daughter, and a wink, and her stomach does less of a flutter and more of a churn.

Chapter 3

Monday

Rebecca shakes Genevieve roughly.

"Gen. Gen!" Genevieve groans, and tries to burrow back under her doona, but Rebecca is tugging it down harder and faster than she can pull it back up.

"Mom!" Gen protests, the cold creeping in from the hallway, from outside. From the situation in the kitchen.

"Where's your sister?" Rebecca's voice is urgent.

"Wha-at?" Genevieve rubs her bleary eyes. "How should I know?"

It's now nearly 9 a.m. Two hours have passed since Rebecca found the front door open, and impatience and irritation have finally given way to something more urgent.

"Get up," Rebecca instructs her youngest daughter, rifling in her cupboard and throwing a tee shirt and some leggings at her. Genevieve holds them up in confusion. They're not appropriate for a Melbourne spring morning, no matter that it's nearly summer. And they're certainly not appropriate for a school day.

"They're gone," Rebecca continues, looking through Genevieve's wardrobe like she might find some clue in there. "Leroy. Tabby. Leroy's car. But something's not right. I can feel it."

Hustling Genevieve through the house, shivering in the thin tee shirt Rebecca had handed her, she points to the mobile phones and wallets triumphantly. "See? Tabby would never go anywhere without her phone. And. Charlie." Here she glances at the little form underneath the sweater she had hastily thrown over him while she made phone calls, trying to find her daughter and husband.

Her eyes linger there, uneasily.

In her state of agitation, she completely forgets how one ought to break such news to anyone, especially to her teenage daughter.

Genevieve is still half asleep, and is struggling to make sense of her mother's words, which are being thrown at her, staccato-like. Bam. Bam. Bam. Bam. But when her eyes—following Rebecca's—fall on the shape under the sweater, she falls silently to her knees. She glances up at Rebecca, a question in her eyes, but she doesn't need a response, and her mouth gapes slightly, tears welling in her eyes, and she doubles over, a silent scream emanating from her open mouth.

She doesn't touch the sweater, just keens silently beside the little body on the floor.

Something about her daughter's grief shakes Rebecca out of her quest for an explanation. Genevieve is a thoughtful, sensitive, quiet teen, and Rebecca is surprised by the force of her pain.

No, that's not right. She's not surprised by the force of it—she's surprised that Genevieve is showing it. To her mother.

Rebecca has her own pain about the dog, but it's been swallowed up by more important things, like where her husband and other daughter are, and why they left in such a hurry that they didn't even shut the front door.

She kneels beside Gen, putting her arms around her shuddering, small frame. "I'm sorry, I'm sorry," she whispers, mortified by her insensitivity. She holds Gen tight, keeping her close until her shaking slows and stills.

"What happened to him?" Gen hiccups, her voice painfully small.

"I don't know, sweetheart. But something's wrong. I'm going

to call the police. I've already called everyone who I can think of who might know where they are."

She'd been methodical—Tabby's friends. Trent Witherall's parents. Nate. The school.

Miss Ambrosia, the cafe where Tabby works on Saturdays —only to be told that Tabby hadn't worked there for over four months.

Where was Tabby going on Saturdays, then?

Where was she getting money from?

Rebecca mentally kicks herself. She'd looked into GPS tracking when she'd bought Tabitha her first smartphone. For a while, she'd obsessively checked her location, but Tabby was always exactly where she said she'd be. Even after that interview with Ms. Paisley, when Rebecca was watching her closely, checking her location again daily—well, she'd gotten slack. She thought Ms. Paisley had it wrong. Tabby was never over in Richmond, where Trent lived. She was always with her best friend Freddy, studying, or else at work.

Rebecca had stopped checking. She really didn't think Tabby was the type to sneak around.

Now, though, she wonders what data she'd be able to access. Tabby's phone was right here. Didn't Google Maps keep data on everywhere you'd been? Was that true? And if it was, please dear God let Tabby's passcode be the same as it always was—the day she got Charlie, her twelfth birthday present. But he had arrived a week early, so it wasn't like she was using her *actual* birthdate, which Rebecca had told her a hundred times would be foolish, anyone could guess it.

Now, she grabs the phone off the table, presses the home button. Nothing. The phone is dead, and she scours around for a charger, usually lurking in every second power point, so many phones seemed to populate their home.

Personal phones. Work phones. Kids' phones.

Old, discarded phones.

Finally, she spies a cord hanging out from under the microwave, and plugs Tabby's phone in. It takes forever even for the little red battery symbol to blink on. Impatiently, she turns away from it.

"Did you know Tabby had quit Miss Ambrosia?" she asks Genevieve, trying to be gentle, but it's hard to keep the urgency, the accusing tone out of her voice.

The girl has pulled Charlie's stiff little body onto her lap. So different from Tabby, Genevieve is short and dark-haired, her brown eyes now staring vacantly into the distance. Charlie was Tabby's dog, but Tabby shared him generously with her little sister. She made sure to give Genevieve turns walking and feeding him, so the dog loved them both eagerly, joyously. Right above her, in fact, is an enlarged photo of the three of them. Charlie is clutched between the two girls, the love on their faces palpable through the camera lens. Tabby is crouched down—she's easily a foot taller than Gen. Her long, blonde hair is sun-bleached and messy, cascading over a slim, tan shoulder. Her blue eyes sparkle, staring right at you out from the wall.

Rebecca shivers. Leroy loves that picture. "Bottled joy" he called it, insisting that it was the one they frame, but it's always made Rebecca uneasy. Tabby looks older than she ought to in it. In a tank top and tiny shorts, she looks worldly, seductive. When she'd snapped at Leroy that perhaps that was why he liked it, he'd looked at her strangely. She still can't quite fathom the look that he gave her.

"They look like happy kids," he'd said, and she wondered if he could sense her jealousy, if that was why he was so restrained. God, she was basically accusing him of lusting after her teenage daughter, he was well within his rights to fly completely off the handle. Instead, that strange look. Like he didn't even know who she was in that moment.

It wasn't as simple as the ageing mother envying the

blossoming of youthful beauty. Rebecca herself was beautiful, she had no doubt and no insecurity about that. Tabby even looked a lot like her, really. Taller and slimmer, but their features were similar, their striking blue eyes.

No, it wasn't that. But it was hard to put her finger on the pang that the picture gave her, every time.

She wished she'd put her foot down, ordered a different print.

Now, though, she focuses back on Genevieve, who solemnly shakes her head.

Rebecca has no reason to doubt her. Gen has always been compliant, cautious, responsible. Tabby is more like her, Rebecca—impulsive, flamboyant. Sure of herself.

Or at least, she used to be.

Is she still flamboyant?

Things have changed, Rebecca knows that. But they've changed so slowly, so incrementally, that she hasn't paid that much attention. Now, though, she realizes that the word *flamboyant* no longer applies to her eldest daughter.

Genevieve, on the other hand, was never flamboyant. Genevieve is steady. Calm. Rebecca trusts her absolutely.

Rebecca casts her mind back to the Saturday just gone. Tabby had left on her bike at about 11 a.m. as she always did. She covered the lunch shift, making coffees and toasting fancy baguettes for a little café one suburb over from them. Or at least, that was what she was supposed to be doing. Rebecca was sure, in fact, that Tabby had boasted of a promotion not that long ago. Managing that shift. Definitely not more than four months ago.

So where had she been going every Saturday for four hours?

"Did you call Freddy?" Gen's voice is faint. Rebecca thinks that she hasn't grasped the seriousness of the situation. All she can think about is the damn dog. And the dog definitely needs thinking about, but right now, Rebecca just wants to know where Leroy and Tabitha are.

"Yes. I spoke to Fred. They haven't seen her this weekend. Freddy had already left for school by the time I called."

Fred and Frederica. For the hundredth time, Rebecca thinks *how vain. Silly,* even. To choose a name for your kid that's basically the same as your own. The amount of times there's been confusion over who is being referred to when you say "Freddy" is ridiculous.

Tabby and Freddy have been best friends since grade four, and Fred, the father, has promised he'll get Freddy to call Rebecca when she gets home from school, in case she knows anything. The way he says it makes Rebecca's stomach churn again.

In case she knows anything.

But Rebecca shoves that feeling aside and calls the police.

Chapter 4

Monday

By the time Nate arrives, the police have already been at Rebecca's house for an hour.

A bored-looking officer stops him at the door, asking for identification and a reason for being there.

"My daughter is bloody missing with *that man!*" He has to stop himself from shouting the last two words, his voice rising unusually high.

Rebecca looks over at him, disdain written all across her face. Even disdainful, she's still a striking woman, with her aquiline nose and astonishing blue eyes. She's fitter than when they were together, too—always shapely, she's now toned as well, and her posture is that of a lioness, queen of her terrain.

The officer's ears prick up at Nate's tone, though. "We don't have any reason to suspect anything suspicious at this stage, sir," he says. "But can you tell me why you refer to Mr. Giovanni in that manner?"

Nate can't though. He's never gotten along with Leroy, but do you usually get along with your replacement in the husband department? Leroy is too smooth, too handsome, and Nate is sure he'd be a player. The thought of him living with his teenage daughters is a constant thorn in his side. When Leroy had first moved in, he'd had to be very firm with Rebecca about some boundaries.

Leroy can't shower the girls.

He can't be in the bathroom with them.

At the time, they'd been ten and twelve, and Rebecca had just nodded and smiled sarcastically at him, but he could see how close she was to rolling her eyes. Because of course the girls didn't need any help in the shower, and of course even Rebecca would have thought it weird if her new boyfriend had wanted to spend time in the bathroom with her tween daughters. Rebecca was clearly humoring him. But she didn't know men the way that he, Nate, knew men. Tabitha was a knockout. Even at twelve, men did double takes on the street. She looked like she was a model, with those long, lean, tanned legs and waist-length beach-blonde hair. She didn't look away, either. She'd fix those smoldering eyes on whoever stared, her face deadpan, neither shy nor embarrassed nor egotistical.

He often wondered what went on behind her eyes, but he never asked.

She was going to break hearts, though, and Nate would be damned if he'd let a grown man spend any time with her naked.

Now, though, he's forced to backtrack. Because what could he say?

The man would have to be blind to not ogle her, to not notice her in a sexual manner?

No. He was being ridiculous. He knew that. He was just paranoid. You hear so many awful things these days. It was a terrible time to have a daughter.

To be a woman, he corrects himself. *It was a terrible time to be a woman. Or had it always been a terrible time, and now they were just starting to shout about it?* #MeToo had shaken him. And then there was the "incident" on Messenger. Here he cringes slightly, the police officer watching him curiously. It was all too difficult to think about, and he's whittled it down to a simple concept, one which was, however, impossible to enforce: *he did not want men thinking about his daughter in a sexual manner at all.*

Ever.

For the rest of her life.

Did all fathers feel like this? It was a constant mild panic, a sense of tension he could never quite shake. How dangerous the world might be for someone so beautiful.

Now, he wishes he'd asked what Tabby was thinking behind that blank expression when men stared at her. At the time, it was too uncomfortable. Embarrassing, even. What do you say to your daughter about men his age staring at her on the street? He always felt mortified, as though he was part of that group, like he needed to collectively apologize, like he was tainted by their stares, too. Like she might think less of him because weren't they all just a little bit like him? On the surface, at any rate. He couldn't quite put his finger on it. But it was awful and uncomfortable and he pretended it wasn't happening at all.

Now, he wishes he had some idea what her views were on middle-aged men. He wishes he'd been more proactive in talking to her. Guiding her.

Protecting her.

He shakes his head at the police officer. "Nothing, sorry," he says. "I don't trust my ex's new husband, that's all."

"But it's just a gut feeling, isn't that right, Nate?" Rebecca interjects, her voice jeering at him ever so slightly. Nate ignores her.

"Is there any news?"

"Well, no one has been able to locate Mr. Giovanni or Tabitha, but given there was no sign of forced entry, and Mr. Giovanni's car is gone, it does suggest that he and Tabitha have gone somewhere together. We do understand that Mrs. Giovanni feels that that is extremely unlikely, but at this stage, I'd suggest waiting until tomorrow to see if this all sorts itself out. These things usually do. Alternatively, if you want to file a missing person's report, we need you to come down to the station." The officer snaps his notebook closed with an air of finality, nodding to his colleague, a silent agreement that it was time for them to go.

"What about the dog?" Rebecca asks, her voice high. She has one arm wrapped around Gen, and Nate moves forward to give his youngest daughter a hug. He strokes her hair and pulls her head onto his chest, murmuring gentle words to her. Gen starts crying quietly again, but Nate can't tell if she's worried about Tabby or if she's crying for Charlie.

"Yes, the dog is concerning." The officer consults his notebook, as though that will help him clarify what has happened here, what the solution might be. But he doesn't add anything else, and Nate grits his teeth.

"What happened last night?" Nate turns to Rebecca, his voice tight. "Did you have a fight? With Tabby? With Leroy? How was she yesterday? Did she seem okay?"

Rebecca's face closes. "She was fine. Wasn't she, Gen? Except..." Here she glances at the officers uneasily. "Apparently she quit her job months ago. But she's been pretending to go every Saturday like usual. Did you know that?" Her tone is accusatory, as though Nate being privy to something she wasn't privy to was the worst thing about that piece of information. She sounds defensive, *and so she should be*, thinks Nate.

Saturday is Rebecca's day to look after the kids. *What else was she not keeping track of?*

Nate shakes his head slowly. "So where was she going?" he asks, his eyes conveying the challenge he would never dare to say aloud: *Why weren't you looking after her properly? Why weren't you paying more attention?*

But the police officer interrupts them. "We'll be off now. But do keep in touch and get back to us if they haven't turned up by tomorrow." He goes to hand Nate a card but Rebecca snatches it out of his hand, her eyes flashing. "Great," she snaps. "Just great. I'm telling you that things were tense between them."

This is news to Nate, and he looks up sharply.

"I am one hundred percent sure they wouldn't go off sightseeing together. And leave their phones and wallets behind. Something is wrong, and isn't it your job to find out what?"

"Whoa, whoa, back up a minute," Nate interjects, nodding to the officers who are heading for the door, despite Rebecca's wrath. He assumes she has discussed this tension with them and their assessment of the situation still stands, so he says, "Thank you, officers. We'll be in touch." Then he turns back to Rebecca. "What's this tension between Leroy and Tab? How long has it been like that? Did something happen?" He knows his suspicions are written all over his face, that Rebecca can see through him, can even probably anticipate the self-satisfied "I told you so" on the tip of his tongue, but he doesn't *want* it to be true. He wouldn't mind being right for once, in this particular relationship, but not about this. Despite his eager jumping on this news, he really does just want to find Tabby and check she's okay.

That she's not fooling around with Leroy, who even Nate has to admit is shockingly good-looking.

Sexy. Alluring.

"It's nothing." Rebecca stares back at him coldly. "He's just been really on board with parenting her, and she resists it, you know? Says he's not her dad. Yada yada yada. Exactly what you'd expect from a sixteen-year-old toward her stepfather setting boundaries."

Nate studies his ex-wife carefully. There's something she's not telling him, but he can't guess what it is. *Is it a subtle dig, that he's not pulling his weight in the parenting department? That Leroy has had to take up the slack?*

"Where is Leroy on Saturdays when Tabby does her vanishing act?" he shoots back, and for a moment he sees a flash of doubt on Rebecca's face. She composes herself instantly though, looking at him pityingly. "My husband is not looking for any extracurricular entertainment, Nathan," she says archly. "We are extremely happy. If you want to know so much about what our daughter gets up to, perhaps you should do a little more with her yourself." And Nate winces, because it's true, he used to have the girls more, he used to have Tabby on Saturdays in fact, but things had come up, life had gotten in the way, and Tabby wasn't even home on Saturdays anyway, so what did it matter if they were at Rebecca's house just one extra day a week? He still had them two days a week, and for most of the holidays.

His thoughts are interrupted though, by a small sob from Genevieve, and Nate realizes with a guilty start that he had forgotten she was even there, listening, and maybe Rebecca was right, maybe he *was* a shit dad.

Who would focus on making accusations rather than comforting their daughter?

"Hey, hey," he says, his face softening, and he reaches for Gen again, pulling her small, compact little frame into his arms. "Let's think about a funeral for Charlie, hey? We'll have it when Tabby's back. But we could make some plans, now. Maybe choose a tree to plant?" Nate's mind is working overtime. He's never been a fan of dogs, but he knows Genevieve is going to need a lot of support over this.

And also, he wouldn't mind taking her out of Rebecca's house and asking a few more questions about what she saw last night.

Not least because he might have been parked outside her house for a good portion of it.

Find out more at www.samcewen.com.

AUTHOR'S NOTE

This idea for this book came to me while watching The Staircase, and the deeply uncomfortable way that I experienced Candace (Kathleen Petersen's sister)—brittle, strident and almost nonsensical (her claim of victory that Michael 'confessed' following his eventual Alford plea, when it was very clearly a tactical move, not the confession and truth which she so longed for). It bothered me that even had a jury convicted him a second time, not Candace nor anyone else would truly know the circumstances that led to Kathleen's death. The whole story revolved around Michael, Kathleen and their children, but there are so many more stories around every family than the one that ends up in the limelight.

I was also mulling over *The Sociopath Next Door* by Martha Stout, which I highly recommend as well.

I also wanted to explore how difficult it can be to make changes in families, even small ones—how when one person starts doing something differently, there is enormous pressure to step back into line and do things the way they've always been done.

Readers are often curious about what Bethany was up to at the end - I wrote a blog about this. If you'd like to read it, please head over to my website (www.samcewen.com) and subscribe to my newsletter, and it will be sent to you automatically.

ABOUT THE AUTHOR

S.A. McEwen writes nuanced and gritty psychological/domestic thrillers exploring relationships, especially within families... with a particular interest in how the dark gets in, and the complex things that drive us toward or keep us out of connection with each other

She is a qualified social worker and educator in youth mental health, and lives in Melbourne with two gorgeous boys and a puppy.

If you've enjoyed her writing, please get in touch and say hello! The links are listed below.

Get notified when I **release a new book** via my newsletter here: www.samcewen.com.

facebook.com/authorsamcewen

amazon.com/author/samcewen

bookbub.com/authors/s-a-mcewen

goodreads.com/samcewen

patreon.com/samcewen

ACKNOWLEDGMENTS

To Sarah MacPherson—do you know, we have now known each other for more than thirty years?! You make me laugh even when it's grim. I love you. Thank you for reading ten zillion different endings for this book and not losing patience. Still loving me and leaving funny comments, even! You are a wonder.

To Stephanie Mendis—I'm so glad I chose social work, because I got you. Thank you for reading, even with COVID. And for getting on and off that damn train with me for ten-odd years. (Choo-choo!)

To Dani Guy—thank you so much for reading an early draft and providing such lovely, thoughtful feedback (and pulling me back from the brink of despair!) It was so lovely to meet you. In person, next time!

To my beta readers—Amy Vox Libris and Kirsten Moore. 'Grateful' really doesn't cut it. You are amazing. Thoughtful, attentive, clever and kind. Thank you for your care with my book, and your wonderful ideas and feedback.

To Erica Russikoff from Erica Edits—thank you. I trust your judgement so much. Your attention to detail and care with your edits is extraordinary. I am so grateful I get to work with you.

To Elizabeth Mackey for this glorious cover—thank you. I adore it.

And to all of you reading this book—thank you. I really appreciate it, and I hope that you enjoyed it. x